Usin...
fou...

Allison opened the safety deposit box....

The box held one sealed envelope. No name was on the outside. She slit the seal and took out a single sheet of paper. She scanned the document, then read it carefully. With a trembling hand, she returned the box to its proper place in the vault and put the envelope in her purse. The document she'd found had solved the mystery of why Harrison Page had left her a fortune and now Allison wished she didn't know, for her life was shattered.

She wanted to pray, but a wall of anger and hurt feelings separated her from God, and the only prayer she could muster was a plea for guidance.

"Dear God," she prayed aloud, "I don't know if I can bear this alone...."

Books by Irene Brand

Love Inspired

Child of Her Heart #19
Heiress #37

IRENE BRAND

This prolific and popular author of both contemporary and historical inspirational fiction is a native of West Virginia, where she has lived all her life. She began writing professionally in 1977, after she completed a master's degree in history at Marshall University. Irene taught in secondary public schools for twenty-three years, but retired in 1989 to devote herself full time to her writing.

After a long career of publishing articles and devotional materials, in 1984 her first novel was published by Thomas Nelson. Since that time, Irene has published fifteen contemporary and historical novels and three nonfiction titles with publishers such as Zondervan, Fleming Revell and Barbour Books.

Her extensive travels with her husband, Rod, to forty-nine of the United States and twenty-four foreign countries, have inspired much of her writing. Through her writing, Irene believes she has been helpful to others and is grateful to the many readers who have written to say that her truly inspiring stories and compelling portrayals of characters of strong faith have made a positive impression on their lives.

Heiress
Irene Brand

Love Inspired®

Published by Steeple Hill Books™

STEEPLE HILL BOOKS

Steeple
Hill™

ISBN 0-373-87037-X

HEIRESS

Copyright © 1998 by Irene Brand

Printed in U.S.A.

Do to others as you would have them do to you.

—*Luke* 6:31

Chapter One

Chicago wasn't at its best on a snowy January day, but Allison Sayre had lived in Illinois's largest city all her life and she was accustomed to the capricious climate. The inclement weather hadn't caused her mournful face and melancholy mood. Today, Allison had started delving into the past and she had reached a momentous decision. If she ever intended to bury Donald's memory, today was the time to do it!

Allison glanced around the bedroom that she had occupied the first twenty-three years of her life until a year ago when she had moved into a nearby apartment. Scattered around the room were the mementos of her defunct romance, a lifetime relationship that had ended two years ago with a "Dear Jane" letter. She took the note out of her Bible and read it, although the words had been seared into her memory since the day the postman had delivered the message:

Allison,
I can't go on with the marriage. I'm sorry.

Donald

Donald Brady had been the boy next-door, occupying a brick bungalow identical to the one owned by the Sayres along a row of modest single-family dwellings built in the 1930s. He and Allison had started kindergarten together and continued their education at the same schools. It had been easy to change from friends to sweethearts. Donald had entered the navy after his graduation from high school, while Allison had attended the University of Illinois at Chicago, an easy commute from her home, and they had set their wedding date for the week of her graduation. Donald had had a month's leave for the wedding, and she had no idea anything was wrong until she received his note.

As Allison had looked at the wedding dress spread out on the bed, the pain of rejection and resentment was as sharp today as it had been on the day Donald had jilted her. Days went by now without a thought of Donald, and she would think she had forgotten him until something happened to stir her memory. A photo album had been her downfall today, and she was sitting on the floor with it spread out before her when the door opened.

"What are you doing?" her sixteen-year-old sister, Cleta, asked as she glanced at the littered floor. "You've about wrecked this room."

"I started out to rearrange the chest of drawers and closet, but my cleaning turned into a journey down memory lane." She took a tissue from her pocket and blew her nose.

"Why, Allison—are you crying?"

"A little, I guess."

"No wonder you're crying. Your beautiful wedding dress!"

Cleta ran to the bed and carefully lifted the garment from its paper wrappings. Allison remembered how many hours her mother had slaved to make this gown of white slipper satin styled along colonial lines. The yoke of nylon marquisette was outlined with folds of lace-edged satin and caught at intervals by clusters of pearlized orange blossoms.

Tiers of lace trimmed the hemline of the pickup skirt, which ended in a court train edged with matching lace.

Cleta carried the gown to the mirror on the closet door and held it in front of her. "What are you going to do with it?"

"Sell it, if Mother agrees. I have no intention of marrying now, and even if I did, I wouldn't wear that dress."

"Maybe I could wear it at my wedding."

"I doubt it—not without a lot of alterations."

Allison and her sister were alike in many ways, but lanky, large-framed Cleta had already grown several inches taller than Allison, who had a light, trim figure that moved without effort. The siblings had thick chestnut hair, but Cleta's eyes were a dark brown, while Allison's amber eyes beneath dark lashes turned warm as liquid gold when she smiled—a trait she had exhibited rarely since her romance had ended.

Cleta lounged on the floor beside Allison. "What put you in such a mood anyway? Pictures in the album?"

"Since I haven't been busy chaperoning you and Tim while Mother and Dad have been gone, I decided to clear out this room, for I didn't take time to do it when I moved into the apartment. I found too many things that reminded me of the past." She turned several pages in the album. "You've seen most of these pictures."

"I've not seen this one," Cleta said, pointing to a photo. "Who's this handsome guy standing between you and Donald? Looks like you're in a football stadium."

"When we were sophomores, Donald and I and several other teenagers from our church went to a Young Believers Crusade in Indianapolis, which was held in Market Square Arena—a combination sports and entertainment center. There were young people from all over the world witnessing to their faith. It was a wonderful experience and one that broadened my concept of how to live a life pleasing to God."

"But who is this?" Cleta said, tapping the photo of the golden-haired Apollo who had excited her interest.

"That's Benton Lockhart, a plenary presenter at the crusade. He was a college freshman, and one of the most vibrant, motivating speakers I've ever heard. All the girls were crazy about him."

"Including you?"

"Including me," Allison acknowledged with a laugh. "But of course he didn't know I existed. I was just a face in the crowd to him. I haven't seen him since that time, or even heard of him, although judging from his charisma, I fully expected him to become a well-known evangelist."

"Too bad you don't know where he is—maybe you could still use that dress," Cleta said as she stood up and ran her hand over the shiny fabric. "I hate to see you unhappy. Why did Donald have to marry someone else?"

Noting the distress in Cleta's eyes, and to cover up her own unhappiness, Allison joked, "Oh, you bring Benton Lockhart around, and I'll put on that wedding dress in a hurry."

The telephone rang, and Tim called from the living room, "It's for you, Cleta,"

Cleta scuttled across the hall into her bedroom, leaving Allison with her memories. She knew she should be happy that Donald had had the courage to tell her the truth rather than marry her when he loved another woman, but two years hadn't made her pain any easier. Donald was her past, and she had to stop mourning for him. Remembering the words of the Greek philosopher Epictetus, Allison opened her Bible and wrote on the frontispiece: "He is a wise man who does not grieve for the things which he has not, but rejoices for those which he has."

She had many reasons to rejoice. Charles and Beatrice Sayre had been good and understanding parents, and she got along well with her siblings. Since graduating from college Allison had worked for a religious book publisher in Chicago, and although there wasn't much room for advancement at that firm, she had received good training, which would be helpful in finding another job.

"I'll stop grieving and rejoice," she said solemnly, and the words were a vow.

Bowing her head, Allison prayed, *God, I claim a verse from Proverbs for direction.* "Trust in the Lord with all your heart and lean not on your own understanding. In all your ways acknowledge Him, and He will make your paths straight." *Lord, I do claim You for my guide. If You will direct my decisions, I can throw off the unhappiness that has gnawed at my heart for two years. Direct me into new paths.*

With a lighter heart, Allison ran downstairs and found eighteen-year-old Tim lying on the couch watching television. A midterm high-school graduate, Tim would begin classes soon at the University of Illinois at Chicago.

"What do you say to eating out tonight at the Pizza Shop and taking in a movie? I'll pay."

Tim hesitated and glanced at the phone. "Aw, Sis, can't we eat here at home?"

In mock concern, Allison went over and rubbed his forehead. "Are you sick? I've never known you to turn down free pizza before. Mother placed you in my care this weekend, I can't have you getting sick."

Tim pushed her hand away. "If you want pizza, have it delivered."

Cleta entered the room. "Now, Allison, don't annoy Mr. Millionaire, or when he comes into his riches he won't share with you."

Tim raked his long brown hair back from his face and revealed dark, serious eyes. "All right, poke fun at me if you want to, but I'll bet you're just as curious as I am. I wish Mother and Dad would call."

Allison sat down in a chair opposite the couch. It had been four days now since their parents had gone to Columbus to attend the funeral of Beatrice's only brother, Harrison Page. They hadn't returned at the expected time, nor had they telephoned. Beatrice had called when they arrived in Ohio, but no word had come since then.

Allison knew very little about her uncle. His wife had been an invalid several years before she died and the couple had no children, so the disposition of his considerable wealth was often a matter of family speculation.

When Allison went into the kitchen to prepare their evening meal, Tim turned off the television and followed her.

"Surely he left us something. He must have had lots of money, and after all, I'm the only nephew Uncle Harrison has, and you and Cleta are his only nieces. What else would he do with his money if he didn't pass it on to us?"

"I don't know," Allison said, "but I can't believe that he would remember us in his will when he didn't have anything to do with us when he was living. I've seen him only two times—when our grandparents died."

"But Mother heard from him," Tim argued.

"A card at Christmas with a hundred-dollar bill in it. The rest of the time she didn't know if he was living or dead."

"Surely I'll get enough to buy a new car."

"Only a car?" Cleta taunted him. "I thought you were expecting his whole publishing company."

Tim went out to the backyard and slammed the door, but he rushed back in when the telephone rang and slumped into a chair when he found Cleta talking to one of her friends.

"I wish I'd paid more attention to Uncle Harrison when he was alive," Tim moaned.

Allison was rummaging in the refrigerator to see what leftovers were available. "Have you considered that Aunt Sarah may have had relatives he knew better than he knew us? Maybe they'll inherit."

Tim groaned, dropped his head on the table and wrapped his arms around his head. Cleta hung up the phone in record time for her, shoved Tim away from the table and laid out the plates and silver.

"I'll admit I'd be pleased if we did get some of his money," she said. "It would ease Dad's load. I know he dreads the expense of sending Tim and me to college."

"Don't spend the money until you get it," Allison warned, although she knew that her sister's observation was true.

Since Allison's plans of taking the family out for dinner had been foiled, she settled on food that her mother had prepared before leaving. She sliced some roast beef, browned boiled potatoes and tossed a garden salad. They could eat the rest of the apple pie for dessert.

Allison had just gotten the dinner dishes rinsed and put in the dishwasher when they heard a car entering the garage. Tim rushed to the door between the kitchen and the garage, and the girls were right behind him.

Charles was opening the car door for Beatrice, and he said, "Your mother has had a rough time, so don't pester her. You can help me unload, Tim." He put his arms around Cleta and Allison and gave them a hug. "We've missed you. Has everything been all right here?"

"Yes," Allison said in her low, melodious voice, "but we're happy you're home." Charles Sayre was a brawny man, jovial and friendly, always ready to listen to his children's problems. Allison had missed him.

Beatrice greeted her children with a slight, sad-faced smile. "Mother," Allison said. "I'm sorry it's been a sad experience for you." She put an arm around her mother, who was standing as rigid as a statue.

"He was my only brother. What else would you expect?"

Allison gasped, for never before had her mother been so curt with her. It was almost as if Allison had done something to annoy Beatrice. How could that be? She hadn't seen her for a week.

Beatrice turned abruptly and walked into the house, passed through the kitchen and into the living room. Again

Allison was stunned. It wasn't like her mother not to comment on the tidiness of the house. The three siblings had always worked hard to earn their mother's praise, and the house looked as neat as it had when their parents had left. Beatrice Sayre was the dominant personality of the family, and although she could be tender and understanding in times of distress, she exerted a rigid discipline over her children. Charles made the money, but Beatrice managed their finances so that the family lived comfortably.

Charles was laughing when he followed Cleta and Tim into the living room. They struggled with the luggage, and he carried a large plastic bag, out of which he pulled three teddy bears. "Here, I brought you some presents from Columbus."

Cleta squealed and grabbed the white bear with a red ribbon around its neck.

"Aw, Dad, I'm too big for a teddy bear," Tim said, but he picked up the large brown bear.

Smiling, Allison said, "Looks like I'm left with the black one. Thanks a lot, Dad." She didn't want to dim her father's joy by not being appreciative, but she was concerned about Beatrice's attitude. What had happened in Columbus to distress her mother? How could she be mourning for a brother with whom she'd had so little contact for years?

Tucking the brown bear under his arm, Tim said, "The bear is nice, Dad, but I'm interested in other things. Give us the scoop. How much did we get?"

Charles dropped his head, refusing to look at his children. Beatrice stared at the floor, her face ashen, so it was easy to guess from their dismay that the Sayres hadn't been mentioned in the will. Cleta and Tim certainly looked woebegone, but Allison wasn't surprised. Was she the only one in the family who hadn't expected a windfall? Crushed as she had been by Donald's perfidy, Allison hadn't given any thought to Uncle Harrison's illness and his subsequent death.

With a sigh, Beatrice fastened her eyes on her son. "*You*

didn't get anything!'' She pulled a large envelope from her purse. ''According to Harrison's lawyer, with the exception of a few bequests to some of his employees, my brother bequeathed his entire estate to Allison. He gave us a copy of the will.'' She started to hand the document to Allison, but Tim grabbed it from his mother's hand.

''But why Allison? Why her and not me?''

Charles took the will from Tim and gave it to Allison, whose hand was shaking so badly she couldn't hold the envelope and it dropped to the floor.

''Harrison must have had his reasons, but he didn't choose to tell us. Stop being selfish and congratulate your sister for her good fortune,'' Charles said.

''Well, if I can't have it, I'm glad that he chose Allison instead of Cleta. You'll divide with me, won't you, Allison? Cleta never would. How much is his estate worth?''

''We don't know. Since neither Beatrice nor I was named in the will, we had no right to inquire. Harrison's lawyer did give us that copy of the will, but Allison will have to go to Columbus to find out all the details.''

Allison felt as if she were observing the scene in their living room from another sphere. Beatrice looked as though she would burst into tears at any minute, and that troubled Allison. Had Beatrice herself expected the money? Charles watched his wife with anxious eyes. Tim wore a petulant expression. A broad smile brightened Cleta's face.

After Allison's first wave of surprise passed, an excitement started building within, and she picked up the envelope, opened it and began to read the will, noting immediately that the document had been validated three years ago on her twenty-first birthday.

''Isn't that a coincidence!'' she exclaimed. ''Signed on my birthday. Uncle Harrison couldn't have known that.''

No one answered, and she continued to read. After she passed the introductory legal jargon, the wording was very simple. Five people were listed for bequests based on a percentage of Harrison's total estate, with the balance to be given to "my niece Allison Sayre." This balance included the Page Publishing Company, a home in Victorian Village and whatever investments and securities Harrison owned at the time of his death.

"Oh, this is great," Allison said. "Just this morning, I prayed for God to give new direction to my life, and here it is, offered to me on a silver platter."

"I don't want you to take it," Beatrice said quietly.

Her family stared at her, speechless, and Charles was the first to find his voice.

"Not take it?" he shouted. "Why would you want Allison to turn down an estate that might be worth several million dollars?"

Beatrice regarded her husband in amazement. "Charles, think a minute. It's the only sane solution."

"Mother," Allison said, "why can't you be happy for me? Ever since Donald married and started bringing his wife next door, I've been miserable here in Chicago. This will give me something else to think about. Are you disappointed because he didn't name you in the will?"

"I didn't expect anything from Harrison, but I don't like the idea that he favored you over the other children. That isn't fair. Besides, you're not mature enough to take over his estate."

"I'm not a child anymore, and I've had some experience in the publishing business. Perhaps that's the reason he chose me."

Cleta spoke for the first time. "I think you should take it. If the money had been left to me, I'd rush out of here for Columbus so fast you couldn't stop me. Not take a few million dollars! Mother, you must be joking."

"We've tried to teach you children that money isn't everything, but if you're determined to accept it, Allison, then promise me that you'll liquidate it the minute the estate comes into your possession. I don't want you to go to Columbus."

Trying to think of a way to answer her mother, Allison

hesitated as she glanced through the document again. She read the names of the others that Harrison Page had listed: Celestine Handley, Adra and Minerva McRamey, Thomas Curnutt and Benton Lockhart.

Benton Lockhart! Surely not the Benton Lockhart she had once known and had never forgotten. A photo of that dynamic young man had brought him to mind today, and here was something else to evoke his memory. Seeing that name convinced Allison that she would definitely go to Columbus and at least find out what was involved in accepting Harrison's property.

"That's a promise I can't make right now, Mother. I must go to Columbus and find out what is involved. Maybe I won't want to live there, but I have to find out for myself. Will you go with me to investigate? I don't want to go alone."

Beatrice stood, and her visage was stony. "No, I won't go with you. This move may very well ruin your life, and I won't be a party to having you wreck the life-style we've worked for years to achieve."

She stalked out of the room, and as Allison heard her steps, heavy and deliberate, on the stairway, she turned to Charles questioningly.

"I'll go with you," he said quietly. "After being gone this week, I can't be away from work long, but I'll arrange for a couple of days, as you will have to do, and we'll take a plane for Columbus. I believe you've made the right decision."

The following Sunday, Allison and Charles waited at O'Hare Airport for a plane to Columbus. Sleet pelted the large windows in the waiting area as Allison tried to be patient. The plane was already an hour late, which meant that their arrival in Columbus would be well after dark. It was a good thing they had allowed two days for the trip instead of only one. Their appointment with the lawyer, Thomas Curnutt, was scheduled for nine o'clock tomorrow morning, with a flight back to Chicago in midafternoon. Allison was eager for the meeting, but she knew she couldn't hurry the plane, so she took a book from her purse and started to read. In a short time, passengers from the incoming jet came through the walkway, and soon the call was given for loading. It was obvious that the airport authorities were moving the planes as fast as safety rules permitted to avoid a big buildup if the airport had to be closed because of the weather.

Their plane arrived in Columbus two hours late, but since no one was meeting them, it didn't matter. Heavy clouds had hidden the ground all the way across Indiana and Ohio, but as they approached Columbus, the plane reached a lower altitude and Allison saw the wide fertile fields of western Ohio give way to a metropolis spread around the banks of the Scioto and Olentangy Rivers, and as they neared the airport, she was amazed at the cluster of tall buildings in the downtown section. The city wasn't as large as Chicago, but it displayed an interesting skyline, and Allison looked eagerly at this capital city that might soon become her home.

Intermittent rain was falling when the plane landed, and since they hadn't checked any luggage, Charles motioned Allison toward the lower level of the terminal, where ground transportation was available. Her father arranged for a van to take them to a downtown hotel, and it was almost seven o'clock when they registered and took the elevator to adjoining rooms on the third floor.

"Will a half hour give you time to freshen up for dinner?" Charles asked, and when Allison nodded, he said, "Come into my room when you're ready."

Allison was ready in fifteen minutes, as was Charles, and as they waited for the elevator to take them to the restaurant, Allison said, "I'm not hungry."

Charles gave her a hug. "I know that, but you're going to eat anyway. Stop being nervous—this is going to work out fine."

Tears welled in Allison's eyes. "I hope so, but I'm scared."

"I know that, too," he said as he gently squeezed her shoulder.

Charles, who always had a healthy appetite, ordered a full meal, and when Allison asked for a salad only, Charles said to the waiter, "Add a bowl of vegetable soup and some crackers to her order. Also, we'll have pie for dessert."

He reached across the table and took Allison's hand. "Listen to me, Allison. Harrison should not have loaded all this on you without telling you first, but that was his way. The man was self-centered, and while he seems to have had an excellent head for business, he didn't know much about dealing with his family."

"Why didn't he ever come to see us?"

Charles shrugged and leaned back so the waitress could arrange their beverages and salads. He took Allison's hand again as he said a prayer of thanks for their food.

"You know very well that I'll miss you if you leave Chicago, but I honestly feel that your future lies here in Columbus."

"I've been very unhappy for two years. I couldn't live at the house anymore and see Donald bringing his wife home to visit. It helped to go into the apartment, but it will probably be better if I leave Chicago."

Sternly, Charles said, "It's time for you to stop this yearning for Donald. You would have had a miserable life married to a man who was in love with another woman."

"I decided last week while you were gone that I was going to bury the past."

"That's good. When Donald refused to marry you, he was simply living by the Golden Rule, the way I've taught you children to live, and it's time for you to forget him and go on with your life. Frankly, I question you ever had a deep love for Donald—he was just a habit in your life. You two were friends and little more, I think. He was your first boyfriend, Allison, but I don't think you and Donald shared the strong feelings necessary for a good marriage."

Allison stared at her father as if he didn't know what he was talking about, but perhaps he was right. He hadn't steered her wrong yet.

The next morning Charles ordered a taxi to take them to Curnutt's office on South High Street.

"And they call Chicago the windy city," Allison said to Charles as she noticed the effect of the strong wind sweeping across High Street where it intersected with Broad. People could hardly stand against its power. Stoplights and shop signs risked being blown from their moorings. Pigeons with ruffled feathers, strutting along the street looking for crumbs, staggered drunkenly from the force of the blasts, and passengers waiting at the bus stops were sprayed with liquid as foam coffee cups were torn from their hands.

"It's a nice city, though," Charles observed. "Smaller than Chicago, but enough like it that you wouldn't notice a great deal of difference."

Before they reached the stone statehouse in Capitol Square, they observed the sprawling Nationwide Insurance Plaza and passed under the connecting mall bridge between Lazarus and Jacobson's, the city's two large department stores. The stately city hall building was on their right as the taxi dodged in and out of traffic on busy High Street.

The attorney's office was in a two-story brick building, which had been a dwelling at one time. Charles paid the taxi fare, took Allison's arm, steered her along the sidewalk and up the two steps to the front door. She sighed deeply.

"You're prettier when you smile," Charles said jokingly, and Allison forced her features to relax. She couldn't smile, but she did look pleasant as she inspected her image in the glass panel of the walnut door. A sign on the door said Open. Come in.

There was no turning back now. A blast of heat hit their faces, and it felt good after the chill morning air. They were in a narrow, heavily carpeted foyer with a circular stairway leading upward. The door to the left was marked Receptionist, and a woman well past her youth greeted them with a pleasant, "Good morning." She was dressed in a black suit, and her elegance blended with the lavish office, which must have contained every modern office machine on the market. Thomas Curnutt obviously wasn't a struggling young lawyer.

"I'm Charles Sayre, and this is my daughter Allison. We have an appointment with Mr. Curnutt."

"Won't you be seated for a few minutes? I'm Mary Curnutt, and my husband was delayed with a client at the hospital this morning, but he telephoned just a few moments ago that he would be here soon."

Another delay, Allison thought with a sigh. If the Lord was trying to teach her patience, she was in the right classroom. Although it had been only eight days since she'd learned of her inheritance, the wait had seemed endless.

Alert to her moods, Charles muttered, "You've waited this long—five minutes more won't make much difference."

She flashed him a smile. How many times in her life had this best of all fathers jollied her out of the dismals?

The phone rang, and under cover of the secretary's conversation, Charles said, "I can't understand you. You've suddenly become a millionaire. That's supposed to make you happy. You were excited at first. What's happened?"

"I'm disturbed about Mother's reaction. If she wanted me to have the money, I'd be dancing around light as a feather. I can't be happy if I make others unhappy."

Charles waved his arm in an impatient gesture. "Forget your mother. There comes a moment in all our lives when we can't do what our parents want us to. Your mother will get over her peeve, but it will take time. Just be patient with her. And another thing, my only purpose here is to give you support. You'll have to do the talking, so loosen up."

When the secretary terminated her conversation, she said, "I believe I heard Mr. Curnutt come in."

The door behind the secretary opened, and a well-built man of medium height entered the reception room. He had glossy dark hair, streaked with gray, and brown eyes, and Allison judged he was about sixty years old. He advanced and shook hands with Charles.

"I'm sorry to keep you waiting, Mr. Sayre," Curnutt said in a deep-toned powerful voice, and he turned to Allison. "And this is Allison, I presume."

Allison took his outstretched hand. He sounded as if meeting her was his greatest pleasure, and Curnutt's presence affected her like a gentle breeze on a soft, spring day. She felt safe in his hands, and much of her nervousness dissipated under the influence of his warm, radiant personality as he stood aside to let Allison precede him into his office. The office had the air of a cozy living room, with comfortable leather chairs grouped about two coffee tables. The focal point of the room was a window overlooking the backyard, where cardinals and chickadees fought for sunflower seeds in a well-filled bird feeder. Tall maple trees marked the property line, and a fountain, now wrapped in a protective cover, would provide a pleasant addition to the scene in summer.

The attorney seated Allison and Charles beside one of the low tables, and Mrs. Curnutt brought in a silver tray containing coffee and tea urns and a plate of homemade cookies. Charles poured a cup of coffee and handed it to Allison, but she declined. She wouldn't have considered putting food or drink into her queasy stomach.

While Curnutt opened a locked file and took out a well-filled folder, Allison clenched her fingers and commanded them not to tremble. *God, I need some help,* she prayed, and instantaneously she remembered a verse that she'd heard over and over at funerals. She almost felt as if this were her funeral—at least it was the death of her old way of life, so the words were welcome. "Do not let your hearts be troubled and do not be afraid."

She felt Charles's eyes upon her, and she was smiling when Curnutt sat down and laid the folder on the table between them.

"Mr. Curnutt," Allison began in a steady voice, "the inheritance from my uncle came as a complete surprise to all of us. I know nothing about his affairs."

He nodded. "I was aware that Harrison had not made his intentions known to you, and I advised him that he was making a mistake, and especially after he became ill, I insisted that you should be told, but he refused."

"Then he wasn't sick when he first made this will," Allison said, taking the document from her purse.

"That's correct. Harrison and I have been friends for years, and he had never mentioned a family until he came in here three years ago and asked me to draw up his will."

"He must have been a strange man. He didn't keep in contact with us, either."

"He was a lonely man, I think, because he was attentive to his ailing wife. He worked hard at his company, but he had no social life." Curnutt spread open the file. "Since I knew you were coming, I've prepared a portfolio of his worth so we could start probating the will upon your arrival."

"Since I know nothing about his assets, tell me what I need to know."

He smiled at her. "You should know, Miss Sayre, that you've become a very wealthy young woman. Page Publishing alone is worth more than a million, his three-story Victorian home could be listed for close to a million, and I estimate that his stocks, bonds and other assets will round out your total inheritance at nearly three million dollars."

Sweat popped out on Allison's hands, and she suddenly felt faint. Curnutt's smiling face faded before her, and Charles placed a hand on her shoulder and shook her gently.

"I'm all right, but it's overwhelming. You see, Mr. Curnutt, my mother wants me to sell the house and the publishing company and take cash for everything, and that's a lot of cash! She doesn't want me to move to Columbus, for she says I'm not mature enough to take over Uncle Harrison's business, and I suspect she's right."

Curnutt shook his head and handed her a sheet of paper. "This is a copy of the codicil to your uncle's will, and I neglected to give it to your parents last week. Perhaps Harrison had second thoughts about saddling you with so much responsibility, but a year ago, he made these provisions— you must manage Page Publishing Company for at least three years before you can sell it. And you will notice the stipulation that if you do not choose to abide by these provisions, you will not inherit, the business will be shut down and his assets will be liquidated and given to Mount Carmel Hospital."

"So I take everything he had or nothing?"

"That's right."

Allison left the chair and walked toward the window. The cardinals flashed brilliant in the morning's sun as they flew gracefully from the tall maples down to the feeder, grabbed a seed and winged back to their perch. Unlike birds in the wild, they had become dependent upon these handouts, and she wondered if she could accept Harrison's money without becoming a slave to it. Unlike Tim, who was far too interested in material possessions, money had never been that important to Allison. Even when she considered leaving her present job, it wasn't to earn more money—she simply wanted an opportunity to learn more and be more productive.

She sat down on the cushioned window seat and looked at Curnutt. "Tell me something about Page Publishing Company."

"Harrison started the business about thirty years ago. They specialize in printing curriculums for colleges and secondary schools. When Harrison started out, he did some trade publishing, but the business is really a printing company now, for they don't deal with the authors personally. Rather, they do contract printing for a number of publishers. They produce books in Spanish, French and German, and they're shipped all over the world. It's a stable business."

"What do you think I should do, Daddy?"

"The decision is yours, honey, but if you want some advice, I'd say go for it. You've had some experience with the publishing world. You'll never know what you can do until you try. I've always heard, and I believe it, that when God closes one door of opportunity, He opens another. The Donald door is closed—you know that—so if God has provided a new pathway for you, be cautious about closing it before you step through. But," he repeated, "the decision is yours."

Allison stared at the floor and, with the toe of her shoe, traced the outline of the hexagon shapes on the carpet. Curnutt and Charles didn't rush her.

"May I take some time to deliberate?"

"Certainly," Curnutt said, "but I wouldn't hesitate long. Will it help you make up your mind if I take you to Page Publishing and the house Harrison owned?"

"I'm not ready for that yet. I want to go back home and make my decision there. I'll telephone you within a week."

The attorney closed the file before him. "Very well." He gave her a look of admiration. "May I say that it's a privilege to work with such an exceptional young woman."

Allison's look of surprise was genuine. "Exceptional? Me? I've always considered myself a very ordinary person."

"You aren't, Miss Sayre. I don't know of anyone—young or old—who would hesitate a minute if given an opportunity to have several million dollars handed to them. Let me repeat, you're exceptional. I would be interested to know why you are so cautious."

"I haven't really thought it out, but I suppose I'm hesitating for a number of reasons. I'm afraid I will make a failure and lose everything. Also, I told you my mother doesn't want me to move to Columbus, and I don't want to be at odds with her. And what will so much wealth do to my values? My parents have taught me to avoid selfishness and greed, and I've had everything I want on a moderate income. Will I be greedy to take so much wealth? No doubt the hospital needs it more than I."

Curnutt smiled at her and shook his head. "As I said before, exceptional."

Allison was silent as they traveled from Curnutt's office to the airport, and Charles didn't press her to talk. As the plane lifted into the air and she looked down on Columbus, now illuminated by the noonday sun, she said, "Daddy, I don't think I can handle it."

"I don't care what you do, but you're worrying needlessly about some things," Charles said sternly. "I've told you that Beatrice will come around. She loves you. She won't want to be estranged from you. And about running that business—millionaires don't make all their own decisions—that's why they employ accountants and lawyers. Besides, the employees at Page Publishing will do the work. Your job will be to see that they're doing it right."

Those words, meant for comfort, did little to assuage Allison's apprehension. How could she supervise employees when she didn't know what they were supposed to do?

Chapter Two

Still wavering between going to Columbus and rejecting the inheritance, Allison gave her employer two weeks' notice and told her landlady that she would relinquish her furnished apartment in another month. More than once Allison picked up the receiver to telephone Thomas Curnutt to tell him that she wouldn't accept the legacy and authorize him to transfer the assets to Mount Carmel Hospital, but something always held her back. Was it the unseen hand of God preventing her from making a mistake? At last, she telephoned Curnutt and told him that she would arrive in Columbus in late February, and he assured her that he would immediately set in motion the necessary steps to transfer Page's assets to her.

Still plagued with misgivings, she began to pack her belongings. Allison wanted to move back home for the few weeks she had left, but when Beatrice still refused to discuss Allison's plans for the future, she knew it wouldn't be pleasant for any of them. Whether or not Charles intervened Allison didn't know, but when Allison telephoned that she intended to move within a week, Beatrice did ask her to stay with them during her remaining days in Chicago.

Tim and Cleta came to help Allison pack the loaded boxes into her six-year-old sedan, and there wasn't room for everything, but she gave a box of knickknacks to Cleta, enabling them to stow the remainder in the back seat and trunk.

As they shifted boxes to make more space, Tim said, "You won't have to drive this old car much longer, Allison. What kind of new car will you buy?"

"I haven't thought about a new car. I've been too busy burying the past to think about my future."

"You're afraid to think about it, aren't you?" Cleta said.

Allison looked in amazement at her perceptive sister. "Maybe, but I have been busy."

After Allison turned the key into her landlady, she said, "If we can all three wedge into the front seat, let's drive around the city. Chicago has always been home; I rather hate to leave it."

Along the lakefront, they enjoyed a view of the public parkland stretching along the shoreline, its broad beaches and lawns covered with a few inches of snow. They drove through downtown Chicago, with its spectacular skyscrapers, fashionable shops and many department stores. Entering the financial district, they noted at least six major banks, the Chicago Board of Trade, the City Hall-County Building and the blue-tinted Illinois Center. Only a few walkers braved the frigid weather to exercise in three-hundred-acre Grant Park. Allison had spent a lot of time with Donald in this downtown area, but she had also enjoyed days of pleasure with her family at the same places, so she focused on the family gatherings rather than her dates with Donald.

As the time approached for her departure, Allison felt her excitement intensify, yet she would have anticipated the adventure much more if her mother had not been displeased. Allison had deduced that Beatrice was not angry with her, for she prepared all the foods that her daughter preferred and insisted that Allison store anything in her bedroom that she didn't want to move to Columbus, and she arranged a dinner party for the family and Allison's best friends at a downtown restaurant and bought tickets to a performance of the Chicago Symphony. Allison winced at the cost of the evening, but she had to accept the outlay of money—for she knew it was Beatrice's way of apologizing for her attitude. Allison decided that her mother was reconciled to the move, for she made no overt display of unhappiness, although Tim and Cleta shed tears for a couple of days before her departure, and Charles, his face solemn, would often hug Allison tightly without saying a word.

Although eager to be on her way, Allison dreaded their final parting, but she forced a cheerful attitude until, at the last minute, Beatrice embraced her eldest daughter and wept convulsively. Her grief spread until the whole family was sobbing, and when Allison finally drove away from the house, her eyes were swollen and red. Beatrice had gone into the house rather than watch Allison leave. She realized that her mother would miss her, but Allison still felt puzzled at her mother's reaction. It wasn't as if Columbus were a continent away—there was no reason they couldn't visit often. Children couldn't stay in the family home forever, and it wasn't like Beatrice to act this way.

Allison planned two days for the trip to Columbus, but driving conditions were favorable and she arrived at the luxurious hotel along High Street where Thomas Curnutt had made reservations for her early Thursday afternoon. Over the past month, she had often wondered if this change in her circumstances was real or if she was dreaming, but if she needed proof that she was now classed among the wealthy, it came when she reached the hotel complex and a valet took her old car and parked it beside the Cadillacs, Lincolns and Mercedes belonging to the hotel's other patrons.

As she followed another valet carrying her small bags into the reception room, Allison had never felt more out of place. Recalling a poem that Charles, from his childhood memory, had often quoted, she thought, *"Lawk a mercy on me, this is none of I."*

Dressed in jeans, wearing a heavy parka and fur-lined boots, she certainly looked out of place, and she breathed a sigh of relief when the door of her room closed behind her. Even here she felt overwhelmed as she viewed the large room with king-sized bed, lavish draperies and bedspread, thick carpet and modish furniture. How she wished she were still in Chicago!

After she telephoned her mother that she had made the journey safely, Allison contacted the attorney's office and made an appointment for the next morning. Still, she had several hours on her hands before bedtime. She wouldn't consider going to a dining room in this building for dinner, especially when the few dress garments she owned were packed away in the car. She contemplated room service for her meal, but she couldn't cower in the room for hours. So exhibiting a nonchalance she didn't feel, Allison took the elevator to the lobby, happily noting that many people were dressed in casual attire, and went out to take a look around the shopping district.

Trying to envision what the city would be like in spring and summer, Allison snuggled into the warm parka, tucked gloved fingers into her pockets and merged with the natives. After she reached Capitol Square, she slowed down and looked in the shop windows, wondering if she should buy some new clothes. She wouldn't spend an inheritance she hadn't received, but she did have some Christmas gift money that she had been carrying in her billfold for weeks.

In a large department store, Allison tried on several dresses before choosing a two-piece brick matte jersey skirt and a matching tunic with vee-necked top. She also decided on a tailored navy suit with a long, fitted jacket and straight-cut skirt. Though the style was a bit more severe than her usual taste, she thought it looked businesslike and made her appear older. Taking over Page Publishing, she'd need all the help she could get.

Leaving the clothing department, Allison stopped to look for a new nail color, for she wanted to work on her nails tonight. Packing and the rush of moving had been hard on her hands. She had spent all her gift money, so she didn't buy anything new, deciding instead to use what she had in her cosmetic bag at the hotel.

The shopping had consumed Allison's extra time and dusk was falling when she left the department store. She stopped for a meal at a nearby Chinese restaurant, and it was completely dark by the time she finished eating. The air was considerably colder, so Allison hailed a taxi to take her back to the hotel.

Dressed in her new blue suit, Allison didn't hesitate about breakfasting in the luxurious hotel, and she asked the concierge to order a taxi for her at nine o'clock. She would leave her car parked at the hotel until she could make other living arrangements. After seeing the cost of the room for one night, Allison knew that her bank account wasn't adequate to spend many nights here, and she figured it would be a long time before she had any access to funds from her inheritance.

The fast-driving taxi driver arrived at Curnutt's office before she had her mind composed to talk to the attorney. One minute Allison was excited and optimistic about the adventure she was facing, and other times she was clammy with fear and indecision.

The latter emotion predominated when she cautiously entered the lawyer's office. She thawed somewhat under Mary Curnutt's welcome and the attorney's outstretched hand, but when she sat facing him and Curnutt started discussing the legal ramifications of her inheritance, Allison swallowed hard and said, "You can't imagine how inadequate I feel to be taking over this estate. You're wasting your time explaining all those things to me. I don't understand

much of what you're saying. Can't *you* just take care of
what has to be done?''

"I can do what I think is best if you're willing to trust
me that far.''

"I have no one else to trust, so please settle this estate
as you would if it had been received by one of your children.''

"Very well. I promised Harrison that I would assist you
in any way possible. Also, I will have his accountant refer
any financial matters to me for the time being. Within a
few months you will be more qualified to make decisions.
For the present, you will have all you can do to take over
the management of Page Publishing. I'll take you there today.''

"Do I have to go so soon?''

"Yes, I believe so. The employees are quite edgy. Several of them have contacted me trying to find out what is
going to happen to the business, but I had no right to divulge the contents of Harrison's will without your permission. It isn't fair to keep them in the dark any longer.''

Allison referred to the copy of Harrison's will that she
carried. "Who are the people named in his will?''

"Of course you know who I am, and I'm flattered that
Harrison chose to remember me.'' He read the names from
the will. "Adra and Minerva McRamey are the caretakers
at Harrison's home. They've been in his employ for years.
Minerva took care of Harrison's wife, and of him before
he chose to enter a nursing home. The McRameys are in
their sixties.''

Curnutt adjusted the nosepiece of his glasses.

"Celestine Handley is an employee at the company. She
has been Harrison's secretary for years, and I question that
he would have managed half as well if she hadn't been
there to support him. I'm sure she will be just as helpful
to you. Benton Lockhart came to Page Publishing Company
out of college and proved his worth right away. He is com-
petent and steady, faithful and devoted to his work, and

self-sacrificing for the company. When Harrison became ill two years ago, he made Benton his assistant, and after Harrison was no longer able to come to the office, Benton took charge and has been in charge since. He's a calm and collected individual and the publishing company has expanded under his leadership.''

The lawyer tapped the document significantly. ''All these people have been valuable employees to Harrison, and they deserved to be remembered in his will.''

''I wasn't implying that they shouldn't have been, but if I encounter them, I want to know why my uncle regarded them so highly.''

''You'll probably see all of them today, so it's well that you know something about them.''

As she folded the document and returned it to her purse, Allison said, ''I knew a Benton Lockhart once. I've been wondering if it's the same person.''

''I didn't know Benton until he came to work at Page Publishing.''

''Then he isn't a native of Columbus?''

''No. I believe he came from somewhere in Indiana.''

''Then it could be the same person, for I met the Benton Lockhart I'm talking about at a youth crusade in Indianapolis. He was the most fantastic spiritual speaker I've ever heard. I had expected him to go into the ministry, but I haven't heard of him since that time.''

''To my knowledge, Benton isn't a churchgoer, and although we meet socially from time to time, he's never impressed me as a man with any spiritual side to his nature.''

Curnutt telephoned the publishing firm and made an appointment to see the entire staff at one o'clock, and while he talked, Allison was conscious of a deep disappointment. She had been hoping to renew the acquaintance with the Benton of her youth.

''That will give us time to have lunch,'' Curnutt said when he finished the phone conversation. ''There's a nice café in German Village that provides a light lunch that you'll enjoy. If you don't mind, Mary can come with us.''

Allison replied that she didn't mind in the least.

The Curnutts were delightful company, and as they traveled along the tree-lined brick streets, Mary commented on the unique atmosphere of the tiny Dutch-single and large Dutch-double houses of an earlier century.

''German Village consists of more than two hundred acres and is listed in the *National Register of Historic Places.* A good way to see it is to take a walking tour because one can get a greater appreciation for the window flower boxes, patio gardens and ornate wrought-iron fences.''

''There are several special events here during the year to celebrate our unique German heritage,'' Thomas added. ''This is a part of Columbus that the casual tourist doesn't see. You'll enjoy visiting this area.''

The small restaurant was decorated with red-and-white gingham tablecloths and café curtains. They ate their lunch of bratwurst on a sesame bun, hot potato salad and a fluffy cherry chiffon pudding, while outside, on the sidewalk, a small gaily costumed Alpine band played toe-tapping music, and Allison was able to ignore the stressful afternoon she faced.

After they returned Mary to the office, the attorney maneuvered his Mercedes through the busy noonday traffic and followed High Street north of the capitol, where he turned east on Broad until he reached a five-story buff brick building with Page Publishing Company etched in a stone slab across the front of the structure. Curnutt turned into a narrow driveway between two buildings and parked in the company's private lot.

''Did Uncle Harrison own the building?''

Curnutt nodded. ''And land is at a premium price here, too,'' he said as he came around the car and opened the door for her. Allison was doing her best to remain calm, but she felt so weak that she actually welcomed Curnutt's hand on her arm as he assisted her from the car. What awaited her at this meeting?

"There's a conference room on the first floor, and that's where the employees are to assemble. We'll meet them first and take a tour of the facilities after they go back to their work."

They walked down the hallway toward a buzz of excited voices that stopped immediately when Curnutt tapped on a half-closed door. He motioned Allison into the room filled with men and women gathered around oblong tables. Allison sat at a table near the door where two other women were already seated. She smiled timidly at them, and they acknowledged her by lifting their hands in silent greeting. She felt ill at ease, but she ran her hand over the fabric of her new suit, thankful that she was dressed appropriately in the latest fashion. Everyone's attention focused on Thomas Curnutt when he stepped behind a podium in the front of the room.

"I know that many of you have been uneasy about the future of Page Publishing Company, and were even before the owner's death, but I was not at liberty to divulge any details about his affairs. Now I can tell you that Harrison left the bulk of his estate to his niece Allison Sayre, who accompanies me today." He paused as a murmur of surprise interrupted him. "That includes this company, so Miss Sayre has become the new owner. She has had two years of experience in the publishing world in her hometown of Chicago. Perhaps you would like to welcome her."

The applause was perfunctory, hardly cordial, and Allison felt her face flushing. Her embarrassment was so great that she missed Curnutt's next words and focused only when she heard him say, "Perhaps Miss Sayre has a few words for you."

Even with her back to them, Allison felt every eye on her, but with a prayer for courage, she stood on trembling legs and, with as much grace as she could muster, turned to face her new employees. Everyone's attention was riveted on her, and she didn't see any sign of welcome, though some of the people looked amused. And no wonder—her youth and inexperience must be apparent. Others seemed in a state of shock, as Allison was. She hurriedly judged there were about forty people present, and not one of them as young as she. A few of the men's faces were belligerent and she figured they would refuse to work for her.

Surmising that the less said the better, and praying that her voice wouldn't tremble, Allison began, "I arrived in town yesterday, so as yet I know nothing about the situation here. I have nothing to say to you now, but please plan for a staff meeting here on Monday morning. By that time, I will have made some plans."

After she sat down, gloomy over her inadequate words, Curnutt stood again.

"I'm sure that Miss Sayre will appreciate the same faithfulness and cooperation that you gave Harrison Page. We'll take a tour of the plant this afternoon, and the supervisors should provide any information that will facilitate Miss Sayre's adjustment. You may return to work now, except I would like Benton and Celestine to remain for a few minutes."

As the employees filed out, Allison turned eagerly to see which one was Benton Lockhart. A middle-aged woman remained seated, as did a strong, broad-shouldered young man with a close-clipped beard that matched his tawny hair. When the other employees were gone, Curnutt closed the door into the hallway.

"I asked you to remain to give you copies of Harrison's will since both of you are named in it. He left each of you 5 percent of his total estate, and since I estimate his assets are nearly three million dollars, that should be an ample amount for both of you." When he handed them the envelopes, he said, "I'm counting on both of you to assist Miss Sayre as she takes over the reins here."

Celestine dabbed at tearful eyes with a tissue, but she smiled at Allison as she left the room. Benton hadn't moved and Allison walked toward him. He observed her approach with cool, steady gray eyes sparkling with tiny golden flecks that matched the mellow tints in his hair.

"I'm wondering if you're the same Benton Lockhart I met several years ago in Indianapolis."

"I've been in Indianapolis several times, so that's possible."

"You wouldn't remember me, but the man I met spoke at an evangelical youth crusade. If you were that person, I want you to know you made a tremendous impact on my life."

Benton's gray eyes didn't change expression, but Allison sensed a chillness settle around him, and his lips twisted in a sardonic smile that didn't reach his eyes.

"Let me assure you, Miss Sayre, that I am not the same man you heard speak in that spiritual crusade." He looked past her at the attorney. "If that's all, Mr. Curnutt; I have a client calling in five minutes."

Allison's disappointment was intense. One of the things that had bolstered her during her goodbyes in Chicago and assuaged her fear of taking charge of her uncle's affairs had been the thought that she might see Benton Lockhart, who could provide the encouragement and guidance she needed during this tumultuous period of her life. Now that her hopes had been dashed, she couldn't take much interest in the tour of the building.

As Benton moved toward the exit, his glance caught and held Allison's, and he held out his hand. She was hardly prepared for the jolt that shot up her arm when she met his outstretched fingers, or the warmth in his voice when he said, "I hope your ownership of Page Publishing will be as prosperous and rewarding as it was for your uncle." With a nod in the lawyer's direction, he left the room. Was he or was he not the Benton Lockhart she'd once known?

Behind the conference room was a well-equipped kitchen. "This is used by the employees for preparing their lunches," Curnutt explained. "The conference room doubles as a dining room. On special occasions the management has food catered for the staff.''

The rest of the first floor was the shipping department, which was supervised by Calvin Smith. A man in his thirties, Smith's careless good looks were accentuated by bold, baby-blue eyes and thick brown hair. He shook hands with Allison and welcomed her to the company.

''Miss Sayre's advent has deflated Lockhart, hasn't it, Mr. Curnutt? He has enjoyed being top dog around here.''

''He didn't seem deflated to me,'' Curnutt said quietly as they moved on, and Allison wondered if Benton would resent her ownership.

Taking the service elevator, Curnutt said, ''Let's go to the top and start down.''

The fifth floor was used for storage, so they spent little time there; the fourth floor housed the printing shop, and although she knew very little about it, Allison was impressed by the functional electronic equipment. ''Obviously Page Publishing has the very latest in electronic ware,'' she said.

''Thanks mostly to Benton Lockhart. Harrison was more conservative in his methods, and as most people of our generation, he understood very little about the computer world. To give him credit, he knew his limitations and followed Benton's advice. Benton has an engineering degree, as well as a degree in computer science.''

The bookkeeping and billing departments were on the third floor, and numerous computer stations were grouped around the room. ''Harrison placed key people as supervisors in each department,'' Curnutt explained, ''and he didn't try to learn the whole business himself, nor should you expect to. As long as the company was making a decent profit, he assumed the employees were doing the job they were assigned to do. I know you're worried about how to manage the business, but you shouldn't encounter any problems. Meet regularly with the supervisors from each department, ask for weekly reports from them, and as you study them, you'll learn all you need to know. Perhaps until you know what's going on, the supervisors should be accountable to Benton and Benton will be accountable to you. Any firing or hiring in the lower ranks should be handled by the supervisors.''

"But shouldn't I have the final word in case of controversies between employees?''

"That's debatable. You remember that Moses of biblical history was trying to handle all the controversies between the Hebrews, and his father-in-law convinced Moses that he should observe a chain of command. The company belongs to you, but I'd be mighty careful about meddling in situations between the supervisors and those who work for them.''

Three offices constituted the second floor, which was the main entrance into the building. The customers came first to Celestine's office, a large room that contained several chairs for customers, her neat computer station and rows of filing cabinets. The room was carpeted and heavy draperies hung at the two windows and muffled the noisy traffic on Broad Street. Benton's office was to the left, and since he was busy with a customer, Curnutt told Allison she could talk with him later.

Celestine Handley was dark haired with wide cheekbones, and although her skin exhibited some lines of middle age, she was still a beautiful woman. Her dark-green eyes were clear, steadfast, unfaltering, and Allison felt that with this woman's support, she could take on the mantle that Harrison Page had cast upon her.

Celestine opened the door into the owner's office, where a large portrait of Harrison Page hung behind the desk. Allison had forgotten what he looked like, for she hadn't seen him for ten years, but she recognized him immediately, and his resemblance to her mother was startling. The office furniture in the room was worn, but still in good repair. Celestine went behind the desk and opened a drawer. She handed a key ring to Allison.

"Miss Sayre—" she began.

But Allison interrupted. "Please, call me 'Allison'. Being addressed as 'Miss Sayre' makes me feel ancient." Turning to the attorney, she said, "And you, too, please. That way, I won't feel such a stranger."

"Of course," he agreed.

"Allison," Celestine started again, a smile lighting her brilliant eyes, "these keys belonged to your uncle. There's a key here to everything in this building. I don't know that Mr. Page had any occasion to use them, but it was simply a symbol of his ownership. He could investigate anything he wanted to." She dropped the large set of keys back into the drawer and handed Allison a ring with two keys on it. "These are the ones you should carry. They open the front and rear entrances and your office door."

"This will be your office, Allison," Curnutt said. "Don't you want to try on the owner's chair for size?" He smiled at her.

"No, not today," Allison said, and her facial features felt frozen. Almost as if it were an animate object, the massive leather chair terrified her.

Perhaps sensing Allison's stress, Celestine said, "Do you have time for a cup of coffee or tea?"

When the attorney assented, Celestine motioned them to a cozy corner of her office. They sat in easy chairs, and Curnutt took up the morning newspaper, placed conveniently for the company's visitors. He offered Allison a section of the paper, but her mind was too muddled to concentrate on reading.

Celestine opened a nearby louvered door into a small kitchenette. "I have coffee ready, and hot water for tea," she said, "but we have juice and soft drinks, too."

Allison wasn't normally a coffee drinker, but the stress of the day was wearing on her, and she needed a stimulant of some kind. After Celestine served Curnutt and Allison with coffee and placed a fruit tray on the table before them, she prepared a small tray, tapped on Benton's door and

served him and his customer. Allison munched on some
grapes, sipped the hot coffee and contemplated the day's
activities. Perhaps the situation wasn't as bad as she had
suspected. She had detected no outright hostility among the
employees, and in time, she might win their confidence.
Celestine, who displayed all the charm of a hostess in her
own home, had done much to put Allison at ease.

While Celestine was busy at her desk and Curnutt was
absorbed in the newspaper, Allison reviewed her conversation with Benton Lockhart. She wished that she had
brought the album containing the picture of the Benton
she'd met in Indianapolis, for, in spite of his denial, she
thought he was the same person she had met there. His
neatly trimmed whiskers did cover most of his facial features, but one of the things she had most remembered about
Benton had been his tawny hair and warm gray eyes.

*Let me assure you, Miss Sayre, that I am not the same
man you heard speak in that spiritual crusade.* That could
be interpreted in various ways—it could mean that he was
the same person, but his attitude had changed, or it could
mean that he had not been there. She couldn't figure it out.
And what good would it do her if she did learn the truth?
It wouldn't be wise to delve into the man's past. If she
learned how to manage this firm, it would be with the help
of Benton Lockhart; she couldn't antagonize him.

After Celestine answered the phone a couple of times
and searched out some files, which she delivered to Benton's office, she joined them with a glass of juice in her
hand. "I suppose Columbus seems like a small town to you
after living in Chicago," she said.

"I didn't realize what a large area Chicago covered until
I saw it from the airplane when we flew down here a few
weeks ago to see Mr. Curnutt. We live in the suburbs and
do most of our shopping in the area where we live. We go
to downtown Chicago only for special events. But I think
Columbus is a fine city, and I'm sure I'll like living here.
Could you advise me about finding a small furnished apart-

ment? I want something fairly close to this business and
not too expensive."

Curnutt laid aside his paper. "Allison, I know it's difficult for you to comprehend, but you're a very rich woman
now and you don't have to be conservative in your choice
of living quarters. It will be several months before you have
complete control of Harrison's property, but I'll instruct the
bookkeeper here to put you on the payroll, and you'll receive a bimonthly salary as do the employees. Harrison
drew a modest salary, just enough to take care of his expenses, and allowed the rest of the profit to build up the
coffers of the company. I would suggest that you do the
same for the time being. Do you have any way to anticipate
your expenses?"

"I made twenty thousand dollars yearly at my previous
job. On that I lived in my own apartment, had a car and
saved a little money."

"We'll double that amount until you see how much you
need."

Allison pulled at the collar of her blouse, feeling as if
her breathing had been hampered. Forty thousand dollars a
year! Her father had supported a wife and three children
on less than that. Why would a single woman need so
much?

"But about your living quarters," Curnutt continued, "I
had assumed that you would live in Harrison's home, which
is yours now."

"Oh, yes, Allison, you must consider living there," Celestine insisted. "It's a wonderful house."

"Didn't you say it was a three-story home? I don't need
that much room, and wouldn't the upkeep be expensive?"

He smiled, and she knew he was amused by her conservatism, but her parents had had no choice but to be conservative; otherwise they couldn't have supported a family
on one salary so Beatrice could stay home and take care of
the children. Even with riches at her disposal, it was a habit
she wouldn't lose easily.

"I'm sure your uncle would be pleased with your attitude toward wealth, for he wasn't a big spender himself, and you're right, the house is expensive to maintain. Although Harrison didn't make any stipulation whether you should sell or keep the house, I suggest that you live there for a period of time before you make the decision. It is a large house, but the caretakers occupy the third floor and take care of cleaning and maintenance, so it shouldn't be a burden to you."

"Even sight unseen, I'm willing to take your advice, but I would like to see the house when it's convenient for you to take me."

He checked his watch and took his appointment book from his pocket. "We can go right now. I have a dinner appointment at six o'clock, but we have time." Turning to Celestine, he said, "Please telephone Minerva that we'll be there in fifteen minutes."

The lawyer traveled on High Street until he turned left on Buttles, drove past Goodale Park to Neil Avenue, where he turned north again. The quiet atmosphere of the area and the Victorian homes on both sides of the street made Allison feel as if she had stepped back in time. Would the Brontë sisters wander out of one of the doors on their way to church? Perhaps Mary Todd Lincoln would be peering from a window, anxiously waiting for her tardy husband. Craning her neck to see each house they passed, Allison was impressed with the asymmetrical brick-and-stucco homes, many massed around a central tower or spire, marked by steeply pitched roofs and narrow arched windows accentuated by hood moldings.

Curnutt drove a couple of blocks before parking the car at street level. He pointed to a massive brick building.

"This surely isn't it!"

"Harrison Page bought this house about twenty-five years ago. After his wife died, he devoted his time to decorating and furnishing the home as it would have been when it was first built. The house is yours now, and I hope you'll be pleased with the results of his efforts. Shall we go in?''

''Allow me to sit here for a few minutes and take this all in. Yesterday I thought of a nursery rhyme about an old woman whose appearance was altered, and she kept saying, 'Lawk a mercy on me, this is none of I!' I don't even feel like myself. Nor do I know my own mind. Am I grateful to Uncle Harrison for gifting me with all these material possessions, or should I resent his interference with a life-style that has been sufficient for twenty-four years? Ownership of this house is more daunting than ownership of the publishing company. I don't know how I can cope with this change in my life.''

Curnutt gave Allison a fond look that she didn't see, but he was pleased with her, and furthermore, he knew now that Page had made the right decision to convey his estate to this woman, although Curnutt had counseled against the move. In the few hours he had known Allison, he had observed the same qualities in her that had made Harrison Page a respected and wealthy man—determination, loyalty to duty, conservatism and intelligence. He silently thanked God that he had been given the privilege of introducing this young woman to a new world—one in which she would undoubtedly make mistakes, but also one in which he believed she would ultimately triumph.

Allison's eager eyes took in every detail of the huge house. A brick pathway from the street traversed a small lawn, and two large marble urns stood beside the three stone steps that provided access to a wide porch with a crested roof supported by six round Ionic wooden columns. The porch was surrounded by a wooden railing sustained by elaborately turned balusters. Two slender junipers, their tops projecting above the porch roof, stood like sentries on each side of the steps, and groupings of low evergreens and shrubbery were arranged around their trunks.

The three-storied redbrick house was divided into three

sections. On the left was a rounded turret crowned by a conical spire. The middle section was dominated at the second story by a curved leaded glass window in a floral design capped by a stone lintel, and to the right, uncovered by the porch, bay windows marked both the first- and second-floor levels. Several brick chimneys projected like sentinels from the steep gray slate roof. Such a home was worthy of a president or even a king; it couldn't be hers.

Her eyes shining, she said, "It's a beautiful building. I'm ready to go in now."

With all the eagerness of a man playing Santa Claus, Curnutt opened the car door for Allison. Tingling with excitement, a broad smile lighting her face, Allison walked briskly up the steps and stopped before double walnut doors embellished by curvilinear floral designs in clear leaded glass. Above the doors was an oblong leaded window that matched the door panels. Curnutt reached around her and turned the old-fashioned doorbell.

As though she had been waiting, the right door was opened by a tall, angular woman with high cheekbones accentuated by steel gray hair pulled back and tightly wound into a small bun at her nape. Dressed as she was in a trim gray dress, she could easily have stepped out of the Victorian era.

"Welcome, come in," she said in a pleasing voice that sounded as if she meant it. Behind her hovered a portly man dressed in a flannel shirt and denim overalls.

Allison and Curnutt stepped into the warm, high-ceilinged foyer, which Allison realized was larger than the living and dining room put together of her family's house back in Chicago. Allison's eyes were drawn immediately to the spiral stairway with graceful scrolled railings that terminated on a landing on the second floor. A brass chandelier with tiers of crystal pendants hung from a leaf-filigreed ceiling medallion. Burgundy carpeting covered the stair treads, and the foyer floor of darkly varnished hard-

wood was brightened with two Oriental rugs. The walls
were a neutral tone of pale blue.

The foyer was long and narrow, with four steps at the
rear of the hall leading to the kitchen area. To the left of
the doorway was a massive walnut hall tree, with several
hats suspended from the hangers. Facing them was a
longcase clock that melodiously chimed the hour.

Sizing up every detail of the house, Allison hadn't
moved since she'd set foot in the hallway. She was brought
out of her trance by a gentle tug on her arm.

"Allison, I want you to meet Adra and Minerva Mc-
Ramey. They're important fixtures in this house."

Trying to shake the cobwebs from her head, Allison said,
"I'm pleased to meet you. I apologize for being impolite.
I've never been in this grand a house before."

She shook hands with both of them, and Adra's rosy face
beamed at her.

"We're glad to see you, Miss Sayre. Mr. Page was a
quiet man, and he never talked about his family. We knew
he had a sister somewhere, but we sure didn't know he had
any kin as pretty as you. How come none of you ever
visited him? After his wife died, Harrison was lonely, and
there was plenty of room in this big house."

"As far as I know, we never had an invitation to visit
him. It always puzzled me why he and Mother weren't
more friendly."

"We're glad you're here now," Minerva said. "What do
you think of the house?"

"If the rest of the house is anything like this foyer, I
want to keep it." She gave Thomas Curnutt an anxious
look. "That is, if you think I can afford it. The taxes and
upkeep on a building of this size must be horrendous."

"Nothing you can't afford if you want to live here. Let's
continue our tour. The living room, originally called the
parlor, and dining room are to the left. Harrison spent a
great deal of time and money furnishing these rooms with

genuine antique pieces of the period. Even the lamps and vases and such are antiques," he added.

A fireplace fronted with gray marble, with a slab of matching marble as a mantel, over which hung a lighted picture of a woman in formal dress of the Victorian era, was the focal point when one entered the room. A brown leather sofa and two soft armchairs upholstered in flowery chintz were grouped around a large oval coffee table placed on an Oriental rug. A delicate brass chandelier with a few crystal prisms hung from a ceiling medallion over the coffee table. A nineteenth-century wooden bench covered with needlepoint was to their right, and a grand piano stood along the wall that looked out on the street.

"This room seems as if it has never been used."

"Mr. Page didn't entertain much, and he spent all his time in the office across the hall," Minerva said. Motioning to the adjoining room, she added, "He did like his meals served in the dining room."

She led them into the dining room, designed with a fireplace identical to the one in the parlor; a portrait of a wigged Victorian gentleman hung over it. A glittering crystal chandelier shed a soft glow over an oval oak table covered with an ecru crocheted tablecloth. Eight cane-back chairs stood around the table, a hutch displayed a set of English bone china and a corner cupboard contained a dazzling array of deeply cut crystal. A garish tree-of-life wallpaper accented the wall above the dark three-foot wainscoting.

Opposite the parlor and dining room was Harrison's office, masculine and overwhelming with its dark wooden furniture, walnut paneling and parqueted floor.

"This could do with a bit of bright color," Allison said.

"I agree with you, Miss," Minerva said, "but Mr. Page was a rather somber man. You'll like the library next door."

"Oh, yes," Allison said when she entered the library, as bright as the noonday sun. A glazed chintz lounge stood between two windows hung with balloon curtains. A needlepoint rug covered the floor. Two wicker chairs were upholstered with the same chintz as the lounge and a floral-patterned fabric was draped over the bay window, which looked out to a landscaped garden area. Several needlepoint cushions were displayed throughout the room, and the seats of many small chairs were upholstered with a variety of patterns, ranging from small-scaled flowers with muted backgrounds to a few that portrayed parrots and other tropical birds in bright floral settings.

"Who has done all this handwork?" Allison said, admiring a cushion that had a lifelike representation of a macaw. She appreciated the many hours of painstaking work that had gone into the crocheted doilies and other finely done handwork in the house because her mother always had a needlepoint project under way.

"I've done a lot of the crocheting, but Mrs. Page did the intricate work," Minerva said. "Being an invalid, she devoted most of her time to creating with her needle."

Noting that there was a desk and chair in one corner of the library, Allison decided this was where she would spend most of her time, rather than in the more formal rooms.

The kitchen had all the modern conveniences—waste disposal, microwave, dishwasher—and Allison clapped her hands in joy when she saw the rounded dinette adjacent to the kitchen. Located in the turret, the dining area was lighted by three curved windows accentuated by airy lace curtains. A round pedestal oak table placed on a ceramic tile floor had four matching chairs around it. A potted African violet bloomed profusely in the middle of the table, and other plants stood on the window ledge.

Allison drew back the curtains and looked out on a high laurel hedge that hid the house next door. Two white iron benches were grouped around an oval matching table, and a tall Greek statue overlooked the scene.

"Oh, what a lovely place! When we look out our kitchen window at home, we see the house next door." Donald's house, she thought quickly and pushed the memory aside. "I'll love having my meals here."

"Do you have time for a serving of banana cream pie?" Minerva asked.

"I am in a hurry," Curnutt said, "but I'll never turn down your pie."

They sat in the dinette alcove, and while they waited to be served, Allison said, "This is the most fabulous home I've ever seen. I'll try it for several months anyway. It may prove too much for me, and I may feel lost here. Our whole home in Chicago isn't a quarter this large. It scares me in a way, but I do feel at home already."

When Minerva brought the pie and a beverage, Curnutt pulled out the extra chairs and said, "Sit down, Minerva, and you, too, Adra. You should be involved in any plans we make for this house."

Adra declined pie, but drank a cup of coffee.

"First of all, Allison, when do you want to move in?" the attorney said.

"Why not tomorrow? I don't see any reason to pay for a hotel room when this house is standing empty."

Minerva nodded approvingly.

The attorney turned to the McRameys. "I assume that you're willing to stay with Allison under the same arrangements you had with Harrison."

"More than willing," Adra said. "We like it here."

"What are the arrangements?" Allison asked.

"They are paid a salary of one thousand dollars a month, which is all they can earn and still draw their Social Security, but they have free room and board, so it's a good deal for them. In return for this compensation, Adra takes care of the outdoor work and does general maintenance work. Minerva is the housekeeper, and she did Harrison's cooking."

"That sounds like more of a bargain for me than for you," Allison said. "This house is too large for one woman to take care of. You should have additional help."

"A cleaning service comes in twice each year to wash the windows and give everything a thorough cleaning," Minerva said, "but I manage well enough the rest of the time, though you're sweet to be concerned."

Curnutt looked at his watch. "Let's see the rest of the house. I don't want to be late for my appointment."

They climbed the wide stairway, Allison in the lead, with the three adults trailing her, each eager to point out interesting things about the house.

Mrs. Page had occupied the turret bedroom and Allison liked it best. A white delicately scrolled iron bed with pale-blue dust ruffle was covered with a handmade quilt. The small desk, rocking chair, bookshelves, nightstand, dressing table and a storage chest at the foot of the bed were all white wicker. The rocking chair was cushioned with a delicate fabric, and richly ruffled curtains enlivened the windows that overlooked the back lawn.

"And my own private bathroom, too," Allison exclaimed when she saw the room with modern pastel-blue fixtures. "This is a suite any woman would enjoy, and it looks like paradise to me."

Two other bathrooms and four bedrooms were located on the second floor. The third floor, occupied by the McRameys, was reached by a narrow stairway that opened from the kitchen or through a small door from the second floor.

"Those steps are steep to climb several times a day, aren't they?" Allison said as she scanned them.

"I don't mind the walking," Minerva said, "but there's a service elevator that Mr. Page put in several years ago for his wife's convenience, so we don't have to walk if we don't want to."

"There's a full-sized basement for utility purposes," Adra offered.

"I've seen enough for one day. I'm so excited now that I probably won't be able to sleep tonight."

Allison glanced around the upper hall one more time,

and Curnutt looked at his watch as the hall clock struck five times.

"For the present, just plan on preparing my dinner," Allison said to Minerva. "I'll take care of my own breakfast and pack a lunch to take to work with me. I'm used to looking after myself. And if it's all right, I'll move in tomorrow morning. I will have lots of unpacking to do, and that will give me two days before I go to work on Monday."

"Which room should I prepare for you, Miss Sayre?"

"I want the one previously occupied by Aunt Sarah. And will both of you call me 'Allison'? I want to consider you friends rather than employees, for I have a feeling I'm going to need all the friends I can find before this first year is over."

Curnutt and Allison rode in silence back to the hotel, and when he stopped his car in front of the entrance, he asked, "Do you want me to help you move?"

"No, that isn't necessary. I didn't unpack my car, and Adra can help me when I get to the house."

"I'll check with you tomorrow to see how you're adjusting. I hope you can sleep tonight."

"I doubt that I will. Right now, I've been elevated to the heights, but I'm levelheaded enough to know that only a little jolt can topple me to the other extreme."

He patted her on the hand. "Allison, you'll be fine. I predict that within a year you'll know as much about Page Publishing as Harrison did."

His encouragement was welcome, for while she didn't feel as desolate and afraid as she had this morning, Allison knew she was heading into an uphill marathon.

Chapter Three

When she reached her room, Allison kicked off her shoes,
dropped down in the lounge chair and pulled the lever to
elevate her feet. She welcomed this evening alone to sort
out her thoughts and impressions. Right now, her mind was
a hodgepodge of crystal chandeliers, opulent furniture, cut
crystal, chintz wall hangings and leaded-glass windows.
How could she get past all that glitter and grapple with the
real issues that confronted her?

It would be easy to succumb to the worries and frustrations of coping with Page Publishing Company, working
with an investment broker to keep from losing her uncle's
money and supervising numerous employees, as well as
living in a fabulous home that plunged her mentally into
the nineteenth century. To be so overwhelmed, in fact, that
she could forget about the important things in life. At this
point, she was more worried about losing her identity and
her purpose in life by becoming Miss New Rich than she
was about managing a million-dollar business.

God, she prayed aloud, *I can't cope with this alone.
Show me how I can bring myself down to earth when I tend
to lose sight of my eternal destiny.*

Allison reached for the Bible on the table beside her and turned on the table lamp. For the next hour, she pored over the Scriptures, searching for the doctrines she must heed to stay on the right path, and she was amazed at the abundance of Bible passages that dealt with her immediate concern— how she could balance an abundance of worldly goods with the riches of God's blessings.

"Remember the Lord your God, for it is He who gives you the ability to produce wealth."

Had her uncle followed this precept? Did he recognize the power of God in his life? How she wished she knew more about her benefactor.

"Cast but a glance at riches, and they are gone, for they will surely sprout wings."

A good proverb to remember. Though she desired to be heavenly minded, if she didn't keep her feet solidly on the earth and tend to important matters of business, her riches would certainly take wing.

"The abundance of a rich man permits him no sleep."

How true! She hadn't enjoyed a restful night's sleep since she had learned about her inheritance.

"Do not store up for yourselves treasures on earth."

Ah! There was the principle that concerned her. The rich young ruler had been told to sell all he had and give the proceeds to the poor as a prerequisite for discipleship. Did that principle apply to Allison Sayre, too? She had wanted to sell everything, but legally she couldn't. She tried to think of rich people who had also been faithful followers, and she considered many wealthy entrepreneurs such as the Carnegies and the Penneys who gave vast sums for benevolent purposes. Nicodemus and Joseph of Arimathea had both been rich, yet they weren't told to give up their wealth. Apparently there was a need for rich people in God's kingdom, but it wasn't easy she surmised when she read, "How hard it is for the rich to enter the kingdom of God."

I'm getting discouraged, God—all I can find are warnings to those who are rich. I gained this wealth through no

*effort of my own. I don't even want the responsibility of so
many riches, but since I do have it, can't You give me some
assurance that it was Your providence that brought me
where I am now? Surely there are some Scriptures to encourage me.*

Looking a little further, Allison came upon the passage
"For if the willingness is there, the gift is acceptable according to what one has, not according to what he does not
have." She suspected that Paul had written those words to
people who were poor, but couldn't it apply to her, as well?
She was willing to use her riches to advance God's kingdom and to benefit others. Shouldn't that count for something? Her greatest comfort came when she read Paul's
admonition in his letter to the Ephesians: "work, doing
something useful with his own hands that he may have
something to share with those in need." She had often fretted in the past when she lacked the funds to contribute
abundantly to worthy causes—missionaries in foreign
countries, those afflicted by natural disasters, the plight of
the poor in the city of Chicago. Now she would have
money to give to charitable causes. What would she do with
the opportunity?

Deciding that she must stop anticipating the future and
deal with individual problems as they arose, Allison read
one more verse: "I can do everything through Him who
gives me strength." Did she need any more assurance than
that? She closed the Bible and prepared to go for the evening meal. After the tasty lunch she had eaten and the pie
Minerva had served a few hours ago, Allison didn't want
a large meal. Rather than eat in the dining room downstairs,
she leafed through the visitor's guide on the desk and decided to go to a pizza house a few blocks away.

She freshened her makeup, drew a comb through her
shoulder-length hair and telephoned the concierge to order
a taxi for her. The elevators were crowded and the taxi was
waiting by the time she got downstairs, but within ten
minutes she was entering the restaurant. While she was

studying the menu on the wall behind the counter, she heard her name.

"How are you tonight, Miss Sayre?"

Benton Lockhart was standing in line behind her.

"I'm fine, but puzzling over what to order. I've eaten more today than I usually do, and I'm not very hungry."

"You might want to try the buffet, which features a variety of pizza, several salads and a small selection of desserts. You can choose as much or as little as you want. That's what I have when I eat here."

Taking his advice, Allison ordered the buffet, and as she paid the cashier, wondering if she should be so bold, she said, "If you're dining alone, Mr. Lockhart, would you mind if I join you? Perhaps we could talk a bit about Page Publishing after we've finished."

"It will be my pleasure," Benton said evenly, without hesitation.

But Allison wasn't sure he wanted to join her.

He lifted both their trays and asked, "Where would you like to sit?"

"The section to our left doesn't seem to be crowded."

He motioned for Allison to precede him toward a booth near the buffet counter. With a minimum of conversation, they filled their plates, and as they started eating, Allison said, "Perhaps I should apologize for interrupting your meal, but I do need to talk with you, and this seemed like a good opportunity. It's obvious that you have a busy schedule at the office."

"Yes, busier than usual today. I didn't get finished until an hour ago, and I wasn't keen about going to the apartment and preparing dinner. I often stop here when I don't want to cook."

"Then you aren't married?"

"No," he said bluntly, definitely closing that subject.

Allison took a bite of double-cheese pizza, and talking was halted for the moment. As the meal progressed, Allison became more and more uncomfortable, for guiding the con-

versation was left to her. Benton would answer when she
made a comment, but he initiated nothing. Although she
wanted to know lots of things about him, especially if she
had met him before, he seemingly had no interest whatever
in her. Much of the time they ate in silence, a silence that
Allison found intimidating.

For dessert Allison took a small wedge of fruit pizza
topped with kiwifruit, strawberries and peaches, and asked
the waitress for a cup of tea. Benton ordered a serving of
apple cobbler topped with a double dip of ice cream, and
he smiled slightly. "I don't usually have such a large appetite, but I didn't take time for lunch today."

"Do you always work such long hours?"

"Since Mr. Page fell ill I average ten hours each day at
the office."

"Perhaps now that I'm here I can take some of the work-
load off you. Naturally, I don't expect to learn everything
I need to know at once, but surely I can be of help to you
if you'll tell me what I should do."

"But you have the roles reversed, Miss Sayre. You're
the employer—you will be telling *me* what to do." Did
Allison note a bit of sarcasm in his comment? She couldn't
tell. The Benton Lockhart she had met years ago would
have been easy to read, but it seemed impossible to get
behind the facade dominating this man's personality. So
maybe this wasn't the Benton she had once known.

She finished the dessert, pushed the bowl to one side and
pulled the cup of tea in front of her. She smiled and said,
"I'm not foolish enough to think I can assume the management of Page Publishing for a long time. After I came
to Columbus and found out the extent of Uncle Harrison's
holdings, I was terrified and asked Mr. Curnutt if I could
just sell everything and get out from under the burden, but
there's a codicil to the will that I can't sell the business for
three years."

"I had no idea what provisions Mr. Page had made for

his holdings. He was a very private person, as you may well know.''

Allison shook her head. "You knew him much better than I did. Our family rarely saw him. How long did you work for him?"

"Five years. I worked in all the departments before I became Mr. Page's assistant."

"So you know the business from top to bottom?"

"I suppose you could say that."

"May I depend upon you to teach me the things that I need to know?"

"I'm yours to command, Miss Sayre. I'll do what you tell me to do."

Allison frowned. "I don't like that type of relationship. I've never 'bossed' anyone, and I don't know how it's done. In fact, I don't want to come across as a boss, especially to people who have worked a long time for my uncle."

"You have no choice. Since you seem to want advice…" He paused and looked expectantly at Allison, and she nodded. "Whether you wanted it or not, you have become the administrator of a company with thirty-five employees. You cannot fraternize with your workers. If you do, you're going to have people asking for favors, and you'll create more ill will than the good relationships you're hoping to foster. You will have to treat all your employees on an impersonal basis."

"That sounds like a rather lonely life."

"Make friends outside the company."

"Even Celestine? I've already asked her to call me by my given name."

His widening smile made his face relaxed and generous. "Celestine is in a different category—she mothers all of us. We can always count on her to smooth over the ill feelings."

He dropped a tip on the table and stood up. "I have to be on my way, Miss Sayre. I'm expecting a telephone call

at ten o'clock, and I must be home by then. May I drop
you off at the hotel?''

"No, thank you. I'll finish my tea before I call a taxi."

"Very well. I'll see you at the office on Monday."

Allison stared down at the teacup and blinked her eyelids
to hold back the tears. She thought Benton's behavior was
downright rude, but she had to admit she had brought it
upon herself. She shouldn't have asked to join him. After
working ten hours, he had probably had enough of Page
Publishing for one day, but that didn't keep her from feeling lonely.

After returning to the hotel, Allison took a sheet of sta-
tionery from the drawer and wrote a short note to her sister,
Cleta:

> Don't say anything about this to the others, but please
> look in that photo album I showed you, remove the
> picture of Donald and me with Benton Lockhart and
> mail it to me. You'll know which one I mean.

This encounter tonight had almost convinced her that she
had not found the Benton Lockhart she had admired, but
she wanted to take another look at that photo.

Adra was watching for Allison the next morning, and
moving quickly for a man with his age and girth, he hustled
down the front steps when she pulled up to the curb in
front of the house and opened the right-hand door.

"You can park in the driveway to the left of the house,
Allison. That belongs to you, and it will be a lot safer than
if we try to unload here on the street. Neil Avenue has a
lot of traffic on Saturday mornings."

He closed the door and she eased the automobile into
the narrow driveway that led to a one-car garage separated
from the house.

Minerva opened and closed the kitchen door as Adra and

Allison emptied her car and carried her things upstairs. When they'd finished, Allison said, "Should I put my car in the garage?"

"Our truck is in there now, but we can move it out," Adra offered.

"Oh, no, my car is used to sitting out in the weather." She locked the car doors, and they went into the warm kitchen, where Minerva had some hot chocolate for them.

The sun shone through the windows while they sat at the round table in the alcove, and the friendliness of these two people softened the hard core that had been around her heart since last night's episode with Benton. They chatted as if she were family—they didn't seem to think an employer-employee relationship was so important.

The McRameys had no children, and they had sold their farm and moved to Columbus several years ago. "I miss being in the country," Adra said, "but our property was right at the edge of the city and developments kept edging closer, making the property so valuable that we couldn't afford to pay our taxes. So we sold out, and when we were looking for a place, we were directed to Mr. Page. He needed some help and we needed a home. It's been a good life for us."

"What was the nature of Uncle Harrison's illness? No one has told me."

Minerva tapped her chest. "Heart trouble. He had a series of heart attacks that damaged his heart. The last few months he had to have oxygen and constant monitoring, and he chose to go to the nursing home, although we would have taken care of him."

"I believe Aunt Sarah's trouble was multiple sclerosis?"

"Yes, she was very young when the doctors diagnosed her. She was an intelligent woman and talented, but she hardly left the house after we came here, and he stayed close by her in the evenings, waiting on her hand and foot," Minerva said. "He acted guilty sometimes, as if he blamed

himself for her sickness and couldn't do enough to make
up for it. She died seven years ago. His life wasn't easy.''

"I wish I could have known them," Allison said as she
stood up. "I must get busy if I'm unpacked and ready to
go to work on Monday. My time will be limited after that."

"If there's anything we can do, let us know. I cleared
everything out of the closets and chests in your room and
the other bedrooms have empty closets. For storage, there
are rooms on the third floor we don't use."

"Perhaps we can store the boxes up there after I've unpacked."

"Just let Adra know. I'm simmering a pot of soup in our
apartment. Plan to eat lunch with us, and I'll prepare your
dinner down here. There's a small door you can take from
the second floor to access our stairway. Come on up when
you're ready to eat."

Allison had organized her garments by seasonal wear and
marked the boxes accordingly. She unpacked her winter
clothes and hung them in the room she would occupy, and
carried the boxes of spring and summer clothing into one
of the spare bedrooms. She would leave them packed for
the time being. She stopped at noon and took the stairs to
the McRameys' quarters.

The small stairway opened into their living room, a central squarish area that accessed the other major rooms. The
kitchen was marked by a spire that served as a skylight
over the McRameys' table. Their two bedrooms featured
dormer windows. After lunch Minerva took Allison into the
storage area—odd-shaped rooms that provided plenty of
space. The rooms were crowded with castoffs, and Minerva
said, "When you have time, you may want to go through
here and throw away a lot of stuff. Some of it is junk and
should never have been stored."

Rubbing her hand along a dusty dresser, Allison said
with a laugh, "If it's been here for years, I'll not worry
about it now. If I learn how to manage Page Publishing,
I'll have all I can do for a long time." And she was deter-

mined to learn the business, whether or not Benton was willing to help her. "I'll have my sister and brother come for a visit sometime and turn them loose up here. They'll carry away everything my mother will let them have." She had been thinking about her parents off and on all day, and she said slowly, "My mother didn't want me to move to Columbus."

A note of wistfulness must have crept into Allison's voice, for Minerva's arm circled her shoulders. "Mothers are like that," she said. "We all have to cast off on our own eventually. You'll be all right."

"I want to spend some time looking around this house, getting to know what is here. Perhaps that way I can learn something about my aunt and uncle."

"A good idea. You'll find lots of reminders of them."

"I'm going to telephone my parents and tell them where I am, and then I'll get busy again."

She went into the library to phone and was relieved when her father answered, for she felt better able to cope with him than her mother.

"I've moved into Uncle Harrison's home, Daddy, and I want you to have my telephone number."

"Are you living there alone?"

"No, a fine couple who have worked for Uncle Harrison for years will be staying with me. I like them, and we'll get along well, I'm sure."

"Do you like the house?"

"It's unbelievable, and not as I would have expected a hundred-year-old dwelling to be. It's in excellent repair. Uncle Harrison had it refurbished over the past several years. There are ten rooms besides the third floor where the McRameys live, and a full-sized basement—certainly more room and luxury than I need, but Mr. Curnutt thought I should live here for a few months before I make any decision about selling it."

"It won't hurt you to have some luxury for a change. Before I call your mother to the phone, tell me this—how are *you,* and I don't want any of this, 'I'm fine, Daddy.' I want to know the truth.''

"Scared to death. I met the company's employees yesterday—all thirty-five of them—and I've scheduled another meeting early Monday morning. I don't know what to do, but I'm depending on Mr. Curnutt to help me. The woman who was Uncle Harrison's personal secretary for years is friendly, and I think I can depend on her for advice."

"I'm sure you can," Charles said, and yelled for his wife.

Allison sniffled a little after talking to her parents, but she did some more unpacking and spent several hours wandering around the house, looking in drawers and closets and checking out the books and magazines the Pages had read. She found a Bible belonging to Aunt Sarah, but nothing that revealed whether or not Harrison had been of a religious mind. She merely passed through his office, for she wasn't ready yet to see what was stored in his desk drawers or check through the filing cabinets. The closets in his bedroom were still full of clothes, and she supposed it was up to her to do something with them. While she liked some things about her inheritance, she wasn't sure that she was pleased with the responsibilities her uncle had handed her.

When Allison discovered that Minerva intended to serve her dinner in the huge dining room, she objected. "I will not eat in there. That small table in the kitchen will be fine for all my meals."

"The Pages liked their evening meal to be rather formal."

"I'm not used to that kind of living. Hopefully, I'll have guests later on, but other times I'll eat in the kitchen. It would please me if you and Adra would eat with me."

"We eat our largest meal at noon and don't have much for supper. We'll take dessert with you sometimes."

After dinner, Thomas Curnutt telephoned and invited Allison to go to church with his wife and him the next day.

"Mary also wants you to come to our home for the noon meal."

"I'll accept both invitations with pleasure."

"Then we'll pick you up at nine o'clock."

The McRameys went to their quarters after clearing the kitchen, and the large house became so quiet it was spooky. Rather than watch television in either the office or the library, Allison went to her room and hooked up the portable television she had brought from Chicago. Propped up in bed, she watched her favorite shows until eleven o'clock. She looked at the buzzer at the head of the bed which Minerva said "will bring us on the run."

Lying awake for a long time, Allison was alert to the sounds around her. The house was heated by a hot-water system, and the radiators hissed and crackled as the boiler pumped heat throughout the house. It seemed ridiculous for this huge house to be maintained for one woman. A two-room apartment would take care of her needs adequately. Not that she didn't love the place, but it worried her when such an outlay of money was unnecessary.

Sirens sounded in the distance and cars passed often on Neil Avenue. A brisk wind was blowing sheets of icy rain against the windows, but Allison did feel safe and protected. Her mind was muddled with all the things she had learned about this house today, but she felt more at home now than she had this morning when she had moved in. If that was any indication, perhaps her first days at Page Publishing would not be as frightening as she anticipated.

When Allison couldn't go to sleep, she snapped on the light and reached for her Bible. Starting one's life in a new direction was intimidating, but also exciting. She hadn't thought once today about Donald, which was a step forward in her determination to forbid his memory to dominate her life. Since she had trusted her future to God many years ago, she had tried to be sensitive to His leading, and though she thought she was still trusting during the Donald episode, she had been feeling sorry for herself rather than accepting the loss of Donald as God's will for her life. She was finally able to admit that the situation had worked out for the best.

Allison had the opportunity for something better now, and she was determined to follow God's leading more closely than she had before. As she leafed through the Bible, she came to the Golden Rule: "Do to others as you would have them do to you." Could she make that her motto for living? Not only in her personal relationships, but even managing Page Publishing—would that principle be applicable there? She had to have something to say to the employees on Monday; perhaps she could use the Golden Rule as a challenge.

Before she turned off the light again, Allison read another verse and prayed with the Psalmist: "Send forth Your light and Your truth, let them guide me."

The day with the Curnutts was enjoyable. Their church congregation was large, but the people were friendly, and Allison looked forward to finding a church home there. Thomas and Mary, as they'd asked her to call them, lived in a modern home in Bexley, a suburb of Columbus. The meal consisted of baked chicken breasts topped with Swiss cheese and dressing, green peas as a side dish and a vegetable salad. For dessert, Mary served German chocolate cake.

Allison asked them to take her home by midafternoon. She went upstairs, removed her church clothes, dressed in wool slacks, heavy socks and boots, put on an insulated, hooded hip-length jacket and headed for Goodale Park a few blocks away. The park was rather bleak now, but Allison could visualize the beauty that spring would bring. Cardinals, chickadees and nuthatches flew among the bare tree branches, so there was some color to be seen, but the fountain was drained for the winter, and no one else walked in the park.

Allison was glad for the solitude. She had enjoyed an

idyllic weekend. It had been fun to move into the house, she had appreciated the day with Thomas and Mary and she liked having Adra and Minerva fussing over her. Her parents weren't the kind to do much coddling—at least with their daughters they hadn't been, although Tim got away with too much—and the McRameys had filled a need she didn't know she had. She walked back and forth on the pathways until she was chilled.

The rest of the day passed slowly, and Allison went to bed early and soon slept, but she awakened before the alarm sounded. By five o'clock she had showered and dressed, and though she wasn't hungry, she went downstairs and drank a glass of orange juice and ate a slice of dry toast. At seven o'clock she let herself in the back door at Page Publishing. No one except the janitor had arrived earlier than she.

She went into Harrison's office, closed the door and sat at his desk. She had a meeting at eight o'clock and she had no idea what to say to the staff. Reality had set in. The ball had been tossed to her, and she had to do something with it. Allison thought that she had mastered her fright, thought that on Friday night she had come to grips with the position she had to fill, but it was different this morning. Her hands shook and she struggled to breathe. She dropped her head on the desk.

There was a tap on the door, and Allison lifted her head hurriedly, fearful that it was Benton who would witness her distress. Celestine peered in, and without a word went out and closed the door. Fighting to regain her composure, Allison swiped at her eyes, hoping that Celestine wouldn't tell anyone that she had been crying. The door opened again, and juggling a tray in one hand, Celestine came toward her.

She set the tray, containing a sliced bagel, a packet of cream cheese and a cup of tea, in front of Allison. "Eat," she commanded.

"I can't. I'm too upset."

"Eat. You can't face this day on an empty stomach."

Rather than argue, Allison ate one slice of the bagel and took several sips of tea. Before she started on the other half of the bagel, the phone rang.

"Benton is in his office. He'll answer," Celestine said. "Go ahead and eat."

A light blinked on Allison's phone, and Celestine picked up the receiver, which she handed to Allison. "It's for you."

"Who could be calling me here?" She took the receiver. "Hello?"

"Hi, Sis. This is Tim."

"Tim! Why it's only 6:30 at home! What are you doing up so early?"

"Say, Allison, I've found a great deal on a car, and I wanted to see if you would buy it for me."

Allison was normally slow to anger, but the very absurdity of his call annoyed her. She pushed back the tray. "Do Mother and Dad know you're phoning me?"

"Er, no. I don't want them to know anything about the car until it's bought and paid for."

"Which will be a long time as far as I'm concerned. First of all, I don't want you to telephone me here at the office again. As for buying you a car, no, I will not. I didn't have a car until I could afford to pay for it myself, and you can do the same."

"Allison! I want the car to drive to college. I start my first classes next week."

"You can take a bus to college the same way I did. But I will do this. If you get a job and earn enough money to pay for half the car, I'll loan you the rest of it, but only if Mother and Dad agree."

"I didn't mean to make you mad, Allison."

"Well, you did make me mad, for I have a hard day ahead of me, and I didn't need to be annoyed by you."

When she slammed down the receiver, Celestine was

laughing. Allison was still so angry that she pushed back the chair and paced the room.

"It's not good for me to lose my temper the first day on the job. As you probably gathered, my eighteen-year-old brother thinks he should share in my good fortune. My sister would never have made such a request, but we've spoiled Tim. He has me so rattled I'll botch that staff meeting."

As Celestine removed the tray from the desk, she was still chuckling.

"I don't find it amusing," Allison said somewhat testily.

"I've wondered if Mr. Page made the correct decision in choosing you for his heir, but he could have looked the world over and not found anyone possessing more of the characteristics he admired in people. While you were raking your brother over the coals, you reminded me so much of Mr. Page that I could even imagine he was back in the office. He was very generous whenever there was a need, but if people tried to involve him in a questionable scheme, he would get rid of them in a hurry, almost to the point of rudeness. He was quick to reward employees who did a good job, but the ones who didn't produce didn't get a bonus. He believed that people should take responsibility for their own lives and not expect to have everything handed to them on a silver platter."

"And yet he left me, little more than a stranger, an estate worth three million dollars."

A strange look crossed Celestine's face. "He did, didn't he?"

"And at this moment, I'm not sure I thank him for it."

Celestine set the tray down again. "Perhaps you're not in the mood to accept advice, but I'm going to give some anyway. This first meeting will have a lot to do with your acceptance here. The staff is suspicious of you now, and if you go into that meeting and assume a big-boss manner, pretending to know things you don't, they'll make fun of you. But if you're honest with them, ask for their help and start learning what this company really means, you'll earn their respect. And it won't hurt you to pray. God has brought me through many difficult situations when I asked Him to.''

Allison reached out a hand to Celestine. "Will you pray for me now? I tried to pray this morning, but God seemed silent, and I couldn't make contact.''

Celestine came around the desk and drew Allison into a close embrace, and she remembered Benton's comment about Celestine mothering all of them.

"I have been praying for you, Allison, but I'll pray again." She paused momentarily, as if attuning herself to the attitude of prayer. "God, one of Your children needs assurance this morning. You know, God, that it takes a big person to fill the shoes of Harrison Page, but he's chosen Allison to take that role. Perhaps You have chosen her, too, and she needs to know that at this time. Give her courage, assurance and an extra portion of Your grace as she meets with the employees. Help her cast all her cares on You and to realize that You care for her.''

Celestine released her, and Allison murmured, "Thank you. I don't feel so alone now knowing that we share faith in God.'' She glanced at the clock. "Only ten minutes to get to that meeting, and I don't want to be late.'' She hurried into the powder room adjacent to the office and repaired the damages of the past tumultuous hour.

Allison was calm as she took the elevator downstairs. As on Friday, talking ceased when she entered the room. She said, "Good morning," to everyone in general and sat down behind the podium. When her watch showed nine o'clock, she stood up. Her knees weren't shaking; her hands didn't tremble; her gaze was steady as she established eye contact with her audience; her voice was clear and unfaltering.

"I'm going to lay all the facts before you so that we won't start our relationship with misconceptions. I've been given a job that I didn't ask for, one I wasn't expecting and one I may not be capable of doing. Harrison Page was my mother's only brother, but we saw very little of him. Mother and her children were his only close relatives, and I'm the eldest of the children. Perhaps that was the reason Uncle Harrison chose me to be his heir, but it came as a complete surprise to me.

"My parents didn't want me to leave Chicago, and Mother begged me to either reject the inheritance or sell everything. When I came to Columbus and learned the magnitude of what was before me, I told Mr. Curnutt I wasn't experienced enough to take over this business and I wanted to sell. He informed me that I couldn't sell Page Publishing for three years, so if I don't want to lose my inheritance and you don't want to lose your jobs, we're stuck with one another whether we want to be or not."

She paused to give them time to think about what she had said. She kept her gaze lowered, but she was conscious of the sounds in the room. A faucet dripped in the kitchen, someone was snapping the top of a ballpoint pen, someone else was drumming on the table and one individual coughed discreetly. The tension she had sensed in the room when she entered seemed to have dissipated somewhat.

"Although I've had some publishing experience, I won't pretend that I'm capable of managing this company. I don't know a thing about it, but I'm determined to learn, and if Harrison Page had enough confidence in me to leave me his estate, I'm not going to disappoint him."

She caught Celestine's eye and received an encouraging smile. She glanced in Benton's direction, but he was looking out the window.

"But I can't do it without your help. Unless dire circumstances warrant it, I won't shift personnel positions or make any other major changes for at least a year. I will have to learn the business slowly, so we'll operate on this basis—anyone with a problem, request or question, go to your supervisor first. The next chain of command will be Mr. Lockhart, who will continue in the same capacity he has

served the past year. Any matters that I should handle, he
will refer to me.

"I have much to learn about the operating policy here,
but I intend personally to use the Golden Rule for my mo-
tivation, and I'm asking the rest of you to do the same. If
you don't know what I mean by the Golden Rule, I'll refer
you to a Bible verse that you may have learned in Sunday
school. 'Do to others as you would have them do to you.'
I believe that's a good precept for governing relationships
in business or elsewhere."

Allison couldn't read the expressions on the employees'
faces, but she had their undivided attention. She didn't
know if they were amazed at her words or surprised that
she was taking such complete charge. At that moment Allison didn't care what they thought. Coming down in the
elevator, she had no idea what to say, but once she opened
her mouth, the speech was ready. Divine inspiration? She
couldn't explain it any other way.

"Do you have questions?"

She waited a few minutes, and when no one spoke, she
said, "I will meet with the supervisors and their assistants
the first and third Fridays in each month at eight o'clock.
Full staff meetings will be called when a need arises, but
we will try to notify you well in advance. Thank you. I
appreciate your attention, and I count on you to cooperate
with me as you did with my uncle."

She turned and left the room before the others. While
she waited for the elevator door to open, she heard one
muffled comment: "We might as well still have Harrison
Page—doesn't look as if the new boss will put up with any
shenanigans." Allison closed her ears to further remarks
for she was better off if she didn't know what the employees thought, but it was obvious that she had inherited some
of Harrison Page's characteristics. Her father had often jokingly told her she looked exactly like her mother, although
he was thankful Allison hadn't received Beatrice's volatile

temperament, but somewhere along the line she must have inherited some Page family traits.

She hoped that Benton and Celestine approved of her presentation, but regardless, she had set her course, and though she knew that she would have other moments of doubt, this morning she had done what she thought she should do. Celestine had not yet returned to the office, and Allison was at the small kitchenette, pouring a glass of orange juice, when Benton entered the outer office. He spoke and continued toward his office without making any comment on the meeting.

He halted when she said, "Well?"

His gray eyes were hooded and secretive. "I'll commend you on your speech, Miss Sayre. I believe you made the right approach to win the employees' loyalty. However, no successful business can be operated on biblical principles, and I would advise you to think that over carefully before you implement it."

Allison gasped, but unheeding, Benton walked into his office. He couldn't have chosen a more horrible way to squelch Allison's optimism. He might as well have drenched her with a bucket of cold water.

Chapter Four

Allison went into Page's office—she must remember that it was *her* office now—and sat in the large chair behind the desk, a chair too big for her, physically as well as psychologically, for if her spine was perpendicular to the back of the chair, her feet dangled an inch from the carpet. Looking around the office, she spotted a secretary's armless chair at a small table, and she shoved the huge chair into a corner and placed the smaller one behind her desk. It felt much more comfortable, for it was similar to her office chair in Chicago.

She sat there, her hands folded, and wondered what to do next. When Celestine returned from the meeting, she came to Allison immediately.

"That was a great beginning. Is there anything I can do for you?"

Determined to overcome the shock of Benton's put-down, Allison smiled. "Lots of things, I'm sure, but I'm trying to decide where to begin. Is there an annual report of the publishing company, perhaps an overall look at what was accomplished the previous year? If so, I could probably learn a bit about the company from that."

"Yes, we have detailed reports from each of the departments quarterly, and at the end of the year, all the material is correlated and bound into one volume. I'll ask Benton for a copy. I agree that will be a good place for you to start."

Benton came in soon with a booklet about an inch thick, and Allison groaned. "I can see it will take me a while to go through that."

"You won't be able to digest it all at once," Benton said evenly, as if a half hour ago he hadn't burst her bubble with his harsh words. "Is there any other way I can help you?"

"Please arrange appointments for me with the individual supervisors so that they can apprise me of the scope of work in their departments—perhaps one each day, and that way I can associate what they tell me with the annual report from that department. I will also appreciate suggestions from you if you see anything I need to do. Today, I intend to tackle this desk, remove items that I won't be needing and add things that will make it seem like my own."

"I'm sure that you'll find everything orderly, for the last week he was in this office, Mr. Page knew he wouldn't be coming back and he spent most of that time organizing his desk and the filing cabinets."

"And since I'll rely heavily on you for important decisions, let's have lunch together once each week—a working lunch away from the firm, where we can discuss problems that arise or plans for the future."

He hesitated briefly before he said, "That will be satisfactory with me. Mr. Page and I lunched together frequently." He cleared his throat. "And, Miss Sayre, you must not let your judgment be swayed by my opinions, which are not always right." He smiled, and the smile softened the severity of his face and ignited his eyes with a glimmer of friendliness. "I do want you to succeed here, and you may count upon me to assist you."

Allison returned his smile, and the tension in the office

eased considerably. He might not be the Benton Lockhart she remembered so well, but she sensed that her association with the man standing before her would influence her life as much as the Benton she had once known. She only hoped he would affect her life for good, as the other Benton had done.

Thus Allison began two months of intensive, grueling labor. She went through every file in Page's office; she met with the supervisors; she spent day after day going from one department to the other to observe the work. Celestine was quick with advice when Allison asked for it, and she eased the transition period. Benton gave valuable help, but only when she asked him. The staff cooperated with her, and although she didn't make friends with any of them, Allison thought that she was slowly gaining their respect.

Thomas Curnutt came to the office often, and Allison had to visit his office to sign papers relating to the estate. She accompanied him to several banks on High Street to sign more papers. The Page Publishing account was at one bank, while Harrison had kept his personal assets with another firm. Curnutt introduced her to Page's accountant and financial adviser, who consulted with her frequently, and little by little, she learned how to manage her investments.

Every day Allison went home exhausted physically and mentally. Although at first the large house had overwhelmed her, it had become a refuge, one that she gratefully entered at the end of many exhaustive days. Minerva waited until Allison arrived before she put the finishing touches on the meal, which gave Allison time to change into comfortable clothing and take a walk in Goodale Park before she ate.

Sometimes Allison ate alone in the kitchen alcove, quietly observing the peaceful scene outside the window as winter gave way to spring and successfully blotting out the day's activities. Minerva and Adra ate with her occasionally, but more often joined her for dessert and tea. The McRameys not only provided companionship, but also relieved her of the burden of the house. The household account had been transferred to Allison's name, and when a bill was due, Minerva laid it on the small desk in the library, which Allison preferred to the large desk in Harrison's office. Allison wrote the check and placed it in an envelope, and Adra mailed it. Minerva also took care of the laundry. Allison was cosseted as she had never been before, and although she eventually intended to be more self-reliant, during this time of transition from the old life to the new one she was grateful for the McRameys, as well as for Celestine and Thomas Curnutt.

Six days a week, Allison set the alarm for six o'clock, at which time she awoke, showered, dressed, had a light breakfast and packed a lunch. She was always at the office by half-past seven. Benton also arrived early, but occasionally she was working before he came in, and she didn't leave until after five o'clock. However, the long hours were paying off, because she was slowly learning the structure of the company and assuming more and more responsibility. Celestine and Minerva both fretted about her health, but she slept well, and felt better than she had for two years.

Sunday was the only day she rested. After attending church with Thomas and Mary, she ate a leisurely noonday meal, and since the McRameys were gone Sunday afternoon and evening, she had the house to herself—a solitude she welcomed after the busy weekdays. At Allison's insistence, Minerva left as soon as she prepared the meal, and Allison cleaned the table and loaded the dishwasher. The rest of the day she walked in the park, napped, read and telephoned her parents.

The days at Page Publishing passed quickly.

Although Benton had done everything she had asked of him, he remained aloof, sometimes almost to the point of rudeness, and Allison restrained her rising frustration with him until one incident brought her to the boiling point. She received a flyer about a booksellers convention in San Francisco, to be held during the last week in August, that snagged her interest, and she took the flyer out to Celestine.

"I received this brochure in the morning's mail, and I believe it would be a good place for me to learn more about this industry."

"I agree with you. Benton goes every year and has a display of our products."

"Oh! Then he may think I'm interfering if I attend."

Celestine shrugged. "I don't know why he should. You are the head of this firm now. I think it's your decision alone to go or not." Despite Celestine's words, Allison still felt she should check with Benton about the convention.

The light was off in his office, indicating he had gone for the day, so she decided to ponder the situation before she said anything more about it. The next morning, she was still in the notion of attending the convention, and when she heard Benton enter the building, she asked him to come to her office.

Why did she let this man intimidate her? she wondered as perspiration moistened her palms. He waited before her desk as if he were standing to attention, and stared down at her. She showed him the flyer.

"I received this yesterday and decided it would be a good place for me to learn about the publishing business. When I mentioned it to Celestine, she indicated that you organize a yearly exhibit there for Page Publishing."

"I've gone each year since Mr. Page made me his assistant."

Allison paused, wondering how to phrase her next statement. She didn't think she should ask his permission to go, but she should at least give him a chance to protest should he want to go alone.

"I'd like your opinion on whether it would be beneficial for me to attend, since the business will be closed that week and I have no other plans. Do you think I should go?"

He gave her a frosty smile. "Really, Miss Sayre. It's not for me to advise you. Without doubt, you could learn a great deal by seeing the exhibits and associating with other publishers, but whether you go or not is a decision you will have to make. Now, if you'll excuse me, I'm supposed to call a client."

He turned toward the door, and rising from her chair, Allison felt a surge of anger such as Beatrice occasionally displayed but that Allison had never experienced before. She slammed the flat of her hand down on the mahogany desk so forcibly that her whole arm tingled, but the gesture halted Benton in midstride.

"No, I will not excuse you. You come back here and talk to me as though I'm a human being. I'm tired of having you react to everything I say as if you're some type of robot whose conversation is carried on by a computerized machine. Most of the time any contact I have with you is so stilted that it appears we're characters in a comedy farce. If you resent my being here because you expected to be managing this company yourself, I'm sorry. I'm here through no machinations of my own, but I am here, and I'm going to run this company to the best of my ability. If you don't like me, I'd rather have you come right out and say so, instead of treating me as though I'm an idiot of some kind who can't understand common English."

"I thought you wanted to keep a distance between employer and employee."

"I didn't say anything of the sort. That was your idea."

Allison's heart was pounding, and her voice had become shrill, so she paused to gain some self-control. She heard Celestine enter the outer office.

"As for being the manager of this company, you've been talking to Calvin Smith too much. Mr. Page never gave me any reason to believe that I'd be his successor. He paid me handsomely for my work while he lived."

"I have not discussed you with Calvin. But back to this convention, I didn't even know you were going when I first saw the brochure, but I tried to be subtle and give you an opportunity to gracefully say I shouldn't go to it if you thought I'd be intruding on your turf. Now I'm going to ask my question again, and I want a straightforward answer. Is there any benefit to Page Publishing for me to go to the San Francisco convention, or should I stay at home?"

The golden flecks were prominent in his glowing gray eyes, and a smile played around his lips.

"I'll be happy to answer your question, *Mr. Page.*"

Allison flushed, wanting to give him an angry retort, but she waited for him to continue.

"I've already told you that I consider it beneficial for you to go to the convention—you'll learn a great deal— and I will be pleased to have you accompany me. I'll make arrangements today for you to join the flight I've already booked. I have a room reserved at the hotel where the convention is held, and I'll check to see if the hotel still has vacancies. We will have to leave on a Monday afternoon and return on the following Sunday, so that will take a week of your vacation."

Ashamed of her outburst of temper, Allison said meekly, "Thank you. Is there anything I can do to help you at the booth or to prepare the exhibit?"

"I've already chosen the book samples to be on display and will send them ahead. You can help with arranging the booth when we arrive there. You should have Celestine fax your reservation to the convention offices today. Is that all?"

Allison thought she should apologize to him for losing her temper, but she wasn't completely sorry that she had if that was what it took to get him to be civil toward her. She nodded.

He left her office, and she saw him lift his eyebrows as he looked at Celestine. "Whew!" he said, and laughed as he went into his office.

Allison was glad he saw some humor in the situation. She wasn't amused, but she was terribly embarrassed at her conduct.

Before the day was over, Benton reported that he'd arranged her flight and hotel reservation, and Allison had received a return fax that she was registered for the convention.

Two other incidents marred Allison's first few months of progress. Calvin Smith, the debonair supervisor in the shipping department, had become a problem. She could find no fault with his work, for the department ran smoothly under his direction. Whenever she met him at work, and this was not often, he had been friendly, eager to please and cooperative. Once he came to her office and talked with her personally about new postal regulations that would necessitate another part-time employee. As diplomatically as possible, she told him that he should take the matter up with Benton first, as Benton was his immediate supervisor. Although he acquiesced graciously, she sensed he was displeased. It was obvious that some kind of friction existed between him and Benton, but if once she dealt with one of the employees individually, she would not only be breaking her own policy, she would also annoy Benton.

Then Calvin started telephoning her at home. At first, he would just talk about the day's work, but one Sunday afternoon he tried another move.

"You've been working too hard, you know," Calvin said.

"I can't deny that I'm working long hours, but I believe I'm the best judge of how much work I should do."

"Maybe that's true. But everyone needs to relax a bit. I know of a wonderful new restaurant. I think you'd enjoy it. May I take you out for dinner tonight?"

For a minute she was tempted. She was lonely. She had made friends with several members of her Sunday-school class and she met them socially each month for class meetings. She visited occasionally at the home of Thomas and Mary. But her social life was bleak, almost as insipid as it had been those two years after she and Donald had broken up. Calvin was a handsome man and might provide good company for an evening.

Remembering Benton's advice about fraternizing with employees, she replied, "I do appreciate the invitation, but I'm not interested in dating at this time."

"Did you leave someone behind in Chicago?"

"Really, Mr. Smith, you're getting too personal. I don't think I want to answer that."

With a laugh, he said, "You're right, of course. I was out of line. Don't hold it against me."

A week later he had approached her in the parking lot as they were leaving work and asked her again to go out with him the following evening.

"I told you before that I'm not interested in dating now, but when I do, I don't intend to date anyone from Page Publishing. I can't maintain an unbiased relationship with the employees if I see any of them socially."

"Oh, you'll get over that."

When she shook her head, he said, "But I thought you wanted to live by the Golden Rule. Would you want someone to reject your attentions?" he asked with a smile.

She flushed as she remembered the rejection she'd had from Donald and the pain that had caused her, but his comment angered her, and she said, "I believe I've made my wishes plain, Mr. Smith. So let's leave it that way, please."

He hadn't approached her again and Allison thought she had settled the situation. In spite of her good intentions and brave words, Allison often wondered how she would react if Benton asked her for a date, but she supposed that needn't worry her. Not once had he stepped across the professional line, even the times they lunched together. Their discussions were always strictly about business, although Allison longed for him to show a personal interest in her.

Allison often thought of the picture of the youthful Benton Lockhart that Cleta had sent her. Time and again she had looked at that picture to determine if the slender, smooth-shaven man they had met in Indianapolis could possibly be Benton Lockhart, her bewhiskered, broad-shouldered employee. She had finally concluded that he couldn't be, for not once had she glimpsed any aspect of the glowing faith and love for people that the other Benton had exhibited. No one could possibly change his personality and life values that much.

The other incident also caused Allison to deal with her Golden Rule policy. One afternoon Benton telephoned from his office.

"Miss Sayre, would you have time to step into my office?"

She always had time for Benton, and she went immediately into his office. Anna Harper, the supervisor from the bookkeeping office, was also in the room.

"Mrs. Harper has a serious problem, and I wanted you to hear it from her," Benton said.

Allison turned toward Mrs. Harper. She was a thin, nervous woman in her early forties, with high cheekbones and snapping black eyes. A telltale pulse pounding rapidly in her throat indicated that she was agitated.

"Go ahead, Mrs. Harper," Benton encouraged.

"There's been an embezzlement in our department."

The woman seemed to be on the point of crying, and Allison moved closer and took her hand.

"Don't be upset, Mrs. Harper. Embezzlement—of how much?"

"Five hundred dollars, or at least that's all the auditors have found thus far. I don't know how that could have happened. I try to be so careful."

"I'm sure you are. Do you know the embezzler?"

Her eyes were ominous. "Yes, I do, and I've already fired her. She's cleaning out her desk now, but I think she should be arrested. Mr. Lockhart says I don't have the authority to do that—you would have to start legal proceedings."

"When was the money taken?"

"A year ago," Mrs. Harper said, and she started crying. "I'm so distressed that I didn't discover it earlier."

"Send the woman to me, and please put her dismissal on hold for a few days. If this is her first offense, we may need to give her a second chance after we learn the circumstances. Mr. Lockhart and I will talk with her."

Mrs. Harper seemed shocked at Allison's approach to the situation and she left the office without further comment.

After Mrs. Harper departed, Allison said, "What do you know about the woman?"

"Her name is Reba Hall, a widow, who has been with us three years."

"Has her work been satisfactory?"

"I haven't heard any complaints." A teasing smile lighted his eyes. "You take this embezzlement calmly, Miss Sayre."

"Five hundred dollars isn't much compared with the worth of this company. I know we can't encourage embezzlements, but I don't want to pass judgment until I hear her story."

When Mrs. Hall came in, she was neither embarrassed nor defiant. She sat down in the chair that Mrs. Harper had vacated and waited calmly, as though resigned to her fate. She was a handsome woman, with dark hair heavily streaked with gray, and her eyes were steady as she looked at Allison.

Benton motioned for Allison to proceed.

"Mrs. Harper has brought some very serious charges against you, and I want to hear your side of the story."

"I won't deny that I juggled a couple of statements and transferred the money to my bank account. I had hoped to pay it back before the theft was discovered."

Allison reached for the annual report lying on Benton's desk and flipped through the pages to the salary sheet of the bookkeeping department. "It seems to me that your salary is adequate. You're making considerably more than I did before I came here."

Mrs. Hall smiled wanly. "Perhaps you didn't have a teenager in the house."

When neither Benton nor Allison commented, she continued. "I have three children. The two girls are married and live away from home. When my husband died four years ago, he left me with a fourteen-year-old son, who has never gotten over his father's death. Frankly, I haven't been able to handle him. He wouldn't finish high school and he has a poor choice of friends. A year ago, he got in trouble with the law, and if I hadn't raised five hundred dollars to pay for the damages he caused, he would have gone to prison. He was near enough his majority to be tried as an adult. He didn't have a previous criminal record, and I couldn't bear to see him imprisoned. I didn't have that much money, and no family or friends who could loan me the sum. So, I took it from the company."

"Doesn't the boy work? Do you continue to support him?"

"He won't work, but I can't very well turn him out on the streets. His fate would be even worse."

"Mrs. Hall, I've asked your supervisor to suspend your dismissal for the time being. I want to think about the situation before I make a decision. If you continue to work here, you'll have to make some adjustments."

The woman rose in one graceful movement. "I'm sorry to cause this problem. I won't blame you whatever you decide."

After she left, Allison said, "What do you think we should do?"

"Dismiss the woman and cross off the five hundred dollars," Benton said without hesitation. "If we take her to court it will cost us more than that."

"But I'm thinking of the personal angle. What will dismissal do to her? She can't meet expenses now, apparently."

"If Page Publishing rewards people who steal from us, the business will fold in a short while."

Allison couldn't be satisfied with that solution, and she sat silent, staring at a pastoral painting on Benton's wall.

She snapped the top of the ballpoint pen she held, until
with a smile Benton reached over and took it out of her
hand. Flushing, Allison said, "I didn't mean to be annoy-
ing, but I'm in distress over this. I'll have to think about
the situation over the weekend and hopefully have a decision by Monday. This is the difficult part of being in
charge. No matter what I decide, someone will be unhappy."

"Remember that any decision you make must be for the
good of Page Publishing."

Allison spent a miserable weekend, praying for wisdom,
deviating from one decision to another. At times like this,
she felt her inadequacy to manage a large company more
than ever. She had learned so much in the past few months,
but this situation had given her a jolt.

Sunday was summerlike, and after the McRameys left,
Allison spent most of the time in the backyard, where the
sun filtered through the first lacy leaves of the maple trees.
Usually Allison could find peace in this spot, but her mind
was in a turmoil. What should be done about Reba Hall?
She didn't want to set a precedent that would cause more
trouble later on. She knew that the woman deserved to be
dismissed—legally and ethically she was in the wrong. No
one would ever blame Allison for dismissing her.

The memory of Donald kept intermingling with her concern over Reba Hall, and some words of the Lord's Prayer
kept hammering in Allison's mind: "Forgive us our debts
as we forgive our debtors." For over two years she had
been unable to voice those words. When she repeated the
prayer in unison with a congregation, she merely stopped
when she came to that part, and the omission had caused
Allison many fretful moments. She interpreted those words
to mean that God would forgive her misdeeds only in the
same manner she forgave others. And since she obviously
hadn't forgiven Donald's perfidy, did that mean God had
not forgiven her during the past two years? Since He was
a loving sovereign, she believed He had forgiven her short-

comings, but if she prayed those words, she was actually asking to be unforgiven. Such thoughts made her uncomfortable.

She was ready to acknowledge that Donald in his wisdom had chosen the right course, and she was thankful that he had the courage to break their engagement when he realized that their relationship was nothing stronger than friendship. She had never doubted that she had loved Donald devotedly, but with him she had never known the emotional sensations she experienced when she was in Benton's presence or when their hands touched in the course of a day's work.

God, I forgive Donald for hurting me, and I hope you will give me the opportunity to tell him so and ask his forgiveness for being stubborn and unrelenting. Now, God, I ask for one more favor. Help me to know what to do about Reba Hall.

By Monday morning she had made her decision. She telephoned Mrs. Harper in the bookkeeping department and asked her to send Reba Hall to her office. When Reba Hall arrived, Allison tapped on Benton's door and asked him to join them. Mrs. Hall didn't look as if she had slept for days, and Benton always seemed exhausted on Monday mornings. They were a sad-looking trio.

Even now, Allison wasn't convinced that she was taking the right course of action, and she swallowed with difficulty before she sighed deeply and said, "Mrs. Hall, it hasn't been easy for me to reach a decision, but I believe in giving people a second chance. All weekend, I've tried to determine how I could abide by my Golden Rule policy and still not jeopardize the success of this business. I've not discussed my decision with Mr. Lockhart, for I will take the full responsibility if this doesn't work."

Reba Hall's face brightened a bit, but Benton's was deadpan, so Allison didn't know what he was thinking.

"First of all, I don't intend to dismiss you or press legal charges, but I will suggest that you be transferred to another department, where you will not have access to any finances. I will talk to the supervisor in the print department to see if any employee there could change jobs with you. And from my personal funds, I'm going to repay the five hundred dollars you took from the company, but you'll have to sign a personal note for that amount, which will be payable to me in one year.''

Mrs. Hall gripped the arms of her chair, and her face, which had been pale, flushed and tears came into her eyes. The phone rang, and the noise pierced the dramatic silence in the office. Benton made no move to answer the call, which stopped abruptly as Celestine intercepted the message in the outer office. Allison looked toward Benton, hoping to see some support for her dealings with Reba Hall, and he met her eyes briefly, but he turned away without giving her any indication of his opinion. She was on her own, so she proceeded with her plan.

"I may be meddling now, and it's certainly audacious to suggest a pattern for a parent-child relationship when I have no children and am little older than your son, but it seems to me that unless you exert some discipline over your son, you will never come out of this financial bind. It's obvious the boy is draining you of money, and I think you have a responsibility to do something about it. If you continue in this manner, it's going to spell ruin for both of you. If you can't discipline him, why not find some help and put him in a program that will?''

Reba Hall's face was twitching and tears ran down her cheeks. "I've tried, Miss Sayre. Believe me I have. I'm very grateful to you, and I'll do what I can.''

In a quick, fluid movement, Allison knelt beside Mrs. Hall's chair, took a tissue from the box on Benton's desk and wiped the tears from her face. The woman's hands moved nervously in her lap and Allison covered them with hers.

"My father loved all of us very much, but he kept a tight rein on us. Once when my brother broke a neighbor's window, Dad took away his ball and bat and wouldn't let him play with his friends until he paid for that window. Tim is a little spoiled, but when he gets too far out of line, Dad hauls him back.''

Benton still hadn't said anything, and that bothered Allison. Just once, she wished he would compliment her on doing the right thing. Couldn't she do anything to please him?

''I believe it would be well for you to take a couple of days off while we arrange to change your position. We will telephone you as soon as possible. I'll have Mr. Curnutt prepare a note for you to sign.''

The woman's eyes reflected her gratitude, but her throat was too tight for words. She gave Allison a quick hug, murmured a quiet ''Thank you'' and left the office. Allison said to the still-silent Benton, ''If you have time this morning, we'll have Mrs. Harper and the print supervisor in for a session.''

''I have an appointment now. Shall we make it at eleven o'clock.''

''Very well. I'll ask Celestine to notify them.''

The meeting with Mrs. Harper didn't go as well as the one earlier in the day, for Mrs. Harper was furious that Allison had overturned her decision about firing her employee, but the print supervisor was glad to have Mrs. Hall in his department, for she was known as a capable and conscientious worker. He had an employee who, because of health conditions, could no longer handle the occasional heavy lifting in his department and would like to be transferred, and it was arranged over Mrs. Harper's protest.

Reba Hall was notified to return to work on Wednesday, and she agreed to sign the note. After that episode, Allison was the first to admit that running a business by the Golden Rule wasn't going to be easy, especially when she was dealing with so many staff members. If you made one happy the other was apt to be sad.

The morning had been so frustrating that Allison was

happy it was the day for her to lunch with Benton. She needed some time away from the office, and she looked forward to the event, for he had a knack of coming up with interesting places to lunch—not once had they gone to a fast-food restaurant. She had become well acquainted with German Village because they had lunched in that area many times.

Today, Benton drove to the Short North, an area not far from Allison's home. This section of Columbus was quite accessible to Page Publishing, but they hadn't enjoyed the quiet atmosphere of the Saturn Pizza & Pasta restaurant before.

After they gave their order and the waitress brought their beverages, Allison sipped thirstily at her iced tea and asked for a refill. "This incident has about gotten me down," she confessed, "and I'm tired. Usually I can relax over the weekend, but not this time."

Her left hand was lying on the table and Benton covered it with his. Maybe he wasn't as indifferent to her as he seemed.

"Why don't you take the rest of the day off. You've done nothing but work since you arrived here. Go shopping or just go home and relax."

She shook her head. "I'll be all right after I've eaten some lunch. The decision is made now, and right or wrong, I'll have to live with it. I hope I don't have to deal with anything else like this."

Benton released her hand when the waitress brought their orders, and losing that contact with him saddened Allison.

"I don't believe you need to worry. During my five years with the company, we haven't uncovered another embezzlement. You may never have one again."

With relish she tackled the macaroni-and-ham casserole topped with cheese sauce, for she hadn't had any appetite for breakfast this morning.

"If it will comfort you any—I'll compliment you on the way you handled the situation," Benton said as he ate wedges of pizza supreme. "At first, I disagreed with you, but your concern for Reba Hall, and the way you treated her this morning, proves to me that you have a tender heart, the kind that is needed when working with people. Your compassion complements the acumen you have for managing the business. It's an uncommon combination, but one that I admire."

Allison stared at him, speechless. The Benton Lockhart sitting before her was not the man with whom she had verbally sparred for the past three months. He was smiling, relaxed and kind—characteristics he rarely exhibited. Watching him now, she wondered again if he could be the Benton of her dreams.

When she found her voice, it sounded strained and incredulous. "Do you know that's the first time you've ever shown one bit of approval of anything I've done? I thought you didn't even like me."

He laughed lightly. "I've never given you any reason to believe that I don't like you."

"That's debatable, but at any rate, you've never given any indication that you *do* like me."

"I resented you at first, not because you owned the company, but because you reminded me of things I preferred to forget. However, you've proven that you're a remarkable woman, one I'm pleased to work for. And if it matters to you, set your mind at rest—I do like you."

"But you've been so cold and impersonal in our relationship!"

"Yes, if I remember you once compared me to a robot, but I've avoided interjecting any of my personal wishes to you. The company belongs to you, and you'll never learn how to operate it if I tell you everything to do."

"Maybe so, but working with you has been about as comfortable as cuddling up to a block of ice."

He looked at his watch and pushed back his chair. "We'll have to change that," he said, and the promise was mirrored in his eyes as well as in his words. "But we do have a business to run, so we must leave now."

By the middle of May, activities at the office had leveled off and Allison was feeling more in control of the management, and she decided to take off a Saturday to determine what needed to be done around her home. On Saturday morning, she was leisurely eating a bowl of mixed melon and fruit for breakfast when Minerva came into the kitchen.

"Come and sit down, Minerva. You had mentioned that you usually have a cleaning service to do general fall and spring cleaning. When are you going to have that done?"

"I can arrange that any time it's convenient for you."

Allison waved a negligent hand. "Fit it into your schedule. I want to invite my family down for a visit this summer. And some evening I'm going to ask Thomas and Mary for a meal, but you arrange the cleaning first. The house always looks super to me, but I suppose you see things that I don't."

"When you have time, Allison, we should clean out Mr. Page's room—dispose of his clothing and personal items. I dust around everything weekly, but those clothes ought to be doing some good, not hanging in the closet."

"I'll trust you to get rid of them, or do you need my help?"

"I prefer your help, for the pockets need to be turned out—hard to tell what Mr. Page may have put in them. There are envelopes and boxes that I don't want to be responsible for."

"I will help, of course. I don't intend to go to the office today. Would you want to tackle the job now?"

"Suits me. I'll get Adra to lend a hand. We can pack everything in those cartons you brought your clothes in when you moved here."

"What can we do with them once we have them boxed?"

"Our church sponsors a clothes pantry for the needy, and

they're always in short supply. Mr. Page had some nice things."

Allison savored the last chunk of honeydew melon and took the bowl to the sink. "I favor giving them to the church. Let me change into some jeans, and we'll get started."

It was an all-day job, and though they went through every pocket of Page's clothing, they didn't find anything more valuable than a handkerchief. The boxes yielded nothing except old pictures, and Allison recognized a few that were her mother's ancestors, so she kept those, but regretfully trashed the others.

"Probably some of Mrs. Page's family," Minerva said as she glanced through the discarded photos. "She had a few cousins, but I don't know where they live."

The room looked barren after Adra carried all the parcels to his truck for transporting to the church the next day. Allison had hoped that the unpleasant job would at least yield some clue to the character of Harrison Page, but except for the fact that he had been a tidy man and bought inexpensive but serviceable clothes, the day's work had yielded no helpful information about why this man would name her as his heir.

She surveyed the room. The bed, with a tall, ornate headboard, was made of rosewood, ebony and gilt incising. The dresser looked like something out of the *Gone with the Wind* movie. It had a gray marble top, and was decorated with three-dimensional animals and foliage. A striped Venetian carpet of green, browns and tans covered the floor.

"It would be nice to lighten up this room," Allison said. "I believe Uncle Harrison must have been a gloomy man. Everything is dark in his office downstairs, and the draperies in here are somber and do nothing to lighten this dark walnut furniture. His office at work isn't too bad, although I suspect I can thank Celestine for that."

"Mr. Page was a sad man."

"Someday after work, I'll go shopping for some new draperies and a bedspread."

As they went downstairs, Allison said, "Now that I'm into this, I might as well tackle the office. I know there are magazines stacked in here that should go, but I'm not up to it now. Perhaps tomorrow afternoon, I'll do it."

Rain was pouring the next afternoon, and reluctantly Allison stood on the threshold of Harrison's office. She brought the large trash can from the back porch and started first on an oak cabinet. She discarded most of the contents—household records, copies of Mrs. Page's charge accounts, receipts for utility bills—some as old as twenty years. She tied strings around magazines for recycling. The files containing Page's personal income tax and medical bills she stored in the cabinet and would ask Thomas's advice about keeping them. As she neared the end of the task, she wondered why she felt such a keen sense of disappointment, until she knew that subconsciously she was hoping to learn something in this office about why Uncle Harrison had favored her.

She turned eagerly to the desk drawers, where she found very little, so it seemed that Page had cleaned out everything before he moved to the nursing home. In the center drawer, she discovered a wooden box containing a set of keys and a small brown envelope. The keys were labeled "safety-deposit box." Allison and Curnutt had already gone through two of Page's boxes, but this security box was at another bank. She dropped the keys in her pocket and decided to call Thomas tomorrow to see what he knew about this box. In a small brown envelope was a gold baby's bracelet. As small as it was, it could have been one used by hospitals to identify newborns. Did this mean that Aunt Sarah had borne a child? It was a puzzle.

Allison put the bracelet back in the box and turned out the lights in the office. Afterward, as she lay on the chintz lounge in the library, she wondered about her aunt and uncle. Instead of making them more real to her, this afternoon's findings had wrapped them in additional mystery.

A stack of departmental reports lay on Allison's desk when she arrived Monday morning, and she spent several hours going over them. The supervisor in the print department indicated that the transfer of Reba Hall was working well, and that was pleasant to know. Allison didn't intend to contact her for several months, though she was eager to learn if she was making any progress with her son.

It was early afternoon before she had an opportunity to contact Thomas about the keys.

"I wasn't aware that he had a box at that bank, although he used to keep his household accounts there."

"I suppose I should check it out."

"Yes, take the keys and that document showing you are Page's heir, and you will be given access to the security box."

"I'm curious, so I'll go this afternoon."

"I hope the box doesn't contain anything that will have to be included in the estate or that will delay the settlement."

"If there's anything of importance, I'll let you know."

She was admitted to the bank's vault without any difficulty, and the attendant assisted her in finding what she sought. Taking the box, Allison went into a small alcove.

The box held one sealed envelope. No name was on the outside, but she supposed she was justified in opening it. She used her nail file to slit the seal and took out a single sheet of paper. She scanned the document, then read it carefully. With unsteady fingers she returned the box to its proper place, put the envelope in her purse, signed out at the attendant's desk and plodded to the car in the parking lot. The document she had found had solved the mystery of why Harrison Page had left her a fortune, and now she wished she didn't know, for her life was shattered. Allison's hands shook so much she had trouble inserting the

key into the ignition, but she started the car, drove down
the street a few blocks and parked in a grocery store lot.
Hoping that she wouldn't be interrupted by anyone who
knew her, Allison read the notarized statement again, which
had been drafted on her twenty-first birthday:

To whom it may concern:

Twenty-one years ago, Mary Miller gave birth to a
daughter, subsequently named Allison Sayre. I am the
father of this child, but I was unable to marry the
mother because I had another wife at the time. The
child was adopted by my sister and her husband.

                              (signed)   Harrison Page

Allison had searched the box vainly in an effort to find
something else, but there was nothing more. The brevity of
the statement opened up a whole new quandary. Where was
Mary Miller now? This meant that the woman she thought
was her mother was really her Aunt Beatrice and that
Charles was no blood relationship at all. How could they
do this to her? When she was a child, perhaps it was just
as well that she didn't know about the adoption, but surely
as an adult she should have been told. Was this the reason
Beatrice hadn't wanted her to come to Columbus? If that
was the case, then perhaps her birth mother lived here. Suddenly, Allison was overwhelmed with the desire to find her
own mother.

As the shock wore off, Allison became so angry that she
shook all over. She was angry at Beatrice and Charles for
not telling her. She was angry at her birth mother for giving
her away. She was angry at Harrison Page for his infidelity.

Once the anger abated, the tears started. This move to
Columbus and inheriting Harrison's estate had been enough
trauma, but Allison cried now for the years of happiness as

a youth when she had felt so secure in her parents' home, so thankful to be a part of a stable family relationship. Several of her friends had come from broken homes, and she'd always sympathized with them, thinking it was sad they couldn't have been as secure as she was. But it had all been a lie. For twenty-four years she had lived a lie. She mourned the memories that would never be as happy again.

Allison went home without going back to the office. She couldn't face anyone today, for she knew her face mirrored the agony and sorrow she felt. What was she going to do with this knowledge? When Minerva commented on her early arrival, Allison told her she didn't feel well, and once she took a look at herself in the mirror, she knew why Minerva hadn't questioned it. Her skin was ashen; her amber eyes were red and lusterless; her mouth drooped at the corners; her body was tense; even her long chestnut hair looked stringy and lifeless.

"My, you do look a sight, Allison! What is the matter?"

"Just a little upset. I'm going to lie on the lounge in the library. I'll be all right in a few hours."

"What about dinner?"

"If you haven't started anything yet, I'll just have a sandwich later on."

In the library, Allison flicked through the mail on the desk, distastefully noticing a letter from her mother. She took off her shoes and lay on the lounge, looking out the window at the tops of the trees. Although the document was brief, it did explain many things, particularly why Beatrice hadn't wanted any association with her brother, especially since she wanted Allison to be unaware of the relationship.

She recalled Minerva's comment that Harrison Page was a very sad man and at times had acted guilty around his wife, as if he were responsible for her illness. No doubt the guilt had originated because of the adulterous situation that had brought Allison into the world. It also explained why all Allison's physical characteristics were like Beatrice's. The other two children were more like Charles Sayre than their mother, and Allison had always wondered why she hadn't inherited one trait from her father.

While this revelation explained some things, it left Allison pondering others. Why hadn't Beatrice wanted Allison to know about her real parentage? Why had she opposed Allison's acceptance of Harrison's fortune when it seemed the natural thing for him to do? Why hadn't Harrison done more for her while she was growing up?

Minerva interrupted her musings when she entered the room. "I've brought you some aspirin and a cup of tea. You take these pills, drink the tea and take a nap."

Minerva's cure for all problems was a cup of tea. With Minerva's anxious eyes upon her, Allison didn't have much choice but to swallow the tablets and drink the hot liquid. Then Minerva bade her lie down again, and after she covered Allison with an afghan, she tiptoed out of the room.

Allison closed her eyes, but she couldn't close her mind, which rioted with unanswered questions. What should she do now? Ignore this document and go on as before? After all, it wouldn't make any difference in her inheritance. It would be easier for all if they remained ignorant of her true relationship to Harrison. Probably no one in their family except Charles and Beatrice knew that she was adopted. But what effect would it have on her if she had to carry this burden alone? Living by the Golden Rule, what was the proper course to take? Beatrice and Charles were good parents, and if she revealed to them what she knew, would it hurt them? But she thought of her birth mother and perhaps other siblings, whom she would never know and who wouldn't know her. If she didn't find out, she would wonder all the time if any stranger she met might be a relative. And after all, how could it make her love Beatrice and Charles any less if she found out about her birth mother? She would always regard them as her parents.

She still hadn't reached any conclusion when Minerva

said softly from the doorway, "Feel like eating a bite, Allison?"

She opened eyes that felt hot and bleary and sat up. "Not really, but perhaps I should. I'll rinse off my face and come right in."

Minerva had prepared a club sandwich and a few potato chips on a plate, and a cup of hot vegetable soup. The food was tasty and did help to revive Allison physically. Mentally, she was still in the doldrums. Adra and Minerva sat down for their habitual after-dinner chat and Allison attempted to act normal, but the effort exhausted all the strength generated by the food.

After a decent interval, Allison left them and, using the handrail, pulled herself up the stairs. She intended to telephone her mother, for she couldn't let the matter rest, but she had to allow for the hour's time difference, and also be sure that Adra and Minerva were in their apartment before she called.

She wanted to pray about the situation, but a wall of anger and hurt feelings separated her from God, and the only prayer she could muster was a plea for guidance. Even though she was hurting and the pain was real, she didn't want to wound anyone else. At nine o'clock she dialed her family's number. Beatrice answered the phone.

After a few minutes of chatting to catch up on the news, Allison said, "Mother..." Her tongue faltered on the word, and she started again, "Mother, I've been going through many of Uncle Harrison's things this week, and I discovered something disturbing today."

"Oh?"

Did she detect anxiety in her mother's tone?

"I found a short, notarized document signed by Harrison Page. I want to read it to you. 'Twenty-one years ago, Mary Miller gave birth to a daughter, subsequently named Allison Sayre. I am the father of this child, but I was unable to marry the mother because I had another wife at the time. The child was adopted by my sister and her husband.'"

"How dared he!" Beatrice said.

Allison was surprised at her venomous tone. "Then you don't deny it?"

"How can I when he's been so specific? Besides, I won't lie to you."

"Haven't you been lying to me all my life?"

"No, we have not. We've simply avoided telling you the truth."

"Then may I have the truth now? I believe it's high time someone told me the truth." Allison was trying to control her anger, but Beatrice's attitude reflected on her, as it always did.

"Charles and I had been married a year when Harrison contacted us, telling us the nature of his problem. There seemed to be no thought of the mother keeping the child, and although we were struggling to make ends meet, we agreed to adopt you, but only if Harrison and your mother gave up all rights and promised absolutely to avoid contact with you. Harrison wanted to assume financial responsibility for you, but we refused, knowing that would have given him the right to meddle in your upbringing."

"It would have been much easier for you and Daddy to have had some help."

"We didn't want it that way. You would be all ours, or he could make other arrangements. We conducted those negotiations before you were born, and when you were two days old, you were brought to us. I will never forgive Harrison for breaking his word."

"But he did, so I know now, and I want to know the rest. Where is my birth mother?"

"Why would you want to know? She obviously isn't a respectable woman, and I'm astounded that you would even ask about a mother who before you were born agreed to give you away. Don't ever mention her in my presence again."

It took Allison a few seconds to realize that her mother had hung up the phone receiver.

Five minutes later her phone rang and Allison answered to Charles's voice.

"Oh, Daddy," she cried.

"I wish I could be there to hold you close, Allison, because I know your life has been shattered. I'm sorry I couldn't shield you from this blow, but daddies can only go so far."

"I could have taken this much better if I'd been told rather than finding out in such a revolting manner. Why didn't you tell me?"

"Beatrice didn't want you to know, and I wouldn't oppose her. She's right that you would have been better off not to know."

"Can't you even tell me if my real mother is dead or alive? Somehow this seems very important to me."

"We've never discussed the situation with Harrison after you were born, so there isn't much to tell. Just forget it, Allison. Harrison has left you his fortune, which is only right that he should. And we love you very much. That's all you need to know. Just forget the rest of it."

"I guess you're right. Thanks for calling me, Daddy."

Chapter Five

Allison flung herself across the bed after she talked with her father, wondering how she could possibly cope with her newfound knowledge. For now she would ignore the matter of her parentage. Often Beatrice, in a flash of anger, made statements that she later rescinded. Perhaps in a few months, her attitude would soften and Allison could approach her again. Although for some reason she was desperate to find her birth mother, she wondered if she should mention her discovery to anyone in Columbus. Since Thomas and Celestine had both enjoyed Harrison's confidence, they might know something, but now didn't seem the time to approach them.

"But, God," she prayed aloud, *"I don't know if I can bear this alone. I know You will comfort me, but right now I feel in need of some human support."*

A questionable parentage such as hers wasn't something one would shout from the housetop, but perhaps she should confide in Minerva, who was such an understanding woman and possessed of an abundance of homespun wisdom, which Allison needed at this point. She was sitting on the side of the bed, wondering if she should approach Minerva, when the doorbell rang. She glanced at her watch. She couldn't imagine who would be calling at such an hour, but she walked wearily and warily downstairs.

She didn't turn on the hall light, and reluctant to open the doors at night, she called, "Who is it?"

"Benton," he answered.

Wondering at the reason for his late call when he had never come to her home before, she glanced at the mirror on the hall tree and flinched at her bedraggled appearance, but she had no choice but to open the door. She flipped on the light and unlatched the door.

They looked questioningly at each other for a minute before, with a gesture, she invited him in. He was dressed in jeans and a pullover sweater.

"Is anything wrong?" she asked.

"Not with me, but you don't look so well. Celestine and I were concerned when you didn't come back to work this afternoon, and I thought I should check on you."

She thought he had waited quite a long time to exhibit his concern, and his story didn't ring true anyway.

"Minerva called you, didn't she?"

"Yes," he admitted, "she was very worried. She didn't think you were sick, but she knew something had happened to upset you since you had left for work this morning. She wondered what might have occurred at the office. Since I knew nothing out of the way had happened there, I became concerned, too."

"Let's sit in the library. It's the most comfortable room for me."

She sat on the couch and piled some cushions behind her back. She had come downstairs in her bare feet, and she curled them under her. Benton sat in the chair opposite her, regarding her with a look of concern, but he seemed at a loss to know what to say to her, and she couldn't have spoken if she had tried.

"I haven't come to meddle," he said slowly, "and I was very reluctant to come at all, but for some reason, I felt it

was important that you not be alone this evening. At first
I thought Minerva was overly concerned, but now that I've
seen you, I know you've sustained a terrible shock."

"I had the most awful experience of my life today,"
Allison admitted in an unsteady voice, "but I can't talk
about it."

He moved to the couch beside her. "Did you have an
automobile accident? Did you strike someone with your
car?"

She shook her head and started sobbing. Benton moved
closer, drew her into his arms and cradled her head on his
shoulder. The tenderness and warmth of his embrace, the
concern exhibited as he alternately patted her back and
smoothed down her hair, brought a comfort to Allison that
only made her cry harder. She knew without a doubt that
God had sent Benton to her tonight to share her grief. But
why Benton? Of all the people she knew, he was the last
person she wanted to know about her tainted family background. Not for the first time Allison acknowleged that the
ways of God were beyond her understanding.

The peace generated by Benton's refreshing presence
soon found its way to Allison's heart, and she murmured,
"Give me a few minutes to get control and I'll tell you."

Still patting her back, Benton said, "Take all the time
you need. I have all night."

Ashamed for him to see her tear-streaked burning features, Allison kept her face hidden for a few more minutes,
and then she pushed away from him.

"I'll go into the powder room and wash my face. Forgive
me for all this blubbering. Believe me, I don't cry often,
but I reached the breaking point today."

She hurried into the small room adjacent to the kitchen,
splashed water over her face and gave her unkempt hair a
few quick strokes with the brush. She paused in the kitchen
to fill two glasses with ice and cola, then placed the glasses
on a tray with a plate of Minerva's coconut macaroons.

When she went back to the library, she placed the tray on the table in front of the couch.

Without meeting Benton's eyes, she said, "I don't know where to start."

Benton lifted her chin until she was forced to look at him. "Something has happened to embarrass you. No matter what it is, it won't matter to me. I don't even need to know, but for your own good, I believe you shouldn't harbor whatever it is."

She nibbled on a cookie and sipped the cola while she debated how much to tell him. Taking a deep breath, Allison said, "Yesterday afternoon, while searching through Uncle Harrison's desk, I found a set of keys to a security box—one that Thomas and I hadn't checked. When I went there after lunch today, I found this."

She took the offending document from her pocket and dropped it on the couch between them as if it were a hot potato. "Please read it, but I don't want you to reveal its contents to anyone. I didn't know if I should tell anyone— not even Thomas, but when you came tonight I believe God sent you to be my confidant. If that's a role too heavy for you, I won't be offended."

"I came to help you," he said as he picked up the paper.

After he had read a few words, his eyes, filled with amazement, met Allison's briefly before he finished reading.

"No wonder you're upset. You didn't suspect this?"

"I've always wondered why Harrison Page left his estate to me, but in my wildest imaginations, I never suspected that he was my father."

Hesitantly, Benton said, "I realize this has been a shock to you, but I don't understand the depth of your depression. Admittedly, to father you out of wedlock was not an honorable thing, but no one could be ashamed of Harrison Page as a father. I've never heard even one word against his character."

"Oh, it isn't that so much," Allison said wearily, "but

this knowledge has severely undermined the foundation of my security—my stable, happy home life. I love my father so much that I can't bear to think that I don't have any blood claim to him at all.'' Her lips trembled, and Benton drew her close and kissed her softly on the forehead. With his touch she found the strength to continue. "And I telephoned my mother...or I should say my Aunt Beatrice...this evening, and we had a terrible quarrel. She said Uncle Harrison had promised never to reveal this information, so she's angry, too."

"I wonder why he did—he didn't seem the kind to break his word."

"I have no idea," Allison said, still sniffing a little. "I'm sorry I had to find out, but I should have been told the truth years ago. When I told Mother that I wanted to find my birth mother, she argued about it and hung up on me."

Tears came into her eyes again, and Benton tightened his hold on her.

"Daddy called me and tried to bring some comfort, but not as much as you have. He was too far away. I'll always be grateful to you for coming tonight."

"Now that you know, what do you intend to do with your knowledge?"

"Nothing right away. I do want to find out about my maternal heritage, but not if it causes a rift between me and my adoptive mother. When she gets over her anger, she may not object to my search."

"I believe that's your best choice. I won't mention this to you again, but if you want to talk about it or need any help in your search, let me know. Nor will I speak of it to anyone else." The clock in the hallway struck midnight, and Benton withdrew his arm from Allison's shoulders and stood up. "Are you all right now? If so, I'll go on home, but I can stay longer."

Allison's eyes felt swollen from all her crying, but she smiled at him and followed him to the doorway. "No, I'll be fine now, but I really needed to talk with someone. I was on the verge of confiding in Minerva when you rang the doorbell."

Benton leaned forward and kissed her on the cheek, and with eyes that were still a bit misty, Allison watched his lithe figure as he walked toward his car. She knew tonight marked a turning point in their relationship, and after locking the door, she ascended the stairway with an easy tread and a lighter heart.

Thomas's message was on her voice mail when Allison arrived at the office the next morning: "I wanted to know what you found in the box yesterday. Telephone if it concerns me."

She might as well tell him something, but she was relieved when Mary answered the phone and said that Thomas was out of the office.

"Just give him a message," Allison said. "Tell him that there was only one envelope in the box I checked yesterday, and that it doesn't have anything to do with settling the estate."

One morning a few weeks later Celestine brought some letters for Allison to sign. "I want to discuss a matter with you if you have the time," she said.

Allison smiled. After three weeks the shock of knowing about her parental triangle had lessened somewhat, and Allison was able to smile again, but her mother's identity was never far from her mind. She had tediously gone through the phone book of the Columbus area, looking for a Mary Miller, but she found none. It was bound to be a slim chance anyway, for even if her mother had been from Columbus, in twenty-four years her status would have changed.

"I'm never that busy. I know my time isn't indispensable to the business yet."

"You must stop underrating yourself, Allison. You've come a long way."

"Thank you for those kind words. Now what do you need to tell me?"

"Until Mr. Page became so ill, he sponsored two company events for employees and their families each year, one at Christmas, the other midyear, usually around Independence Day. Last year we didn't do anything, not even a Christmas party, because Mr. Page was so ill, but he instructed Benton to give generous bonuses to the staff. They were happy to have the bonuses, but I think most everyone would enjoy a get-together. Are you agreeable to sponsoring a gathering around the Fourth of July? The company would have to pick up the tab for the expense."

"Yes, of course. I've been so busy trying to learn the structure of this business that I hardly know anyone. I'll have to rely on you and Benton for major plans."

"We've had the summer picnic at our farm a couple of times, and my husband and I would be glad to host the event again this year."

"Why, Celestine! I didn't know you lived on a farm. See, that's how little I know about the people. When I came here, Benton advised me to stay aloof from the staff's personal lives, but I'm beginning to think he was wrong." Celestine had a picture of her husband, Amos, and son, Truman, displayed on her desk, so Allison felt as if she knew them by seeing their faces so often, but Allison hadn't asked questions about her personal life.

Celestine laughed lightly. "You've had enough on your mind without trying to know all about us. But, yes, I live on a farm and commute to work about fifty miles each day."

"Then I value your loyalty to the firm even more. Go on about the picnic."

"My husband, Amos, will pit-roast a beef, which would make plenty of meat for the 150 people who could attend. We should have hot dogs for the children, and we can arrange for catering beverages, baked beans, potato salad, vegetable trays and melon balls. Ice cream and cookies will be enough for dessert.''

''Sounds as if you have it all planned out.''

''All you have to do is pay the bill,'' Celestine said with a broad smile.

''You must have a large farm to accommodate so many people.''

''Amos will have a hay field mown by that time to take care of the parking, and we have a large patio area, where the food will be served. Staff members usually provide entertainment ideas. In the evening we have a campfire, where we roast marshmallows and hot dogs, followed by a fireworks display.''

''What if it rains?''

''We can spread the food out in our triple garage.''

''Your plans sound great. Go for it! I can surely see why Uncle Harrison kept you around for so many years.''

With a shrug, Celestine said, ''Well, I've tried to earn my salary.''

Allison walked with Celestine into the outer office as they continued to plan the picnic, but they were interrupted by a little woman who opened the door and hustled in.

''Is Benton here?'' she asked anxiously.

At that moment Benton came out, and as Allison looked from him to the nervous little woman, well past middle age, she wondered if this was a client. She remembered seeing the woman in the office once before. Allison couldn't decipher the look on Benton's face, but she wondered if it wasn't resignation she saw in his eyes.

The woman darted nervous looks in Allison's direction, and Benton said, ''Mrs. Holmes, this is our new owner, Allison Sayre. She inherited Mr. Page's assets. Miss Sayre, meet Lois Holmes.''

Allison extended her hand, and Mrs. Holmes took it in a weak clasp, while she quickly appraised Allison's person from head to toe.

"You're too young to be running this place."

Shocked by such a tart remark from a stranger, Allison still managed to say lightly, "You're probably right, and I daresay several of our employees agree with you."

When Benton ushered Mrs. Holmes into his office and closed the door, Allison asked, "Is she a customer?"

Did Celestine hesitate slightly before she answered? "I don't think so. She's a friend of Benton's and comes in to see him occasionally."

Mrs. Holmes stayed more than an hour, and as she went about her work, Allison heard the drone of the woman's querulous tones coming from Benton's office. He didn't seem to be saying much.

That afternoon Allison called the staff together for a short meeting to tell them about the picnic, and judging by the enthusiasm with which the news was received, it was a popular event. After Allison announced that she wanted to sponsor the occasion, she turned the meeting over to Celestine for the details. A coed softball game was quickly organized with Benton and Calvin as captains, and a sign-up sheet was distributed for possible participants.

"Amos has suggested," Celestine said, "that some of you might be interested in an exploration of Old Man's Cave. It isn't too far from our home and could be done in the morning, leaving the afternoon open for the ball game. I'll ask Truman to organize a hike in that region."

Allison gained a new respect for her staff as they quickly worked out the details. Someone suggested that because of the distance, the extra traffic during the holiday weekend, as well as a need to conserve parking space, it would be well for groups to carpool. It sounded like a good idea, but Allison wasn't prepared for Calvin Smith to approach her at the end of the meeting.

"Since you don't have a family nearby, I invite you to ride to the farm with my two children and me," Calvin said.

Allison hesitated, but she had no real reason to refuse.

"Thanks for the invitation. I accept. I'm looking forward to meeting our employees in a family atmosphere."

Did she detect a look of triumph in Calvin's face as he walked away? She wished she could have waited and perhaps Benton would have asked her. She hadn't had any special contact with him since the night he had come to her home, but his manner toward her at all times was more tender than it had formerly been, as if he knew and was concerned about the extra trauma she was experiencing in the wake of her newfound heritage. She wanted to question Celestine about Benton's background, but pride kept her from doing that, although she did check his file in the company's records. He was twenty-eight years old, and as far as she could tell had never been married.

The weather forecast was favorable for their trip to the Handley farm, and after a hurried breakfast, Allison dressed in white cotton piqué jean-styled pants and a white cotton knit T-shirt, and carried a cotton denim zip-front jacket patterned with pink roses. She put on heavy socks and white walking shoes, and was ready when Calvin picked her up in early morning. His daughter and son were well-behaved children, and Allison enjoyed the drive through rural Ohio. It was the first time she had traveled outside the city limits, though she had been in Columbus over four months.

The field where they parked was half-filled by the time they arrived and more cars followed them along the narrow limestone road that accessed the farm. Guests were directed to the parking area by Truman Handley, Celestine's smiling son, a man in his early twenties, his well-tanned handsome face framed by masses of dark, wavy hair whose wayward locks hung down over his brown eyes.

Celestine and her husband, Amos, waited at the front of their home—a large, rambling two-storied frame house that had obviously grown through the years. The dwelling was painted white, with a light-green roof, and situated as it

was among verdant fields and low, rolling hills, it was rem-
iniscent of a setting in a Rockwell painting of an earlier
time.

Allison liked Amos Handley at once. He was a man of
medium height, overweight and unconcerned about it. He
had unruly dark hair like his son and poignant brown eyes.

When Celestine introduced Allison, he said in a rich
drawl, "Well, now, so I get to meet the little boss at last.
Welcome to our home, Allison." Instead of shaking her
hand, he gave her a strong hug. "Now that you've found
where we live, we hope this won't be your last visit."

The Handleys turned to other arriving guests, and Allison
wandered toward the tables set up in the backyard where
pastries, mixed fruit, hot beverages and juice were available
for those who had not had time for breakfast. Taking advantage of Calvin's need to serve his children, Allison
thanked him for bringing her and left him to mingle with
the other guests. She wasn't going to spend the day in his
exclusive company. While trying to juggle a glass of juice
and a doughnut on a plastic plate, Allison encountered Benton.

His denim shorts and light-blue knit shirt unbuttoned at
the collar gave a new vivacity to his gray eyes, which
glowed with life. He had never appeared more handsome
and relaxed to her.

"Good morning, Miss Sayre," he said. "Let me help
you with your plate. Several of us are sitting at that table
to the right, and there's room for you."

He took the plate and led the way to the table he had
indicated. Allison felt as flustered as a schoolgirl to have
his attention, although it didn't last long, for after he seated
her, he moved to a chair several seats from her. While
talking with the employees nearest her, Allison was aware
of Benton chatting with others, and his conversation was
both witty and congenial, causing her to wonder again if
he might be the Benton Lockhart she had once idolized.
With pleasure Allison listened to the laughing and visiting

going on around her. This day's entertainment would cost Page Publishing a lot of money, but it was worth it.

When she was taking her plate and cup to the disposal bin, she encountered Amos Handley, his plate overflowing with rolls, and not one speck of fresh fruit did she see.

Laughing at her expression, he said, "Now, Miss Allison, it takes a lot of food to generate all these muscles of mine." He patted his big, solid stomach. "As hard as I work, I can't be a fashion model like you and Celestine."

She laughed with him. "Help yourself, Mr. Handley. I like to see happy people."

A look of sheer enjoyment creased his face as he regarded his plate. "And I'm happy when I have lots to eat."

Then Allison saw Reba Hall approaching, her face wreathed in an expansive smile. A teenaged boy dressed in a T-shirt and jeans walked by her side.

"Miss Sayre, I want you to meet my son, Edmond."

The boy was lanky, and his brown eyes were on a level with Allison's. "I'm pleased to meet you, Edmond. I'm happy you could come to our outing."

His eyes shifted, and he had trouble holding her gaze. He dropped his head, shuffled his feet and said in a low voice, "I appreciate what you did for my mother, Miss Sayre."

"Your mother is a valued employee of Page Publishing. It's our policy to keep our staff satisfied."

"I haven't bothered you at work with my affairs, Miss Sayre, but Edmond isn't living with me now. He's enrolled in a school in northeastern Ohio, where the curriculum is geared to rehabilitate drug and alcohol abusers. My eldest daughter and her family live there, and my son-in-law is overseeing Edmond's recovery. He spends the weekends at my daughter's home. We thought it was important for Edmond to be away from his former friends and to have a role model like his brother-in-law."

Allison turned to the boy, delight on her face. "That is great news, Edmond!"

He lifted his head and met her gaze briefly. "I'm finishing my high-school work, and I'm enrolled in a vocational program of computer repair. My brother-in-law owns a computer outlet, and on weekends, I tinker around his store, getting some hands-on experience. I intend to pay back the money you loaned us."

"We're all proud of Edmond, Miss Sayre, and we appreciate your help and concern. Mr. Page was a good employer, and you've stepped into his role very well. I'm proud to be working for you."

Allison felt like breaking out into a shout of exultation, but instead she sought a swing on the back porch and savored a great feeling of satisfaction as she looked out over the fields of corn waving like an ocean tide, and to the hillsides where a herd of Angus cattle grazed peacefully. The red farm buildings were in good repair and made a good contrast to the white farmhouse and garage connected to the house by a trellised breezeway.

Truman Handley approached her, swiping his unruly hair back from his face. "Come along, Miss Sayre, if you want to go with us to Old Man's Cave. I have the van loaded, but Mr. Smith said you will be riding with him."

Calvin had two other adults in his car, but his children had elected to stay behind for the watermelon-eating contest.

"Will someone tell me where we're going and what we're going to see?" Allison said as the caravan got under way.

"We're having a tour of Old Man's Cave State Park," Calvin explained. "The Hocking Hills have numerous recessed caves, and since the Handleys' farm is only a twenty-minute drive, this will be a good side trip. I've lived in Ohio all my life and have never visited any of these caves."

They traveled along curving, tree-lined roadways until they entered the grounds of the park. A ranger met them at the parking lot, which was shaded with tall pines and broadleaf trees, and divided them into two groups. This separated Allison from Calvin—a move that pleased Allison but not Calvin, if one could judge by the expression on his face.

"One group will start at the Upper Falls and continue downstream," the ranger explained. "The others will go to Old Man's Cave first, then down to Lower Falls and afterward walk to the upper end of the gorge. A ranger will accompany each group, but after his lecture, you can explore on your own."

"There isn't time for too much exploring," Truman warned. "Mother wants us to be back by one o'clock." He looked at his watch. "We should leave the parking lot by half-past twelve."

When the tour started, Calvin said to Allison, "You don't have to go with that group. Come with me."

"Oh, really, I'll be fine. This will give me an opportunity to become acquainted with some of the other employees as we hike."

"Suit yourself," he said sulkily.

Actually, Allison was glad to be relieved of his constant company, but she hoped that her relief wasn't obvious.

City-girl Allison had never had such an experience, and she stared in wonder as she trailed along behind the ranger. Descending a series of steps into a magnificent gorge, they wandered along the small stream until they stopped before a huge recessed sandstone cave. On the mammoth overhang above the cave, huge oak and maple trees grew upright and strong.

While the visitors stared in awe at the cave sprawling above them, the ranger explained, "The first European settlers came into this region soon after the close of the Revolutionary War, and the caves offered shelter for them as they had to Native Americans years before. This particular cave was the home of the hermit Richard Rowe, who lived here following the end of the War Between the States. The rim of the cave spans hundreds of feet around the sandstone curve."

Allison judged the recess measured a hundred feet from the rim to the cave's deepest part. In spite of the hot July sun, it was cool and clammy in the gorge, but Allison sat on a lichen-covered rock and contemplated the beautiful spot. Towering cliffs surrounded the hemlock-shaded gorge, and water trickled from ledge to ledge into a large pool. Several stones had tumbled from the cliffs and lay in the gorge, many of them carved with the initials of former hikers.

The party continued their walk downstream to Lower Falls, a rock projection with a steep declivity, although not much water was falling over it, and the sight didn't impress Allison as much as the caves had.

The ranger said, "When you've looked around here all you want to, return the way we came, and we'll go on the rim trail from Old Man's Cave to Upper Falls."

After she sat down on a fallen tree to take a stone from her shoe, Allison wandered off alone, looking in awe at the towering cliffs and the huge hemlock trees shooting upward from the base of the gorge. Careful to avoid unmarked trails, she continued down the gorge, noticing a sign that pointed to Ash Cave. Preferring to see it rather than the other waterfall, Allison headed down the trail, thinking she would have time to visit the cave and return before the group left. After she walked for fifteen minutes over the difficult terrain and hadn't yet arrived at the cave, Allison decided she should return to the parking lot. Clouds were thickening and thunder sounded in the distance, so she climbed the hill, not wanting to be down in the gorge if it rained.

In a short time Allison realized she was lost, and it not only scared her, but she was disgusted with herself. When she had come to a fork in the trail, she had apparently taken the wrong turn, and she must be outside the park boundaries, for she couldn't hear any other hikers. For an hour Allison searched the woods for an outlet, and finally she sat down, tired, disgusted, hungry and thirsty, even a bit scared, for with the darkening sky, the woods seemed almost sinister. She put a curb on her imagination when she began to envision a Shawnee Indian shadowing her.

Allison could hear traffic in the distance, but she didn't know if she should try to find that road. Considering the high cliffs and projecting rocks, with one misstep she could easily take a plunge and injure herself. Surely Calvin Smith would realize she was missing and come back for her.

She jumped to her feet in joy when she heard someone at a distance shouting, "Miss Sayre." She answered, "I'm coming," and ran toward the sound.

Expecting Calvin to be her rescuer, Allison rounded a curve in the trail, and was surprised to see Benton running toward her.

"Are you hurt?" he called. He held out his arms and she ran to him and was soon enclosed in the safety of his embrace.

Breathlessly, she said, "No, I'm fine, just feeling stupid for getting lost. I shouldn't have gone off by myself. I've never been in a forest, and I had no sense of direction. The woods became frightening when the storm was approaching, and I walked back and forth until I gave up and waited for someone to rescue me. I was overjoyed when I heard your call."

"Lean on me until we get back to the car," Benton said. "We don't have far to go."

He put his arm around her shoulder, and after her harrowing experience, it was pleasant to be supported by someone stronger than she.

"Celestine had a fit when she found out that Calvin had returned without you. He waited for some time, he said, and then decided you had gone back in the van. Knowing his odd sense of humor, he might have deliberately left you up here for a joke."

"Oh, don't say anything to him about it. I don't like his attention anyway, and this will give me an excuse to avoid him."

He gave her a curious look but asked no questions. "Let's hurry back, then. Celestine is very worried, but I told her I'd find you."

"I'm hungry. Did I miss my lunch?"

"Everybody is still feasting, but there will be plenty left for you. Amos roasted a large beef."

When they reached the narrow steps ascending out of the gorge and had to walk single file, Benton removed his arm, but when Allison panted on the deep steps, Benton took her hand and assisted her over the steepest places.

"Maybe you can take a nap while we're driving back to the farm."

Although Allison was embarrassed about being lost, still she surmised it might be worth it to have Benton rescue her. He said he was acting on Celestine's behalf, but she wanted to believe that he, too, had been concerned. The return trip passed too quickly for Allison, for she was content just to be riding by Benton's side; also, she was embarrassed to face her employees.

A cheer arose from the picnickers when Benton deposited Allison on the driveway and took his car back to the parking lot. Amos and Celestine hurried to her side.

"Are you all right?" Celestine inquired anxiously.

Lifting one hand to her flushed face, Allison waved the other hand airily at her employees and said lightly, "No harm done. I don't think any of you were living by the Golden Rule when you abandoned me, though I'll forgive you for leaving me in the wilderness if you haven't eaten all the food."

A laugh eased any tension there might have been. Calvin walked over to her, looking worried. "I am sorry, Miss Sayre. When you were late arriving at the car, I finally assumed you had already returned to the farm."

"'All's well that ends well,'" Allison quoted an old proverb. "That extra hour of hiking just heightened my appetite so I can eat a large lunch."

"Then I'll fill a plate for you."

To entertain the group after their meal, Celestine had arranged for a local dulcimer player. Her husband accompanied the woman with a guitar. Most of the entertainment was instrumental, but the performer sang a few numbers, which Allison particularly enjoyed since the words told her much about the heritage of this part of Ohio. It was amazing how different life was here to what she had experienced in Chicago.

Allison had always known that Ohio was one of the leading industrial states, but through the words of the songs she also learned that in 1803, it was the first state to be carved out of the Northwest Territory, although thousands of years ago, long before the influx of immigrants after the Revolutionary War, Ohio had been home to prehistoric Indians, the Mound Builders, who had left behind burial mounds, forts and other earthen works. The region had been dangerous for the early settlers. They'd had to cope with a series of Indian uprisings precipitated by European nations vying for control of this important area bounded by the Ohio River on the south and east and the Great Lakes to the north.

The dulcimer sounded a series of chords at the close of the presentation, and the singer's soft voice sung a version of Psalm 100 that had been used by the early Germanic immigrants to Ohio:

All people that on earth do dwell,
Sing to our Lord with cheerful voice;
Him serve with fear, His praise forth tell;
Come ye before Him and rejoice.

Allison welcomed the song's reminder that in the midst of their fun and fellowship today, the God of Creation also deserved some recognition. During the hectic months of establishing herself with Page Publishing, Allison felt that she had slipped in her personal devotion and praise to God.

She was grateful to the young woman for reminding her to constantly praise God for his bounty toward her.

The softball game was played in a pasture field, while the spectators ranged themselves under trees in viewing distance. Allison hadn't considered joining either team, as that might smack of favoritism, but she was looking forward to seeing her employees at play. Celestine and Truman were both participating, so Amos Handley, cheerfully admitting that he was too fat to play ball, took it upon himself to entertain Allison. He carried two lawn chairs under his arm and took her to an oak grove on a little knoll that commanded a good view of the playing area.

After watching the game for two innings, Allison was amazed at the skill of the players as well as the ferocity of their competition. When she remarked on this to Amos, he said, "They divided up into teams as soon as they knew we were having the picnic, and they've been practicing. There's a trophy that the captain of the winning team keeps in his office until the next game is played. Benton's team won the last time they played two years ago, and Calvin's players are determined to get the trophy this year."

Allison was pleased to see that Edmond Hall was on one of the teams and playing a creditable game, but her eyes strayed most often to Benton, whose muscular shoulders bulged against the light fabric of his shirt as he swung the bat or cast the ball from the pitcher's mound. Benton hit a home run in the last inning, but his team lost by one point. Calvin and Benton shook hands amiably, but Benton jumped back when Calvin's team sloshed a bucket of ice water on their captain's head.

A disheveled, sweating Celestine, a member of the losing team, joined Allison and Amos as they walked back to the house.

"Too bad—all that work for nothing, honey," Amos teased her.

"Oh, I don't know. I probably sweated off two pounds,

and—" she patted his paunch "—you should have followed my example."

"I prefer to do my sweating on a tractor," Amos said good-naturedly.

"I've had a wonderful time, Celestine," Allison said. "I know it's been a lot of work for you, but it's been good for me. I haven't laughed so much in years. This is my first visit to a farm."

Amos gazed at her in amazement. "Never been on a farm? Young woman, your education has been neglected. Why don't you spend the rest of the weekend with us."

Celestine threw Amos a quick look of caution or concern—Allison couldn't determine which it was—so she hastily demurred.

"Oh, I couldn't do that. I don't have enough clothes to spend the weekend here."

"You can borrow some of Celestine's. She has more clothes than she can ever wear. You could manage for her, couldn't you, honey?"

"Why, certainly," Celestine said graciously.

Allison decided she had mistaken her first reaction to Amos's suggestion. Laughing, she said, "Amos, after all the years you've been married, I'm surprised you don't know more about women. No woman wants to wear another's clothes. And though you're sweet to offer, I'll have to decline your invitation. I don't have my car, so I wouldn't be able to get back in time for work on Tuesday."

Celestine smiled. "I go to work at the same place you do, remember? And our hours are the same."

"Or you could ride in with Truman Monday afternoon," Amos said. "He's enrolled at Ohio State, and he would go right by your home on his way back to the dorm."

"You're about to convince me," Allison said hesitantly. "I'll admit I wasn't looking forward to spending the weekend in Columbus, for I insisted that the McRameys go for a visit with their families, and I would have been alone."

Wistfully, she added, "The Fourth of July has always been a big event for our family."

"Are you feeling a bit homesick?" Celestine inquired sympathetically.

"I guess so, and if it won't inconvenience you, I will stay until Truman leaves on Monday. But I won't borrow your clothing. I noticed the little town a few miles away had a small shopping center. If I can find a way to go in there, I'm sure I can buy something for tomorrow."

"You can use my car to go to the village," Celestine said. "Our guests will take it easy until time for the wiener roast, which will come before the fireworks. You can go shopping now, and probably won't be missed because most everyone will spread out on blankets and take naps."

Celestine's car was less than a year old, and it was enjoyable to drive—certainly having a lot more conveniences than Allison's did. As she drove into town, she contemplated purchasing a new car, but she put temptation aside. She didn't need another car yet.

The shopping center didn't offer much choice in clothing, but they had the type of lingerie she liked, and assuming that they would go to church the next day, she bought a sheath dress made from a sea-foam shade of linen. She also found a shorts set in prewashed denim. The jacket had a notched collar and patch pockets, and the full-leg shorts had a multistitch elastic waist with side pockets. She concluded her purchases with a natural toned pullover cotton top. Not wanting to spend much more money, she entered a shoe store and found an inexpensive sandal.

It was with some relief that Allison was able to tell Calvin that she wouldn't be returning to Columbus with him. He had been cocky and boisterous after his team had won the ball game, but Allison's plans obviously deflated him. Earlier, he had hinted none too subtly that after they returned to Columbus and he had taken his children back to their mother, he and Allison might spend the rest of the evening together. Considering that the fireworks probably wouldn't be over until half-past ten, followed by an hour's drive back to Columbus, Allison wouldn't have considered going anywhere with Calvin at that hour.

Darkness approached early because of clouds rolling in from the west, and again the people walked out to the field where the ball game had been held. Truman and Amos had a large bonfire going, and they sang until the flame died to coals that were suitable for the roasting of hot dogs and marshmallows. For the first time Allison enjoyed S'Mores, a roasted marshmallow and a piece of chocolate pressed between two graham crackers. After they'd eaten their fill, Amos threw some more wood on the fire so that it blazed more brightly.

"While we wait a little longer for complete darkness to enhance the fireworks," Celestine said, "I've asked Benton to relate a legend of our area."

Benton moved forward a little, and the group formed a semicircle around the fire so that everyone could see his face. His gray eyes, mysterious in the dusk, roamed over those before him as he waited for the last conversations to dwindle into whispers and then to cease.

"Today many of you have had your first introduction to the Hocking Hills, and tonight in the flickering light from the campfire in this quiet rural setting, with the noise of the city far away, we can easily revert to a time when primitive man, maybe as long as seven thousand years ago, inhabited these hills and made his abode in the picturesque recessed caves some of you saw today.

"Imagine with me the scent of venison roasting over a fire pit, enticing warriors in from the hunt and causing the gardeners to lay down crude wooden tools and head toward their lodges, set up under a vast sandstone overhang that formed a natural rock cavern. A ninety-foot waterfall cascades from a high ledge, providing a vast well that furnishes water for the tribe. When the well overflows, the water trickles down a small valley."

Benton paused to let his hearers envision this primeval

setting, and it was easy to feel displaced into another era. Katydids droned in the trees around them. Sleepy birds twittered and stirred restlessly, unable to settle for the night with so many humans in their midst. In the distance an owl mournfully intoned, "Hoo? Hoo?" The quiet, plaintive call of a bird could be heard—and the sad sound made Allison thoughtful and humble. Although Benton was speaking of secular matters, the stillness of the night drew her thoughts to God. Above her Allison could see a smattering of stars; a slight breeze rustled the leaves and wafted smoke in her direction, and her mind turned to the Psalmist and his many references to the wonders of Creation. Truly, the heavens did declare the glory of God!

"The first hardy white pioneers settled the region soon after the Revolutionary War," Benton said, continuing his tale, "and by that time, most of the Natives had moved on, leaving behind cavern floors littered with ashes, pottery and carvings, so that the white settlers knew that they were following in the path of those others who had tamed the land. The aborigines were gone, but the gorges, the caves, the trees and other wildlife remained."

Benton continued his narration, recounting the love story of an Indian maiden and her warrior, who were separated in life when he fell in battle. According to legend, they were united for eternity, their spirits destined to hover over the Hocking Hills. Benton's voice easily summoned up the sweet, melodious tone of a girl, changing to the deep, rough tones of the warrior. When he spoke of their love, his expression was warm and tender. The man was a gifted speaker.

Allison joined the others as they thronged around Benton to congratulate him on his storytelling ability, but she walked silently back to the Handley farmhouse, for that hour around the campfire had revealed more than the history of Hocking Hills. There was no doubt in her mind now that Benton Lockhart was the man she had met in Indianapolis eight years ago. During his presentation tonight, he had spoken with the same warmth, fervor, passion as that youth had done. She was happy that she had indeed found the young man she had respected, but the change in him troubled her. What had happened to transform Benton from the genuine, warm person he used to be to one who now hid his true nature under a dispassionate and reticent facade?

The breeze through the window was brisk when Allison awakened at her usual hour on Monday morning, and she burrowed a little deeper under the homemade comforter that Celestine had placed on the bed. The company picnic had been a huge success, and Allison, with her eyes still closed but in no notion of going back to sleep, thought about the past twenty-four hours. The fireworks had been spectacular, and she wondered fleetingly how much the whole celebration had cost her company. Allison had thoroughly enjoyed the picnic, and she knew now that she should have been more involved with her employees rather than taking Benton's advice and keeping a distance between herself and the staff.

Sunday morning had started with a leisurely breakfast in the Handleys' kitchen. Celestine was just as efficient in the kitchen as she was in the office, and she had prepared biscuits and sausage gravy while Allison, following her instructions to where all the serving items were stored, had set the table for the four of them.

Although much of the Handley house still had the stamp of the nineteenth century, when it was originally built, the kitchen was modern and obviously had been remodeled in the past few years. White wooden cabinets were trimmed in a delicate blue. Across the tops of the cabinets was a collection of colorful plates. The latest in equipment was available, including a microwave, dishwasher and trash disposal. The table, constructed of polished maple stood under a skylight that flooded the area with a soft radiance.

As they had sat down to eat, Celestine said, "I don't

take time to cook breakfast on weekday mornings, as I have to leave for work so early, and I usually have a cup of coffee and toast. Amos likes to tend the livestock before he eats, so Hannah prepares his breakfast after she comes to work.''

"Hannah?"

"Hannah Hoptry—a young woman who works for us five days a week. You will probably see her tomorrow.''

"Hannah! That's a pretty name.''

"Hannah is a pretty girl, too,'' Celestine remarked, "although judging from outward appearances, some might not think so. She belongs to a conservative religion where the women dress very modestly—no shorts, slacks or short-sleeved garments. These outward signs of purity are to symbolize the purity within.''

"And in Hannah's case, that is true,'' Amos said.

After she had finished her second helping of biscuits and gravy, Allison said, "I suppose my family is camping this weekend. Dad owns a lot on a lake about twenty-five miles north of Chicago. The family spends a lot of time up there in the summertime.''

"It sounds as if you've had a happy home life,'' Celestine commented.

"Yes, very. My dad has worked at a factory for twenty-five years, so he's had a steady income. Mother stays at home and takes care of the family, but they have managed very well on one salary. Growing up, we didn't have many luxuries, but we had everything we needed. I appreciate what my parents did for me.''

Her thoughts drifted momentarily when she thought about her natural background. In light of that, she was more appreciative of their sacrifice to provide for a child who wasn't even theirs.

After breakfast, they had gone to worship at a small church near the Handleys', and in the afternoon, Amos had taken Allison on a drive around the country, where acres of corn grew in straight rows in weedless fields. Green alfalfa was more than a foot high. Ripening grain spread over the low, rolling hills and dairy herds grazed near well-kept barns. Expensive, modern tractors, combines and other farming implements gleamed in the sun.

In early evening, Truman escorted Allison on a horse-back ride, and considering the fact that she had never before straddled a horse, it was a miserable experience for her. When they returned to the house after an hour's ride she could barely walk, and this morning her legs still chafed and burned.

Allison was ready to get up, and when she heard Amos whistling as he headed for the barns, she eased out of bed, relieved that her hips and thighs weren't as sore as they had been yesterday evening. After a shower, Allison dressed in her new shorts and shirt and went down to the kitchen, expecting to help Celestine with breakfast preparation, but Celestine wasn't there.

At the kitchen sink stood a young woman dressed in a calf-length dark-gray cotton garment with full skirt, high-necked blouse and long sleeves. The woman's glossy dark hair was drawn into a tight bun on her nape. When Allison entered, the woman turned to greet her with a fetching smile, her deep soft-blue eyes glowing.

"Oh, I'm sorry to bother you. I'm Allison Sayre. I expected Celestine to be here."

"I'm Hannah Hoptry, and I do housework for the Handleys. Mr. Handley said his wife was sleeping in this morning, and that I should get your breakfast when you came down. If you'll be seated, I will serve you."

Allison went to the refrigerator, opened the door, took out the pitcher of orange juice and filled a glass. "I get my own breakfast, Hannah—no need for you to bother with me. Go ahead with your work."

"At this moment, cooking breakfast is my work. I don't want to start the sweeper until Mrs. Handley is awake. I'm making pancakes for Mr. Handley's breakfast. Don't you want to have some?"

"All right. I'm easy to persuade when it comes to food."

Hannah took a bowl from the refrigerator, spooned a mixture onto an electric griddle and placed two strips of bacon in the microwave. She asked Allison's preference of beverage and brought a tall glass of cold milk to the table.

"You'll like that milk—from Mr. Handley's own cows."

Allison watched Hannah as she worked, and she had never seen a more serene countenance on anyone. When the plate of bacon and a large pancake was placed before her, Allison said, "Sit down, Hannah, and talk with me while I eat. Amos probably won't be in for a few minutes."

Hannah poured a cup of coffee and sat down opposite Allison.

"Tell me about yourself, Hannah. Do you live in this community?"

Hannah smiled, and the gesture had a magnetic effect on Allison—she had never felt so drawn to any of her girlfriends as she was to this young woman. Hannah wore no jewelry, and her face was free from makeup, but her face glowed with a rosy tinge that couldn't be found in a bottle.

"About five miles away. My dad brings me to work, and Mr. Handley usually drives me home." Hannah observed Allison with admiration. "Those are pretty clothes you're wearing, Miss Sayre."

"Call me 'Allison,' please."

Hannah nodded and continued, "And I like your pretty hair, too." Her voice lowered. "Sometimes I wish I could dress like that."

At a loss for words, Allison stammered, "Clothing isn't that important. Spiritual serenity comes from the inside, and I can tell you have peace of mind and heart."

Amos entered the washroom next to the kitchen, and Hannah picked up her cup and rustled over to the stove to start his breakfast.

"Hannah, I'm going to leave for Columbus this morning, but I hope we can meet again. I would enjoy talking to you."

"I'd like to see you again," Hannah agreed with a smile.

Both Amos and Celestine were genuine in their invitation for Allison to visit them at any time, and since Allison had already decided that one could carry the employer-employee ban on fraternization too far, she agreed that she would visit again. She especially wanted to return and cultivate the friendship of Hannah, whom she considered a most amazing young woman.

Truman proved to be a somewhat reckless driver who reminded Allison of Tim, but she gritted her teeth, hoped for the best and enjoyed the rapid drive back to Columbus. Although Truman was only three years her junior, he seemed like a child to her. When he pulled up in front of Allison's Victorian home, he whistled.

"You don't mean you actually own this place."

"Yes, I do, thanks to my uncle Harrison."

His eyes lighted momentarily with envy. "Must be nice."

"Not necessarily—lots of problems accompany riches. Besides, you're an only child and one day you'll inherit that showplace farm your parents have built."

He laughed, reminding Allison of his father. "Oh, I know it. But since you live in such splendor, surely you won't mind a poor, hungry college boy coming for a meal once in a while."

"Of course not. You're welcome anytime. But don't come unannounced. Either call me or the housekeeper a few hours in advance."

"I won't make a pest of myself, but I will come occasionally. College cafeteria food is pretty awful."

"I know," Allison agreed. "I've had a few college meals, too."

Chapter Six

After their Fourth of July outing, the employees were much friendlier to Allison; in fact, the whole atmosphere in the workplace seemed more relaxed. Knowing that her mingling with them at the picnic had caused the difference, Allison took her lunch down to the first floor occasionally and ate with the staff. When she went to the various departments, she took more time to visit with them.

Allison telephoned her family each week, and when her father had vacation, she begged them to visit her in Columbus, for she knew Tim and Cleta were eager to come. Her mother refused, and although Allison had never mentioned anything more about Harrison being her birth father, she felt a tension between herself and Beatrice when they talked. Even at that, Allison couldn't understand why they wouldn't come to visit her—out of curiosity about the house and other surroundings, if for no other reason. Charles took the family camping, as he always had, and if she had been asked, she would have taken a week away from work to go with them. Perhaps it was all in her mind, but she wondered if Tim and Cleta had been told that she wasn't their sister and they considered her an outsider now. Had they always felt that way about her?

It was Page Publishing policy to close the last two weeks in August and for everyone to go on vacation at the same time. Allison intended to return to Chicago for part of that time, but things had changed for her now, and she didn't anticipate the visit as she once had. As vacation approached the Page employees talked excitedly about their plans. Benton made no comment on what he planned to do, but Calvin was taking his two children to Disney World. Celestine and Amos were flying to Philadelphia to see Amos's sister. Compared with these vacations, a trip to Chicago didn't sound very exciting; therefore, Allison was pleased that she would have the trip to San Francisco with Benton. Her vacation plans became even more exciting when her mother relented and gave permission for Cleta and Tim to visit Allison for a few days during the first week of her vacation.

Allison rushed to tell the McRameys about the visit of her siblings. "I'm really excited, Minerva. I felt guilty about going to San Francisco when the rest of my family wouldn't have the opportunity, but if Cleta and Tim can have a nice trip, I'll feel better. I don't want to be selfish."

Minerva laughed and hugged Allison's shoulders. "No one can accuse you of that."

Allison sent a check to her father to cover the cost of the two plane tickets and began to make plans to entertain Tim and Cleta. She welcomed the opportunity to have them because she was becoming obsessed with the trip to San Francisco. Although she didn't want to admit it, she knew her excitement was so intense because she was going to have a week's trip with Benton Lockhart. The realization disturbed her because, even though her thoughts and dreams were often of Benton, she was hesitant to become involved romantically with another man, and she was well aware of the strong hold Benton had on her emotions. Experience had taught her that love could be too painful, and she didn't want to be hurt again.

At home, she was caught up in plans for the impending visit, and Minerva and Adra were as interested as she was. At Page Publishing, the employees could hardly get through their last week of work before time for vacation, so it was no wonder that she couldn't contain her excitement.

After she read the semiannual financial report of the company for the period ending June 30 and compared it with the previous year's report, it seemed as if the company's income had increased by 15 percent. Not sure she was reading the report correctly, she called Thomas for an appointment, and when he confirmed her deductions and complimented her management of the company, she said, "You know that I had very little to do with it, but I believe the employees are more diligent in their work habits and are more interested in the company prospering since they know that their jobs are secure. During Uncle Harrison's illness, all of them must have been wondering how long they would have a job."

"I daresay you're right, but don't underestimate your own role. You've set a good example for them. Don't think they're unaware of the long hours you spend at work, or that you're still driving a six-year-old car when you've inherited a fortune and that you wear neat but inexpensive clothing. There are very few people, young or old, who wouldn't be flaunting their fortune like a flag. You've stayed in the background and let the workers do their job."

"Well, whatever the cause, Page Publishing has done well this year, and I want to share some of that increase with the employees. I know there are year-end bonuses, but will it jeopardize our financial standing if we give them a vacation bonus, maybe an extra month's salary?"

"Not as far as I can determine."

"Then I'll discuss it with Benton and have him work it out with the accountant."

Benton's door was open when she returned to the office, which meant that he wasn't occupied at the time.

"Have a few minutes for serious discussion?" she queried with a smile.

He looked up, lazily returned her smile, and leaned back in his chair.

"I have an appointment in a half hour."

"This won't take long," she said, and went in and closed the door.

She took the financial statement out of the file.

"It seems to me that the company has done extremely well for the first six months of the year and I want to give the employees a vacation bonus, if you think we can afford it."

"I don't know why it can't be done. What did you have in mind?"

"Perhaps an extra month's salary or a half-month's to be given the day the company closes for vacation. You'd have to figure out how much that would cost us and then discuss it with the accountant. I want to do it, but I don't want to make a mess of our finances."

"You would be setting a precedent, something to be expected every year."

"I could write a letter to be included in each pay envelope to the effect that the bonus is given because of good performance, but should not be expected unless the company's income is adequate. I believe the staff will work harder if they can reap a financial benefit, but I don't want to do anything foolish."

Benton's smiling gray eyes showed his approval of her suggestion, and another emotion that she couldn't interpret.

"It's a good move to promote company loyalty. In Mr. Page's day, if he made an extra profit he invested it in the business someway. Your idea of investing it in the employees will be beneficial to the company in the long run and in keeping with your predecessor's policy."

His approval of her idea filled her with joy and her heartbeat quickened as her gaze met his and she returned his wide, warm smile. At times like these, she wondered if her heart hadn't been safer when Benton was indifferent toward her.

"I hesitate to give you extra work," she said, finally, "but you will know how to handle this efficiently."

"I'll look into it immediately. Our accountant will throw a tantrum with so little notice, but we'll see what can be done."

Lois Holmes, the mysterious woman who often came to see Benton, was fidgeting in Celestine's office when Allison left, and she darted inside Benton's office and closed the door. Allison thought she must visit him at least once a month, and again she wondered at the connection between Benton and this woman.

Benton and the accountant decided that since this was a first-time bonus, and on a trial basis, that a half-month's salary would be sufficient. Allison preferred to double the amount, but she made no protest, and obviously the employees were astounded at even that unexpected windfall. They received their paycheck with the bonus included when they arrived at work on the last day preceding vacation, and on their break, many of them stopped by the office to voice their thanks. When the buzzer sounded at four o'clock, Allison heard shouts resound through the building, and in a few minutes, Benton told her, "Open the window to the parking lot."

She looked out her office window to the employees massed below. Benton and Celestine stood beside her as a round of applause wafted their way. Then the group broke into singing:

> For she's a jolly good fellow,
> For she's a jolly good fellow,
> For she's a jolly good fellow,
> Which nobody can deny.

She waved to them, but her eyes misted as the exodus of cars began. Had she justified Harrison's faith in her? She hoped so, for she believed that happy employees were faithful employees. The Golden Rule had worked.

She turned from the window into Celestine's arms. "You've done a wonderful thing for all of us, Allison, and Mr. Page would have been proud of you. All of us are."

Benton kissed her on the cheek. "A great decision, Miss Sayre. Thank you. The extra money will be a big help to everyone. I'm going to be out of town for a few days, but I'll contact you next week to make last-minute plans for our trip to San Francisco."

After he left the office, Celestine handed Allison an envelope. "Benton's birthday is August 27, and that will be while you're in San Francisco. Will you give him this card? I try to remember his birthday each year."

Allison tucked the card in her purse, deciding she would do something for his birthday, too. "You've just given me an idea, Celestine. When we return from vacation, if you'll print out a list of employees' birthdays, I'll send each of them a personal card on their special day. With only thirty-five employees, it shouldn't be a burdensome task."

Cleta and Tim were scheduled to arrive on Sunday and return to Chicago on Wednesday, so Saturday was taken up with plans for them. Allison helped Minerva prepare their bedrooms, giving Tim the master bedroom, now brightened by new draperies and bedspread, and Cleta the room at the end of the hall; which overlooked the flower beds. This room was furnished with a rosewood bed and dresser, and the posts on the four-poster bed were just a few feet short of the ceiling. Bright, flowered wallpaper covered the walls and the ceilings, and lace curtains graced the windows. Allison had bought a new set of ruffled-hem sheets in a pattern of pink flowers on a sea-foam-green background, with contrasting patterns on the pillowcases. The coordinated comforter, bed ruffle and pillow shams were sure to please Cleta. Allison scattered several colorful cushions around the room.

After the rooms were ready, Allison went to the store and purchased the many snack foods that Tim and Cleta liked, although she probably shouldn't have bothered, for Minerva had been baking goodies for a couple of days and the aroma of cookies and baking bread greeted Allison each day as she came home. On the day of their arrival, the McRameys were as excited as Allison when she left for the fifteen-minute drive to Columbus International Airport.

"Allison," Cleta yelled as soon as she stepped into the airport and saw her sister. She ran toward Allison, stumbling over the strap of the backpack that she was swinging in her hand.

Tears choked Allison—it had been six months since she had seen any of her family, and as busy as she'd been, she hadn't realized how much she had missed them.

"Hi, Sis," Tim said, landing a mock blow on her shoulder. "Flying is neat. Thanks for sending us the money for a ticket so we didn't have to take the bus. It was great fun, although I didn't care much for the lunch we had."

Putting her arms around both of them and steering them toward the baggage claim on the ground floor, she said, "You can load up at the house. Minerva has enough food prepared to feed an army, and she's a great cook."

Cleta had brought two large suitcases, but Tim had stuffed all his belongings in one small bag, and they all talked at the same time while they loaded the luggage into the car.

"The same old car, I see," Tim said critically.

Allison shook her head at him. The boy had a fixation on new cars.

"What are we going to do while we're here? Two days will go in a hurry," Cleta said.

"I've got plenty planned for you."

Tim and Cleta filled Allison in on news from home as they took the back streets from the airport to Neil Avenue.

"You mean you actually own this house?" Cleta said when she pulled into the driveway.

"Uncle Harrison must have been richer than we thought."

"Maybe I can come down here and go to college and stay with you," Cleta said. "OSU is supposed to be a great university, and it's practically in your backyard."

"We'll see," Allison said, not given to making rash promises without consulting her parents.

Allison had never known her brother and sister to be so enthusiastic. They liked everything—their bedrooms, the house in general, the food, the McRameys, the whole neighborhood. It was past midnight before they settled enough to go to sleep.

Allison had planned a full schedule for the next day—she took them on a tour of Page Publishing, they went to the Columbus Zoo and stopped for a couple of hours at the city center, where she gave them a hundred dollars each to spend for whatever they wanted. They were more than ready to return to the Neil Avenue residence by six o'clock and Minerva's dinner.

When they went in through the kitchen door, Minerva said, "Truman telephoned, and I told him I'd have you return the call."

"Who's Truman?" Cleta demanded. "A new boyfriend?"

"Well, he's a boy and he's a friend, but not the way you have in mind. He's the son of my secretary—a student at OSU."

Before she went up to her room, Allison stopped in the library to telephone Truman.

"I'm an orphan," he said piteously, "and I may starve before morning."

Laughing, she said, "So you didn't go to Philadelphia with your parents. I assumed you would."

"No, too much studying to do. I have a term paper due next week."

"I'll take pity on you and invite you for dinner. My brother and sister are visiting, and I want you to meet them anyway."

When Allison saw how well Truman fitted into their family circle, she invited him to go with them on the next day's outing.

"You might be of some help to me. Have you ever been to the Indian mounds down around Chillicothe?"

"Yes, I have—all good Ohio Boy Scouts go there. I should stay home and study, but I can take one day's break."

Truman arrived at eight o'clock, and they went first to the Great Serpent Mound near Hillsboro, Ohio, which was built by the Adena peoples long before the birth of Christ. The burial mound, which resembled a huge snake from the air, measured about a fourth of a mile long. In Chillicothe they checked out historical sites dating back to the time when that city was the state's capital. After they stopped in a city park to eat the bountiful picnic that Minerva had packed, they were ready to start back to Columbus.

"Since we're in good time," Truman said, "let's drive by home so they can see our farm. Mother and Dad are gone, but Hannah is cleaning this week."

"That would be great," Allison said. "Tim and Cleta don't know any more about farming than I did when I came here."

Tim and Cleta enthusiastically endorsed the idea, and Allison checked the road map to find the quickest route to the Handley farm from Chillicothe.

As the farmhouse first came into view and Truman pointed it out as his home, Tim said, "What a neat place to live! Look at all those cows."

When they parked in the driveway, Hannah waved to them from the porch, and Cleta said, "Why would she dress that way? In that long dress she must be sweltering in this hot weather."

"Please watch your tongue, Cleta," Allison said. "Hannah dresses in that manner because of her religious beliefs, which leads to a life-style more conservative than ours."

"She's pretty," Tim said.

"Very lovely, inside and out," Allison said. "I hope she will become my friend, for I like her very much."

After introductions were made, Truman said, "I'm going to take you on a tour of the farm. We'll go by tractor, so it shouldn't take long."

"I'll stay here," Allison said, "since I've already had the grand tour. Will I interrupt your work, Hannah?"

"Not at all. It's time for me to take a breather. Let's sit on the trellised porch, where there's always a breeze. I'll have some lemonade for you when you get back," she called to the three who were heading for the barn.

"They'll like that. We've been out in the sun a lot today."

"I'll go prepare the lemonade and take some cookies out of the freezer. I won't be gone long."

Allison was glad for a few moments to be alone. She had become accustomed to solitude, and while she had enjoyed her visitors, she hadn't had any time to relax. She heard the hum of the tractor as it climbed the hill behind the barn, but she was more conscious of the sights around her. A hummingbird feeder at the corner of the porch attracted tiny birds that winged constantly back and forth, stopping for an instant to take a sip of the pink nectar. Bees buzzed among the geraniums and petunias blooming in the flower bed beside the garage. A saucy mockingbird perched on a fence post and filled the air with his melodious repertoire of birdcalls.

When Hannah returned, she carried a tray holding the ice-filled pitcher of lemonade, five glasses and a plate of cookies.

"The cookies have to thaw a bit, but you can have some lemonade now if you want."

"No, let's wait for the children." She laughed. "Calling them children makes me sound as though I'm in my dotage.

Sometimes I feel that way when I observe the exuberance
of Tim and Cleta. I remember myself as a rather quiet teenager—I'm sure I never had that much energy."

"My father is a farmer, and when we were children, we
worked every day except Sunday. Even as children we had
chores to do."

"It sounds like a good life, though. Sometimes when I'm
hustling around trying to learn all I need to know and coping with all the new responsibilities I've had this year, a
quiet life on a farm sounds good."

With her winning smile, Hannah replied, "And dare I
confess that I envy your way of life, Allison? Mrs. Handley
talks about the publishing company quite a lot, and the way
you've tackled your responsibilities there, and I often wish
I could be in your place." She dropped her head and said
timidly, "I've been doing some writing—that's the reason
I'm interested in publishing."

"How wonderful! What kind of writing?"

Hannah's hands were crossed in her lap, and she still
didn't look at Allison. "Children's stories. I've written little
things for years and read them to my brothers. I would like
to be a writer, but my parents discourage me—they think
it's a woman's duty to marry and have children, and if one
does that, there's no time for writing."

"Many people are housewives and successful writers,
too. I don't know why you couldn't be, also. I'd like to
read some of your work."

Hannah darted a look at Allison, then lowered her eyes
again. The tractor with the three laughing youths whizzed
by the house on the way to the barn, and Hannah stood up
to resume her duties. By the time Truman and his guests
arrived at the porch, Hannah had poured the lemonade and
had the cookies ready on small plates. The talk turned to
horses, cows and big fields of grain, the likes of which the
Chicagoans had never seen. Hannah said very little, seemingly enjoying the conversation of the others. As they prepared to leave, however, when the others had gotten in the

car Allison said quietly, "Hannah, I think you should pursue your love of writing, and I would like to read some of your work."

Hannah's fair skin flushed, and her hands trembled as she fumbled with her apron. "I don't know if I should."

"You can send the stories by Celestine if you change your mind."

When Allison got behind the wheel, Truman said, "Let's follow the secondary roads back to Columbus. It will take longer, but the traffic is slack, and we can enjoy the view."

"That's fine with me," Allison said. "You be the navigator and tell me where to go so I won't have to read the map."

Allison didn't pay much attention to the chatter of her passengers, for she was thinking about Hannah and her writing interest, but thoughts of Hannah fled when they passed a small cemetery about thirty miles from the Handley farm. The fenced cemetery was on a sloping hill, and a weathered wooden sign over the gate read Miller Family Cemetery. Her mother's name had been Mary Miller. Could she find a clue to her ancestry here? At the public library, she had looked through all the phone books in the area, and there were many Millers listed, even one Mary Miller, but when she had tried to call, the phone had been disconnected. She couldn't stop today, but she made a mental note of the location of the cemetery, thinking that she could come alone and see if those burial plots might hold the secret of her past.

Allison had packed her luggage the night before, and she sat in the parlor watching for Benton an hour before he was due. She tingled all over with excitement, and she wondered what was wrong with her. Her girlish crush on the Benton Lockhart of her youth was so mixed up with the emotions that he provoked in her now that she didn't know which way to turn. She must watch herself this weekend. Benton had been helpful the night she had learned about

her real father, and not since then had he lapsed into the
cold, exacting person he had been when she had first arrived in Columbus, but he hadn't gone beyond friendship,
so if she was too forward during this trip, he might revert
to the icy manner he had earlier displayed.

Knowing she could not spend an hour fidgeting and peering out the window, Allison went into the library and
picked up her Bible to continue daily devotions, which she
had skimped on this morning in her rush to prepare for
their journey. She turned to the passage that the minister
had used in his message on Sunday. The Apostle Paul had
been admonishing Timothy, ''Set an example for the believers in speech, in life, in love, in faith and in purity.''
Allison determined to remember that verse during the coming week. Benton's apparent lack of faith disturbed her, and
she wondered if their days together would present an occasion to witness to her own faith in God's saving grace.
If nothing else, she should set a believer's example before
him, and she couldn't do that if she allowed her growing
fascination with him to override her good judgment.

God, she prayed, *You've given me this week. Right now
I don't know what opportunities might present themselves.
Will You give Your blessing on our time together and in
some way make me an instrument whereby Benton might
renew his commitment to You? I feel too weak and unwise
to know how to deal with my feelings for this man, who
really is a mystery to me. Amen.*

Although her feet itched to run to meet him when he
stepped from the car, Allison forced herself to stay in the
library until Benton rang the doorbell. Ignoring the pounding of her heart, she calmly opened the door. ''All ready?''
he asked with a smile.

''All ready. Looks as if we have a pleasant day for our
trip.''

''I'll get your luggage.'' He followed her into the living
room and picked up the two pieces she had packed. Mi-

nerva and Adra came into the hall to bid them goodbye. Minerva kissed Allison, and Adra shook her hand.

"You watch out for our girl," Adra warned Benton.

"She'll be as safe with me as if she were under your care," Benton said with a broad smile. "I can't afford to lose a good boss."

"Pray for us," Allison called to the McRameys as she went down the sidewalk to Benton's car, where he was storing her luggage in the trunk.

When they arrived in the vicinity of the airport, Benton pulled into a parking facility with valet service, and a driver took them to their airline in Benton's car and returned the automobile to the security of the parking lot. With only one round-trip flight to her credit, Allison knew little about flight procedures, but she followed Benton's example as they checked the luggage at curbside and presented their tickets and a picture ID before they entered the terminal.

"We still have an hour before loading time," Benton said. "Shall we have a soft drink? I'm buying."

Allison dimpled a smile in his direction. "I never turn down anything free," she said. "Remember I'm related to Harrison Page."

He put his arm around her shoulders, and Allison's heart soared.

"I never forget that for a moment," he joked.

She realized how much comfort she gained from knowing he knew and understood about her past.

During much of the flight Benton chatted companionably, and he was attentive to Allison's comfort, but there were quiet times, too, when she looked out the plane's window, sometimes seeing only the clouds that resembled down-filled comforters hiding the earth below. Farther west, however, the clouds faded, and she saw the broad fields of the Midwest, easily identifying, after Benton pointed them out to her, the round green circles of the ir-rigated fields and the square township lines, until gradually the level land gave way to foothills and then to the Rocky

Mountains—range after range of snowcapped peaks, blue mountain lakes and rugged rock outcroppings.

Struck by the majesty of the scene below them, she said, "I've never seen anything before that impressed me so much with the magnificence of God's creation. I wish I could stand on one of those vast peaks and cry out, 'My God, how great You are!'"

Impulsively, she turned, wanting to share the earth's glory with Benton, but he was staring straight ahead as if he hadn't heard her, and his stern face left no room for any further praising of God's beauty. Apparently any comment about God or her spiritual beliefs was off-limits with Benton, so where did that leave her good intentions to witness to her own faith this week? Someday she intended to ask him outright about his spiritual beliefs, but she didn't want anything to mar this trip, so she ignored his attitude.

When the steward brought their dinner, Benton was once again attentive to her comfort and was friendly the remainder of the trip, but as they stood waiting for their luggage in the noisy San Francisco terminal, Allison reflected on their flight. She had spent the whole day with this man who interested her greatly, and they'd had a pleasant time, but she realized that for all their hours of visiting, she knew no more about his private life than she had when she had come to Columbus in March. He freely discussed anything that he knew about Page Publishing and the industry, but he apparently had no desire to share any aspect of his personal life with her.

The next four days were busy—Allison helped set up the booth in the large conference center of their hotel, arranging their new products and displaying signs about the services of Page Publishing. Benton introduced her to all perspective buyers and other publishers, and she learned much about the needs and wants of their clients as she talked with the many people who stopped by their display. She took occasional breaks and looked over the stock of other exhibitors. Remembering Hannah's interest in writing, she took particular note of the companies that produced children's curriculums.

The convention closed at noon on Saturday, and their flight was booked for early the next morning. Allison helped pack their display, and Benton arranged to have the parcels taken to the airport for shipping. When he finished, he said, "So what shall we do now? Take in the sights of the Golden City?"

"I would love that."

"Then you should change into comfortable shoes." He looked approvingly at her black-and-white houndstooth blazer and streamlined black crepe pants. She was wearing a white blouse, a gold chain necklace and tiny gold earrings. "You've certainly added charm to our booth this year and we'll have to make this an annual outing, but your heels won't do for this afternoon. We will do some walking and San Francisco is a hilly city."

Before they parted to their separate rooms, Allison took Celestine's birthday card from her purse. "Compliments of Celestine," she said. "I know your birthday isn't until tomorrow, but since we'll be traveling then, let's celebrate it tonight by going out for dinner." Her lips parted in a grin. "I'll pay this time. It will be your birthday gift."

"I already had in mind where I wanted to go tonight, and I'll accept your gift with pleasure if you'll let me choose the restaurant. It's down in the wharf area, on the second floor, with a large alcove where we can look out over the bay. This afternoon we can ride the cable cars, shop in downtown San Fran, visit Golden Gate Bridge and go to the wharf this evening. Would that suit you?"

"Sounds wonderful."

"Then I'll make reservations while I'm in my room and meet you in the lobby in a half hour."

He had changed into a red-and-white striped shirt and white shorts when he met her, and he looked so handsome that Allison was breathless for a moment. She felt rather

dull in jeans and knit blue blouse when Benton took her
arm.

"As of twelve o'clock today, we are off the expense
account of Page Publishing, Miss Sayre. As a matter of fact,
why don't we pretend we've never heard of Page Publishing, and be friends rather than employer and employee."

Allison's heart skipped a beat, but she agreed noncha-
lantly, "Suits me," and added to herself, *that's what I've
been wanting for a long time.*

"Let's go, Allison," he said, taking her hand, swinging
it as they went outside to catch the shuttle bus into downtown San Francisco. They rode the cable cars from point
to point, stopping often to look in the shops, climbing back
on the next car, clinging to the straps for the downhill
plunges. They were as carefree as teenagers, and Allison's
face was wreathed in a perpetual smile.

"Where's the best place to buy gifts?" she asked. "I
had strict orders from Tim and Cleta to bring them souvenirs."

"Why not wait until we go down to the wharf. They
have lots of shops there, and the items aren't as expensive
as you will find in this area. Then, too, we won't have to
carry them all afternoon."

They took a leisurely stroll down Sacramento Street, a
quiet, shady stretch in one of the city's most interesting
shopping districts. It was an offbeat street for the tourists,
but locals frequented the area to buy anything from contemporary crafts to choice antiques and serviceable, quality
children's garments.

After going by bus to the Golden Gate Bridge area, they
walked out on the bridge itself, where they stopped to
watch the many sailboats in the bay and the fishermen lined
up along the breakwater walls. At the wharf area, Allison
bought a carved wooden seal for Tim and a set of gemstone
earrings and necklace for Cleta. She also bought sweatshirts
for each of them, and when she saw the reasonable prices,

she said, "I'm going to buy one, too. I should have at least one souvenir to remind me of our day on the town."

Allison paid for her purchases, and as they left the store, Benton handed her a package. "How about two souvenirs? You can put this on your desk to help you remember our day together."

Eagerly she opened the sack to find a model of the Golden Gate Bridge.

"Oh, I like it," she said. "Thanks so much. I'll enjoy seeing it every day."

As he directed her toward the restaurant he had chosen, Allison knew that she didn't need any visible reminder of this day—one that she would never forget. Everything they had seen and every word and action of Benton were etched indelibly in her heart.

The maître d' escorted them to a table for two in a corner that had an unobstructed view of San Francisco Bay and seated them in two chairs close together so they could both enjoy the view. Sailboats were silhouetted in the gathering dusk and fishing vessels floated toward their moorings into the dock area. Seabirds swung low over the water, looking for food, and the more brazen birds stalked the wharf, picking up choice tidbits of diners' castoffs from the damp boards.

After they gave their orders for a green salad, a seafood variety platter with assorted vegetables, the waiter dimmed the light at their table, and Benton's eyes sparkled as he turned toward her.

"Very romantic," he said lightly. He reached for her hand. "Had a good day?"

"The best ever. Although in the past few months, I've despaired of the change Harrison Page brought in my life, there have been precious moments, too, and this is one of them. A whole new world opened up for me when I came to Columbus, and I needed the change. Chicago was no place for me."

"Care to tell me why?"

Allison didn't want to think about Donald now. "Some other time, perhaps. I don't want to talk about the past and ruin this evening. We're celebrating your birthday, remember?"

Seated as they were with their backs to the other diners, it was almost as if they were alone in a world of their own. Soft music muffled the voices of those in the room and the restaurant employees made no sound as they walked back and forth on the thick carpet. The whistle of an incoming steamer reminded them of the local setting; otherwise, they could have imagined being on a desert island.

Benton released her hand when their salads arrived, but the romantic mood persisted as the main course was served. As they waited for dessert, he laid his arm across her shoulders, and Allison turned toward him. She started to speak, but he cupped her chin in his hand, bent forward and kissed her. Breathless, she couldn't remove her gaze from the gray eyes, warm and tender, that mesmerized her. She was sure he would have kissed her again, but the waiter arriving on noiseless tread, said, "And which one of you ordered the apple pie?"

There was little conversation as they rode in a taxi back to their hotel, but Benton sat with his arm about her. Allison nestled close to him, her head on his shoulder. He took her to the door of her room and with a sigh he said, "Thanks for the birthday dinner, Allison. This has been a wonderful afternoon and evening for me. It seems as if it's the first time I've relaxed for years. Too bad we have to go back to Columbus and end all our fun."

With her heart pounding in her breast, Allison said breathlessly, "End? Does it have to end, Benton?"

A weary, sad look crossed his face.

"Yes... Yes, it does have to end, Allison."

He drew her into his arms and held her in a tight embrace. Without kissing her again, he murmured good-night and left her.

Chapter Seven

True to his word, following their return from San Francisco, Benton was reserved in his dealings with Allison, but he didn't call her "Miss Sayre" anymore. She refused to let his attitude dampen her spirits. For one thing, she was convinced he was attracted to her, for often she sensed Benton was watching her, and she would look up suddenly and surprise a wistful expression that changed immediately when he knew she had intercepted his gaze. Also, he spent more time in her office, briefing her on business matters. She longed to return to the intimacy they had experienced on their business trip, but she forced herself to act nonchalant, while her whole being cried out for his love.

She had mixed emotions about her affection for Benton—for fear of being hurt, she had not wanted to love anyone again, and though in most ways she considered Benton an excellent choice for a husband, his lack of spiritual commitment bothered her. She wouldn't marry a man who didn't share her faith.

She continued to work each Saturday morning, and one Saturday in late September, about noon, Benton entered the building. He was in his office briefly, and then he appeared at her door.

"About through for the day," he said, and his smile was so captivating that she lowered her eyes from his intense gaze.

"Yes, I work only a few hours on Saturday, and I may stop that now since you and Celestine have tutored me so well. I don't feel so stupid about the company anymore."

"You are not stupid about this business and never have been," he asserted.

His words caused her spirits to soar. She wanted his approval.

"Have any plans for the rest of the day?" he asked.

"I'm going home, getting into shorts and spending the afternoon outdoors. We won't have many more days like this."

"Would you be interested in taking in a Swiss festival?"

"Sure, that sounds like fun."

"There's one held at Sugarcreek, northeast of Columbus. It's an interesting drive. Would you like to go up there with me?"

More than anything else in the world, her heart said, but she replied lightly, "Yes, what time do you want to start?"

"It's a hundred-mile drive, so we should start soon and eat lunch en route—my treat this time. Can you be ready in an hour?"

She nodded. "I'll put these papers away and go home now. It won't take me long to change clothes."

He was the Benton of San Francisco, exuding charm and pleasure in her company as they lunched leisurely. It was midafternoon before they reached Sugarcreek, and Benton held her hand as they walked through the streets of the little town, watching the costumed dancers and listening to the polka bands. Swiss cheese was available for convenient snacking. The afternoon was marred by only one incident—

when they entered a gift shop and came face-to-face with Calvin Smith and his two children.

"What a surprise!" Calvin said, and the expression in his eyes didn't indicate that it was a pleasant one. "Miss Sayre, Mr. Lockhart, enjoying a departure into the past."

Uncomfortable, Allison tried to release her hand, but Benton's grip tightened.

"Yes," he said to Calvin. "We're having a nice afternoon. What about you and the children?"

"If I had known that Miss Sayre had dropped her rule of employer dating employees, she could have come with us," Calvin said.

"I don't consider Mr. Lockhart an employee—you know as well as I do that he really runs the company. I'm still learning what's what."

"Come on, Dad," Calvin's son said, and the Smiths went on their way.

Guiltily, Allison looked up at Benton. "Ignore the guy," he said with a laugh. "He's just jealous—he wishes he were in my place in more ways than one."

Benton was a delightful companion, just as he had been that day in San Francisco, and Allison decided that his responsibilities at the company must weigh heavily on him, causing him to be curt and ill-natured at times. They spent several hours wandering in and out of stores and enjoying the scents and sounds of the autumn afternoon.

They stopped at Cambridge on their return to Columbus, and while they were eating dinner, Allison, acting on impulse, said, "Tomorrow is Invite-A-Friend Sunday at the church I attend. I haven't invited anyone yet—would you go with me as my friend?"

"No, I won't. I have other plans for tomorrow, but regardless, I still wouldn't go to church."

"But why?" she persisted.

Benton reached for her hand that was lying on the table. Sighing he said, "Because I tried Christianity for many years and learned that it doesn't produce what it promises.

Since I know that I've not convinced you otherwise, I'll admit that I *was* the speaker at that youth crusade you attended in Indianapolis, but I've changed since then. All the things I believed about God solving our problems and answering our prayers, and that if we were one of His, all things would work out for the best—those things just aren't true, Allison. I hope you never have to learn their falsity in the way I did.''

''But—'' Allison started, before he put his fingers on her lips.

''I don't want to talk about it. You have your opinion— I have mine. If we're going to be friends, don't try pushing your religious beliefs on me.''

Allison was appalled at his answer, and she was silent through the rest of the meal. What could have happened to cause such an about-face in Benton? She had never talked with anyone before who rejected God in this manner. And although it caused her emotional pain, before they left the table, she said, ''If you really feel that way and mean what you have said, I'm not sure I can be your friend, Benton.'' He shrugged and didn't answer, indicating to Allison that being her friend was inconsequential to him. They didn't exchange many words on the return drive to Columbus.

During the next few months, Benton asked her for occasional dates, and Allison debated within herself whether she should continue seeing him, for she knew that it would be disastrous to consider marrying a man who rejected God's leading in his life. She prayed that he would see the error of his ways and revert to the faith of his youth, and because it would have made for strained relations at the office, she continued to enjoy his company.

As winter approached, Allison's outlook for Page Publishing was positive. They were making good profits and employee output was excellent, and when Allison encountered Reba Hall, she reported that Edmond had gotten his GED and was planning to attend electronics school after the first of the year. One day she brought Allison two hundred dollars, which Edmond had saved out of his salary at his brother-in-law's shop as the first payment on the loan she had made to his mother. Allison was so overjoyed that she wanted to return the money, for the Halls obviously needed it more than she did, but she kept it, knowing that Edmund would learn a valuable lesson by paying for his mistakes.

But some problems continued to plague her. Lois Holmes still made her mysterious visits to Benton, and after each visit, he was unusually irritable. Each Monday, Benton came to work looking as if he had been ill. When she questioned him in concern about his appearance one morning, Benton gave Allison a curt reply, so she didn't mention it again. If Celestine noticed anything unusual in his behavior on those days, she didn't say anything, and Allison wouldn't ask.

After he had seen Allison and Benton at Sugarcreek, Calvin Smith had been more persistent in his attention to her. The man was a valuable employee and she didn't want to drive him away, but she didn't intend to go out with him. She had tried to be nice in her refusals, but she knew the day was coming when she would have to give him a firm no, and be prepared to live with the results.

Recognizing her love for Benton and her optimistic belief that they might marry someday, she once again started thinking about her birth mother. With the current emphasis on genetic testing as a disease-preventive measure, she thought it was imperative that she should uncover her maternal ancestry. Benton hadn't mentioned her relationship to Harrison Page again, but it was a comfort to know that one person in Columbus did understand her questions about the past.

One warm Sunday afternoon in November, Allison drove to the Miller Cemetery, which she had located in August. There were about thirty-five graves in the fenced enclosure, some dating into the early 1800s, and she found one simple marker: Mary Miller, died 21-years-of age. There was no date to indicate when the death had occurred, and Allison couldn't tell by the condition of the granite marker how long it had been there. That could quite easily have been her mother, and Allison believed that it was, for if her mother had still lived, surely Harrison Page would have given some indication of it. Perhaps her mother had died in childbirth and that was the reason for her adoption. Allison would like to believe that was the case rather than think that her mother had also rejected her.

She spent more than an hour copying information from the tombstones, but without further facts about her mother's antecedents, there was no way to know if those deceased Millers could be her relatives.

Wondering what procedures to take to find the information, she often considered asking Thomas Curnutt his opinion, but she always decided against it because as astute as he was, he might very well come up with her reason for asking. She did ask Benton for suggestions, and he told her that she could probably find out all she needed to know at the Department of Vital Statistics at the statehouse, but she stopped her search at that point.

When it seemed that she was on the threshold of finding the information, she was reluctant to proceed any further. Now that she knew her ancestry might be readily available, loyalty to her adoptive mother held her back. Perhaps when she went to Chicago for the Christmas holidays, she might persuade Beatrice to tell what she knew about the birth mother and rescind her objections to Allison's search.

Celestine invited Benton and Allison to their farm for Thanksgiving Day, and they both accepted, which would leave the McRameys free to spend the day with their relatives. Hannah had come to help with the dinner preparation, and at Amos's insistence, she sat down to eat with them. After dinner, before Amos drove Hannah back to her home, Hannah called Allison aside and handed her a shoe box.

"I've decided to let you read some of my stories," Hannah said, and she refused to meet Allison's eyes.

"Why, thank you. I'm looking forward to it." The shoe box was quite heavy, and Allison lifted the lid and peered into the box, which was full of tablet sheets with the text in penciled longhand.

"I had no idea you had written so many!" Allison exclaimed.

"Are there too many for you to read? I can keep some of them."

"Oh, no, I want to read all of them, but it may take me a while."

"No hurry. I've been writing these since I was a child."

After Amos left to take Hannah to her home, Celestine and Allison started clearing away the dinner dishes, and Benton and Truman pitched in to help. The kitchen was in order by the time Amos returned, and the three men gathered around the large television to view the football games.

"Do you want to watch the games?" Celestine said.

"Not particularly. Neither my sister nor I is a sports enthusiast, which made us outcasts at home during the football season."

"Let's just sit in front of the open fire and toast our feet."

They pulled two chairs close to the fireplace, kicked off their shoes and leaned back in lounge chairs, their feet soaking up the heat from the slow-burning oak logs. Allison was dozing when she snapped to attention at Celestine's question.

"Have you given any thought to a Christmas entertainment for the staff?"

Allison turned startled eyes toward Celestine. "No. Should I have?" She remembered tardily that Celestine had mentioned two yearly entertainments when they'd planned the July picnic.

"We didn't do anything last year due to Mr. Page's critical condition, so it would be well to plan some function this season."

"We've had such a good year financially that I've asked Benton to suggest appropriate bonuses for year's end, but I hadn't considered a party. Give me some suggestions."

"It doesn't have to be elaborate. You could have a meal catered in the conference room downstairs."

"What have you done in the past?"

"Various things. We've gone out for dinner to exclusive restaurants. We've attended various features at the Palace Theatre. Sometimes we've gone to ice shows."

"Are the families invited as in July?"

"No. Each employee may bring a spouse or a friend, but the children aren't included."

"Would it be acceptable if I hosted a reception at my home? I could have part of the food catered, but Minerva would be delighted to help."

Celestine's eyes lightened. "That would be wonderful. After Mr. Page spent so much time and money to refurbish the place, he never did any entertaining, and our employees would love to see it."

"I would have to get busy with decorations. I hadn't intended to do much because I will be away for the holidays." She turned around, and called, "Benton, Truman, can you tear yourselves away from the game long enough to talk to us for a few minutes?"

Truman came willingly, but Benton was more reluctant.

"There's a commercial on now," Truman said, "but my team is losing, so I'm not interested in watching anyway. What do you want?"

"We've been discussing a Christmas party for Page Publishing, and I'd like to have a reception at my home, but I'll need lots of help with decorations. May I count on you two to help me?"

"Sure," Truman said, "what do you have in mind?" He dropped down on a hassock beside his mother.

Glancing at the television screen, Benton said, "I'll do

what you want me to, but tell me later. *My* team is winning
and I want to watch.''

Piqued that Benton would rather watch television than
enjoy her company, Allison gave Celestine a rueful glance.
Celestine lifted her eyebrows. ''Amos doesn't have any
time for me, either,'' she said, causing Allison to wonder
if Celestine sensed her more-than-casual interest in Benton.

They started back to Columbus in late afternoon, and
darkness had fallen when they reached the house on Neil
Avenue.

''Do you have time to come in?'' Allison asked, trying
not to sound hopeful. ''Minerva made a pumpkin-pecan
pie,'' she said to tempt him.

He pulled up into the driveway. ''You sure know how
to get my attention. I'd love some pie and a cup of coffee,
please.''

They entered the side door into the warmth of the
kitchen, and the coziness of the house affected her as it
always did.

''How good to be home! Hang your coat on the hall tree,
and I'll heat water. Do you want decaf?''

''Yes, please.'' Benton removed Allison's coat from her
shoulders, and his soft breath on her cheek warmed her the
way a gentle breeze did on a summer evening. Her hands
trembled as she ran hot water over them at the sink and
turned toward the stove, and she wished his proximity
didn't always affect her so greatly. By the time the water
was boiling she had placed the pie on the table with two
forks, plates and a server.

''Help yourself,'' she said. ''What you eat, I won't have
to. I'm bound to gain weight the way Minerva feeds me.''

He surveyed her slender, trim form. ''She hasn't hurt you
yet.''

Benton held the chair for Allison, sat down opposite her
and put servings of pie on each plate.

''Umn!'' Benton said on the first bite. ''No wonder Truman shows up here for dinner so often.''

Allison laughed. "Oh, he isn't here very much, but he always telephones ahead, and Minerva delights in feeding him."

"Are you happy here?" he said. "It seems to me you've adjusted well."

"I am happy. I love this house, and I'm learning enough about Page Publishing, thanks to you, that I don't feel intimidated there anymore."

"You never should have felt that way. I think if we hadn't found out already, I'd be convinced that Harrison Page was your father. Your decisions are so much like his that it's uncanny sometimes."

"I've wondered about your parents, Benton. You never mention a family."

"My parents are out of the country now, as missionaries in India. My father is a medical doctor. They have another year of duty before they come home. Needless to say, they're not very proud of the way I've turned out."

"I don't believe that for a minute. You've done well for yourself."

"Materially, yes, but I was speaking about spiritual values."

"You could do something about that."

He shrugged. "You never did tell me why you wanted to leave Chicago," he said, adroitly changing the subject.

Allison toyed with her coffee cup, and without meeting his eye, she said, "I was engaged to the 'boy next-door,' and two weeks before our wedding, he decided he loved another woman more than he loved me. We had to cancel everything, send back gifts and notify guests. It was a terrible time. I couldn't talk about it for a long while, but I've since realized that it was for the best."

"Any man would be lucky to have you, Allison," he said.

His words thrilled her, but she said lightly, "Donald apparently didn't think so. Anyway, I wanted to leave Chicago, where I was reminded of those bitter memories."

"Well, it's good for us that you came here." His gaze was warm and tender. "You've made a difference in all our lives."

Allison was so very happy with the direction the conversation was taking and could have cried when the phone rang.

"Probably my parents calling," she said. She didn't like answering machines, but now wished she had one.

As she left the table to answer the phone, Benton stood, too.

"Enjoy your visit with them." He leaned down and grazed her lips with a kiss. "Thanks for the pie, but I have to leave now."

Knowing that she had no time to spare, Allison approached Minerva the next day about hosting the reception.

"Oh, I'd love to help you, Allison. If you want to have the meat and hot vegetables catered, I can do all the baking and salads."

"We probably would have seventy people—that's a lot of baking."

Minerva shook her head. "No problem."

"We'll need to beautify the house. Do you know if there are any decorations here or will I have to buy everything?"

Minerva scratched her head. "When we first came here, Mrs. Page always had a tree in the parlor, wreaths on the doors and candles in the windows. So those decorations must still be here—no doubt in the attic. I'll have Adra look."

"Let's see what we can find before I go shopping."

Allison went upstairs with Adra to the attic, and they started shoving cartons and old furniture to one side.

"If I put those decorations away," Adra said, "the box will be marked."

After they spent several minutes shifting boxes around and sneezing from the dust they stirred up, Adra called, "Hey. I've found it."

He was standing beside a huge wooden box and Allison helped him push it into the middle of the room, where the light was better. The dust flew when Adra pried open the lid. The boxes inside were also marked, and they found tinsel ropes, several boxes of glass ornaments, electric candles and two large wreaths made of artificial laurel leaves, with sprigs of dried heather interspersed with the leaves.

"Mrs. Page had me hang those on the front doors," Adra said.

"They are still in good condition. We'll use them." Allison looked at the glass ornaments. Some of them were broken, and the paint had peeled on others. "We can get a few small trees and use these ornaments on them, but I want a big tree for the parlor, and I'll buy some new decorations for it."

Adra lifted some of the candles out of their individual boxes. "You shouldn't use these. The wiring is broken in places. It could be dangerous."

"The candles that operate on batteries are the safest to use," Minerva said.

"Let's separate the good items from the bad, and have the latter hauled to the dump. Minerva and I can figure out what we need, and I'll go to one of the department stores after work on Monday and make the purchases. We haven't spent nearly as much on monthly household accounts as Uncle Harrison did, so I don't feel too extravagant buying some decorations."

"You can use them over and over, so it won't be extravagant."

While Minerva and Allison went from room to room to decide on needed items, Adra took the candles and other useless items and discarded them in the trash cans.

It was the middle of December before Allison had all the items purchased, and after work on Friday, Adra took her in his truck to buy the tree. She chose the tallest spruce on the lot, as well as two smaller pines, and swallowed convulsively when she wrote the check for them. That was too much for Christmas trees that would be thrown away in a few weeks. She tried to excuse her extravagance by considering the people driving along Neil Avenue who would see and enjoy the lighted trees, plus the pleasure afforded to the employees who attended the reception, but she hesitated about spending money. She'd been a millionaire for almost a year now, and she still hadn't gotten used to the idea.

Benton and Truman came early the next morning, and it took them and Adra an hour to get the big tree in a holder, moved into the house and stabilized.

"It looks a lot bigger in here," she said worriedly. "I may not have enough ornaments."

They worked until late afternoon, taking a short break for lunch, but they were all pleased with the results. Each bedroom had small artificial trees decorated with the tinsel and ornaments that had belonged to Sarah Page. The top of the cupboard in the dining room wore a crown of fresh fruit and hemlock. They had arranged the fruit by placing the larger fruits, pears and red apples, directly above the hemlock layer. Red and green grapes and tiny red apples were positioned on the top.

The tall, slender tree in the parlor was placed near the fireplace and was decorated with wooden oranges and apples, stuffed calico hearts and horses, crocheted ice crystals and tiny red and white bows. A garland of popcorn was placed over the branches. Allison had also splurged and bought some imported die-cut lithographed ornaments of angels, cherubs and Santa Clauses, and these decorated a three-foot spruce in the dining room. The tree in the hallway was embellished with Victorian cardboard cornucopias filled with tiny candies, which were to be given to each of the guests.

Disregarding Allison's protests, Truman tied sprigs of mistletoe in strategic areas around the house. Potted poinsettias were placed on each stair tread, and clusters of various-sized candles graced the tables and mantels in the parlor and library. The three of them were pleased with the results as they sprawled on the upholstered furniture in the library.

"How about if I take you out for dinner?" Benton said.

"Am I included?" Truman asked.

"Yes, if the lady agrees to go. I'm not taking you out by myself."

Allison looked at her disheveled clothes and fingered her dirty hair. "I really don't feel up to going tonight. I'll take a rain check if I might. How about tomorrow afternoon?"

A cloud came over Benton's eyes. "Sorry, I'm busy tomorrow."

That was another secret about him. Why didn't he ever mention his Sunday activities?

Interspersed with her plans for the holidays was Allison's reading each evening of Hannah's stories, and while she conceded that she was no authority on children's literature, she thought the writing was superior. The plots were based on the experiences of two pioneer children living in Ohio soon after it became a state, and while the stories were not preachy, each episode emphasized a facet of good moral behavior. Allison began to envision a series of children's books. She had scrutinized several series at the convention in San Francisco, and she considered that Hannah's work was equally as good. As soon as Christmas was over, she must talk to Hannah about what she wanted to do with her writings.

Early in November Allison had contributed generously, both from Page Publishing and her own personal account, to the various charities in Columbus that were striving to provide Christmas benefits to the poor of the region, so she felt justified in spending large sums on decorations and catering for the staff party. As she wrote checks for the items, she often thought of how different her life was now from what it had been a year ago. But was it a better life? She had unlimited finances, but she couldn't say that she was any happier than she had been when living on a strict budget. This time last year she was fretting about the loss of Donald; this year she was miserable because she was in love with Benton and he was indifferent to her. Often she wondered how a psychiatrist would analyze her. She'd lived through rejection from one man and now was fast on the way to having her love spurned again. What kind of quirk in her makeup caused her to love the wrong men? Surely just once she should make the right choice.

After she had spent so much money on decorations and catering, Allison pondered a long time whether to buy a new dress for the Christmas reception. But when she considered what she had spent for her parents and Cleta and Tim, she went timidly into an exclusive dress shop and let the saleslady suggest a garment. She was pleased with the dress they agreed upon—a beaded velvet, coffee-colored dress that accentuated the gold tints in her amber eyes. The ankle-length dress had slender straps over the shoulder, with a long-sleeved matching jacket. The beads on the dress front and the shoulders of the jacket were designed in sunburst patterns. Allison smiled at her reflection in the mirror of the dressing room, and thought the effect was well worth the price of the dress. The saleslady contributed a beaded necklace and earrings that matched the fabric of the garment.

After she finished at the dress shop, she stopped at a jewelry store to pick up an item she had ordered there. She had fretted for days over buying something for Benton. He was so unpredictable that he might very well refuse to take it, but she'd ordered the gift anyway and decided that she would present it to him at the reception as a gift of appreciation from the whole staff for handling the reins of business as he had done. She was pleased with the gift—a gold ring with a black onyx stone, on which tiny diamonds formed the initial ''L''—and only hoped that he would be.

It was not so expensive that the other employees would get the wrong idea, or at least she hoped they wouldn't. Driving back to her home, the car filled with packages, Allison decided that being rich did have its advantages.

Allison asked the supervisors and their assistants in the various departments to help host the reception. She arranged to have Celestine stand with her in the vestibule to welcome everyone and then the guests would have freedom to mingle in the four first-floor rooms, where the various supervisors would greet them and see to their needs. Her helpers were to arrive at half-past six, and she was ready a half hour before that.

When she went into the kitchen, Adra whistled.

"Look at this, Minerva," he said. "Our little girl has blossomed into a woman."

"Your 'little girl' is almost twenty-five years old. Hardly a child anymore," Allison said with a smile.

"You look wonderful, Allison," Minerva said. "Don't let him fluster you."

"May I help in any way?"

"Of course not," Minerva said brusquely. "The caterer sent along two girls to pick up the dishes and wash them, so all I have to do is keep the plates of goodies filled. Don't stand in here and soil your dress."

Allison paused by the dining-room table, which had been expanded to its full length, and it was loaded with food. Small hot sausages sizzled over a burner; there were large platters of sliced ham, roast beef and various cheeses, and a container of meatballs. In addition to the salads that Minerva had prepared, the caterer had brought trays of veggies and fruits, and a variety of dips. The desserts were on small tables along the walls, and the beverages were on the sideboard. Black-and-white-uniformed waitresses scurried around preparing to serve everyone. The caterer had also provided folding chairs to accommodate the visitors.

The guests started arriving promptly at seven, and as they

scattered around the house, it didn't seem that the rooms were overfilled at any one time. Celestine helped Allison with the names of employees she didn't know very well. Almost everyone brought a gift-wrapped package, and Allison was amazed to see how many were laid beneath her tree.

At eight o'clock, Allison asked everyone to assemble in the parlor and the dining room. "You are welcome to stay as long as you like," she said, "but in case any of you do have to leave soon, I want to have a short meeting. Mr. Lockhart has a few words to say to you."

How elegant can one be, Allison thought as Benton came to the foreground. He was wearing a black suit, snowy white shirt and burgundy tie. She had never seen anyone who carried himself with more poise and grace. His firm, authoritative voice resounded throughout the room, and when he spoke, everyone listened. She sensed his undeniable masculinity when he stood beside her, and her pulse quickened.

"Actually, I'm speaking on behalf of our boss." He cast a warm smile in Allison's direction and her heart somersaulted. "When she came here almost a year ago wanting to institute a Golden Rule policy, I was opposed to it and told her so. But it has apparently worked, because if our present figures continue to the end of the year, our company will have had the best financial year on record."

He was interrupted by applause that seemed unusually loud in the crowded room.

"And we owe much of that to you," Benton continued, "who in many cases have set aside your own desires for the good of the company or for others with whom you work. At vacation time you received an unprecedented bonus, so you know that Miss Sayre practices the Golden Rule—she doesn't keep all the financial gain for herself. The fact that our wage scale is comparable to any other publishing house's in the country proves that you are amply paid, but you are going to be compensated even more. Our employer has declared, in light of the successful year, an extra half-month's salary as a Christmas gift. The bonus will be added to your next paycheck.''

There was a momentary pause after his announcement, then the applause was deafening. When Benton started to sit down, Allison placed her hand on his arm.

"Just a minute," she said. She held up her hand.

When she had their attention, she said, "All of you know as well as I do who has been the real manager of Page Publishing this year. I came here knowing nothing, and I still have a lot to learn. Not only did Benton manage the firm the last year of Uncle Harrison's life but he has also carried 90 percent or more of the load during this calendar year." She took a small package from the mantel. "For that reason, I bought a special gift for him, and I want to present this, not just from me, but on behalf of all our employees. Although it's an old cliché, I want to truly say—I couldn't have done it without you, Benton." She handed him the box; he hesitated momentarily, then he took it.

"Open it," someone shouted, and others took up the chant.

When the box was opened, Benton put on the ring, where by some luck it fitted the small finger of his left hand.

"Thank you very much," he said. "I do a lot of work at Page Publishing, I'll admit, but I've always been compensated more than I deserved. However, I do appreciate the thought behind this gift. And since all of you would like to examine what you've given me, I'll put the ring in the box and pass it around." He handed the box to Celestine and Amos and added jokingly, "Just be sure it's returned to me."

The staff seemed reluctant to leave, and it was ten o'clock before everyone departed except Benton and the Handleys. Amos helped Celestine with her coat, and he bent down and kissed Allison on the cheek. "A great party, Allison—be sure to invite me to your next one."

"Oh, I'm just paying you back for the one you hosted in July."

Celestine embraced Allison warmly. "It's been such a blessing to learn to know you this year. I thank God every day that He sent you our way. You've made all of us happy, and I pray you will have a good visit with your family during the holidays."

When the door closed behind them, Allison sat down on the hall tree and kicked off her shoes. "Wow! My feet are tired. Three hours of heels is too much."

Benton sat down on the bottom-stair tread. "When do you leave for Chicago?"

"Sunday afternoon—that way I will be home by Christmas Eve."

"I thought you would leave in the morning."

"I won't leave all the straightening up for Minerva. It will take us all day tomorrow to get the house organized again." The caterers were noisily stacking the chairs. "Before they take all the food away, I want to fill a plate. I was so busy hostessing I only nibbled. Would you like something?"

"Thank you. I didn't eat much, either."

Allison brought plates from the kitchen cabinets, which they filled with meat and cheeses, veggies, salads and several of Minerva's pastries. Not wanting to be in the way of Minerva and the caterers, they took the food into the library, where the chairs had already been removed.

"I'll bring glasses of punch," Benton offered.

"Get some big glasses from the kitchen. I'm thirsty."

Allison took a couple of snack trays from the closet, and they pulled chairs close to the fireplace, where the gas logs were giving off welcome heat rays. They were silent until they sated their hunger. When they finished, Allison stacked the dishes on one of the trays. "I'll wash those after Minerva goes to bed."

"I want you to know how pleased I am with the ring," Benton said, and he held it up for closer observation.

"It's a small gift, considering how much you've helped me this year."

Benton put his arm around Allison and led her into the parlor. He retrieved a package from the many piled beneath the tree.

"I'm going soon, but I have a gift for you, too. I had intended to have you open it later, but decided to present it in person."

He took Allison's hand and led her toward the chintz-covered sofa before the coffee table. He pushed the table to one side and drew Allison beneath the chandelier, where Truman had tied a sprig of mistletoe on the day they had decorated.

"We mustn't let Truman's efforts go to waste. I don't believe anyone took advantage of this all evening. Merry Christmas, Allison." He stood looking down into her eyes for a few moments, and Allison slipped her hands on his shoulders and melted into his embrace. He sighed and pulled her closer to him, and she wondered if she could ever be held enough by this wonderful man. How was it that his simplest touch made her pulse race and filled her heart with longing?

"I know I shouldn't hold you close this way Allison, but it's times like this that I realize all I'm missing. I can hardly stand it. Don't hate me, Allison."

Now, what did he mean by all that?

She leaned back and looked at him in amazement, but when she started to speak, he kissed her with such a lingering, emotion-filled caress that she forgot everything except the pleasure of this moment. But just as Allison began to return his kiss, Benton lifted his head and put her gently from him. Taking Allison's hand, he pulled her down beside him on the sofa.

"You've made a great difference in all our lives," he said, speaking of mundane matters, when she was so tense she felt like a hang glider poised to lift off. "I hesitated about buying you a gift for several reasons that seem unimportant right now. I've tried to be indifferent to you, fought against falling in love with you, but I have, and I'm sorry.''

Allison gasped. ''Why would you be sorry? I've loved you since our trip to San Francisco. In fact, my attraction to you started years ago in Indianapolis. Why don't you want to love me?''

He refused to meet her eyes. ''I can't tell you—I can't talk about it.''

A terrible thought came to Allison. ''Are you married?'' Did he hesitate before he answered?

''No, I'm not married.''

She believed him, but she knew that some devastating incident in his past stood between her happiness with Benton.

He handed her the wrapped box. ''I'd like to have you open it now,'' he said with a smile.

Her hands trembled, and her heart fluttered when the open box revealed a ruby pendant strung on a slender gold chain. A mist of tears blurred her vision as she met Benton's gaze. ''It's beautiful,'' she said. ''It's the first piece of good jewelry I've ever had. Thank you.''

''I was prepared to give a little speech citing my reason for buying the gift as appreciation for what Page Publishing has done for me, but it would have been a lie. Although I have prospered at the firm, that's not the reason for the gift. I just couldn't let Christmas pass without buying something for you.''

Allison removed the beaded choker that matched her dress and fastened the pendant in place. ''How does it look?''

''As if it was made for you.'' He leaned back on the sofa and drew her close. ''Sometimes it amazes me when I realized that this time last year I didn't even know you existed. You've changed my whole world.''

Allison was so comfortable in his arms that she refused to think about his earlier comments and the aura of mystery

that surrounded him. She must have dozed, for when the
hall clock started striking, she was startled.

Benton, too, must have been sleeping, for he straight-
ened. "Midnight. I had no idea I'd stayed so late." He
yawned, and he put his arm around her waist as they went
into the hallway. After he put on his coat, he bent to kiss
her again, a quick, sweet kiss, compared with their embrace
in the parlor.

"Merry Christmas, Allison. I hope you have a pleasant
visit with your family."

Despite the cold, she stood in the hallway and watched
him drive away. As she walked upstairs to her room, she
realized that she had no idea what he planned to do for the
holidays.

After the successful Christmas reception and its after-
math, when Benton had admitted that he loved her, Allison's visit in Chicago seemed anticlimactic. All four of the
family met her at the airport, and Allison's heart warmed
when it was so obvious that they had missed her. Their gift
opening was pleasant, for all of them liked the presents she
had brought. Christmas Day itself was shared with the extended family—a couple of dozen cousins, aunts and un-
cles.

The only unpleasant part of the whole holiday was when
Allison again approached Beatrice about her parentage.

"Mother," she said, "you're my mother and always will
be. I appreciate your love and care for me even more when
I realize that you adopted me when I was apparently un-
wanted by my real parents. The fact that I want to find out
about my birth mother has nothing to do with you or our
relationship. I know how to find out the data about my
birth, but I don't want to do it without your consent. Have
you changed your mind about it?"

"No, I haven't. If you find her, you'll have to choose
between the two of us. Either I'm your mother or I'm not."

Allison felt as if she were banging her head against a stone wall. "She may be dead for all we know."

"No, she isn't dead."

"So, you do know who and where she is!"

But Beatrice looked away and wouldn't answer.

"I should know for medical reasons. I went to a doctor in Columbus for my annual checkup, and since I was a new patient, I had to fill out a medical questionnaire. Always before when asked about the medical history of my antecedents, I gave information about you and Dad, which as I know now is false. It gave me such a sense of loss to write down that my maternal heritage was unknown."

In spite of her pleadings, Beatrice didn't relent, and Allison's departure from Chicago wasn't as joyful as her homecoming, for she felt a rift widening between her and her mother.

Chapter Eight

Allison spent New Year's Day with the Handleys, and in late afternoon when Hannah was ready to go home, Allison volunteered to take her.

As they departed from the Handley driveway, Allison said, "I wanted to talk with you privately, Hannah. I've read all the stories you sent me. I'm very impressed. I didn't want to proceed further without your permission, but I believe your work has the potential for a series of children's books."

Bewilderment crossed Hannah's face as she looked wide-eyed at Allison.

"I hadn't thought of anything like that."

"You understand that I'm not an authority on children's literature, but with your consent, I want to have an expert critique your work."

"And if this expert thinks they're good, then what?"

"I couldn't guarantee this without speaking to the advisory board at Page Publishing, but we might print the series."

Surprised at Hannah's sad countenance, Allison said, "I thought you would be excited about it."

"It would fulfill a dream of mine, but I don't know if I'm ready to displease my parents. They want me to get married, and they won't understand my desire to be independent."

Allison could understand Hannah's hesitation—especially since she had vacillated for months about searching for her birth mother simply because she didn't want to hurt Beatrice.

"Give it some thought anyway," Allison said encouragingly.

They had arrived at Hannah's home, and as she opened the car door, she said, "Yes, I will. Will you come in for a visit?"

"Thank you, not now. Snow is predicted for tonight, and I want to return to Columbus before dark."

Two weeks later Hannah sent Allison a note by Celes tine:

> I've decided to let you look into the publication of my stories. I haven't said anything to anyone about this— didn't see any need to start a quarrel if the project doesn't pan out. Let me know.

The next day at work, Allison dialed Benton's office number. Tomorrow was the staff board meeting, but she didn't want to present this matter to the complete staff without having him know beforehand. After he answered, she said, "When you have a few minutes, I have something to discuss with you."

"Come in now. I don't have an appointment for an hour."

Often Allison contrived reasons to be in his presence, but she rather dreaded this interview, so as she picked up a file containing some of Hannah's stories, she drew a deep breath and prayed for guidance. Benton's eyes brightened at the sight of her, as they almost always did when she encountered him, and she wished her pulse wouldn't flutter so rapidly when he looked at her so intently.

"Did you know that Hannah Hoptry is a writer?" she asked when she'd composed herself sedately in the chair in front of his desk as if she were a customer.

"No."

"She told me several months ago that she liked to write, and when I showed some interest, she agreed to let me read some of her stories. I think they're excellent, and after a good deal of thought, I approached her about having them published. I want Page Publishing to do it."

"But we aren't publishers in that sense of the word. We confine our work to contract printing for publishers."

"Is there any reason we can't branch out into other avenues if we want to?"

"What do you have in mind?"

"I looked at a lot of children's books when we were at the convention in San Francisco. Hannah's stories are every bit as good as those, if I'm any judge."

"Which you probably aren't," he commented caustically. "You can do what you want to, but I advise against it."

"I can't see what harm it would be to look into the matter, at least have an editor of children's books look at the stories. Hannah said that her family probably won't like it, but since she's decided to risk their displeasure, I'm willing to promote her career. I'm going to investigate the matter. Will you help me?"

"No, I won't. I don't like to disagree with you about it since you so seldom take the initiative on decisions here, but when I feel that it could be a mistake for the company as well as Hannah, I'm not going to be a part of it."

Their discussion was shortened by some rapid knocking on Benton's door. A frown crossed his face, and he looked at his watch. "She's early, as usual," he muttered.

When the door opened and Lois Holmes fluttered in, Allison excused herself and left, somewhat annoyed that the

woman didn't know any better than to interrupt them. As
far as she could tell, Benton's meetings with Mrs. Holmes
didn't have any connection with Page Publishing.

When she returned to her office, Allison telephoned
Thomas Curnutt. She explained her idea to him, adding,
"Benton says it's a bad idea. What do you think?"

Thomas hesitated briefly. "I'm not sure how to advise
you. It would require a large investment to have the stories
illustrated, marketed and distributed, which won't be easy,
since Page Publishing's customers don't require children's
books. You would have to find other customers, and that
would take a lot of money."

"I don't want to disappoint Hannah."

"Better to disappoint her now than to have the books
printed without any readership. I would think about it a few
weeks."

"I have been thinking about it for a long time. If I could
find a children's writer, I would pay for her opinion. Do
you know of anyone?"

"In that matter, I can help you. One of our Bexley neighbors, Elizabeth Moore, is an author, and she majors in children's stories, mostly printed in magazines, but she would
have enough expertise to give you an opinion."

"I would expect to pay her, of course. Will you give me
her name, or will you contact her?"

"I'll be glad to contact her," Thomas said.

The next morning, Thomas telephoned. "Elizabeth
agreed to review the stories and give you an opinion of
their value."

"That will be great. I'll bring the manuscripts to your
office today, and after she's read them, she can telephone
me either at the office or at home."

The next evening, Elizabeth Moore telephoned Allison.
After introducing herself, she said, "I am impressed by
Miss Hoptry's talent as a writer. I've read most of the stories, and I consider them worthy of publication. What did
you have in mind for them?"

"I want to publish them as a series of children's books."

"That would be possible, probably for preschoolers or at least children through the primary grades, but in addition to a good plot, children's books have to be exceptionally illustrated."

"Do you know an artist who might do the work?"

"I know several. One in particular comes to mind for these stories. I think her style would suit Hannah's writing well. She does the artwork for several children's magazines. In fact, she is the illustrator for some of the magazines I write for."

"If I decide to continue this project, I would need an editor as well as an artist, and I'd like to discuss the production of these books with you and your friend. Think about this, and if you're both interested, perhaps we could set up an appointment to discuss the project."

After Benton had disassociated himself from Hannah's works, Allison hadn't discussed it with anyone at the company, but when she had progressed to this extent, she knew she should present her plans at the next staff meeting. The next morning when Celestine returned after a doctor's appointment, Allison called her into the office.

As she had Benton, she asked, "Did you know that Hannah writes children's stories?"

"Why, no, I didn't," Celestine said, brightening.

Allison explained how she had learned about Hannah's talent and brought Celestine up-to-date on her research into the matter.

"I don't know anything about current children's literature," Celestine said, "but I think you can rely on Elizabeth Moore's recommendation. That would be wonderful for Hannah."

"She hesitates because she thinks her parents won't approve. Do you think that is true?"

"They're very conservative in their beliefs, so they may well object."

"But shouldn't it be Hannah's decision?"

"By all means," Celestine agreed. "She should have the chance to decide. We faced a similar dilemma when we asked her to come to work for us, because her family's life-style differs from ours, but that has worked out well."

"I don't like to risk Benton's displeasure, but I feel it's something I must do."

"Then do it," Celestine said with a smile. "You know you have my support."

"And don't think I don't appreciate it. I don't know what I would do without you, Celestine."

"I fear you're going to have to get along without me for a few weeks, though. My gynecologist wants me to have surgery, and if I do, I'll have to be off work for a month or six weeks."

"Why, Celestine! Is it serious?"

"Nothing more than many women of my age face. I've been having minor problems for several years, and the doctor said today that I should have a hysterectomy. It will be a routine operation. I want to talk with Amos before I give the doctor an answer, and I need to check the schedule here to see when it's most convenient for me to be away."

"Your health is more important than this firm. We'll manage somehow. You and Amos decide when it's most convenient for the two of you."

"There's an employment agency in town that provides secretaries on a short-term basis. If we can hire someone to operate the computer and answer the phone, you and Benton should be able to handle everything else."

The next morning Celestine telephoned the gynecologist, and her surgery was scheduled in two weeks. "I'll have everything done when I leave here," she assured Allison, "and you can always telephone if you need to know something. I won't be in the hospital more than two or three days."

In spite of his hesitancy about the project, Benton was the company's manager, and Allison insisted that he be present when she met with Elizabeth Moore and the illustrator she'd suggested, Pamela Sackett.

When she requested his presence, he said, "Well, you're the boss."

"Yes, I am," Allison said testily, "and I expect you to work for the success of this enterprise as much as you do everything else that goes on around here. Without your help, we won't get anywhere with it, and you know that. Didn't Uncle Harrison ever suggest things that you didn't like?"

He smiled. "Many times."

"Well, what did you do then?"

"Whatever he told me to. He was the boss, so that answers your question. What do you want me to do?"

"I want you to come to the office when I interview these two women, and if I decide to proceed with the book series, I expect you to support me."

Allison liked Elizabeth Moore the minute she met her. Pamela Sackett, the artist, was a reticent woman and had very little to say when they came to Allison's office, but when Allison saw examples of Pamela's work, she knew the woman did have artistic talent.

Allison wasn't sure that Benton had changed his mind about the project, but he entered wholeheartedly into her plans after Allison engaged Elizabeth and Pamela to prepare the manuscripts for publication. The small hardback books were to be marketed as the James and Rhoda series, and they set May 1 for release of the two launch titles, with one a month to be published after that. Hannah already had written enough stories for a two-years' supply, so Allison considered that sufficient backlog to meet their publishing schedule.

Allison made a trip to the Handley farm and talked with Hannah. They agreed that as soon as Celestine had recovered from her surgery Hannah would move to Columbus and live with Allison while she worked with Elizabeth and Pamela to produce the first books.

Thomas drew up contracts for those two women and Hannah, as well. Benton checked out royalty rates for her, and as they tallied the figures, she began to see that Benton had been right about the large amount of money involved.

"Maybe we shouldn't do it," she said worriedly. "What if I lose a lot of money?"

"It's your money to lose," Benton said. "This firm has lost money before. I'll take care of the business end, but it will up to you to handle Hannah."

"Why should she take handling?"

"She's going to be plunged into an environment that is completely foreign to her. I believe she'll be over-whelmed."

Celestine's surgery was set for eight o'clock on Monday morning, and the office felt empty when Allison arrived. Celestine's substitute had spent two days in the office the previous week being instructed in her duties, and she had already made coffee when Allison arrived, but in spite of the habitual routine, the room felt empty without Celestine.

Allison had asked Amos or Truman to telephone as soon as the surgery was over, and when Amos called in late morning, she thought he had a good report, but his tone was worried.

"Allison," he said, "her surgery isn't going well. The doctors have run into complications. They can't get Celestine's blood to clot, and she's losing a lot of blood. The medical staff are concerned, and I wanted you to know."

"I'll be there immediately," she said, then slammed down the receiver and rushed into Benton's office, heedless of the fact that he was entertaining Lois Holmes again. After she repeated Amos's message, she said, "I'm going to the hospital."

He rose quickly from his chair. "I'll go with you." To Mrs. Holmes, he said, "I must leave now. This is an emergency."

With only a word to the substitute secretary about their

destination, they rushed out to Benton's car. At the hospital, they found the ruddy Amos pale and anxious, trying to calm his son, who was stalking around the room in anger.

Benton took Truman by the shoulder and halted his pacing, while a tearful Allison put her arms around Amos. "But what happened?" she said. "Celestine said this was only routine surgery."

"And so it was," he said, "but the surgeon says complications can occur in any operation."

Benton persuaded Truman to go with him for a snack in the hospital's cafeteria, and when they returned they brought coffee for Amos and a cup of tea for Allison.

When Truman resumed his pacing, Allison suggested, "Let's go to the chapel. We can leave word where we are if we're needed." Truman and Amos agreed readily, and to her surprise, Benton trailed along as they went down the corridor to the small room with a vaulted ceiling and a few wooden chairs clustered around a small pulpit. Taped organ music sounded in the background. Allison sat between Truman and Amos and held their hands tightly as all of them looked upward to the highlighted cross between the two stained-glass windows. Benton perched warily on a chair in the rear row of seats, looking for all the world as if he would bolt if anyone spoke to him.

Usually Allison had no trouble making contact with God, but this morning He seemed far away. She remembered the many times Celestine had encouraged her through difficult situations, and she wanted so much to help her friend now. But Celestine was in the hands of the surgeon and God, so the only way Allison could help Celestine was to comfort her loved ones.

Since Allison didn't know what petition to make on Celestine's behalf, she started simply, "Our Father, who art in Heaven…" Amos joined his bass voice to hers, and with a few sobs, Truman prayed with them. Allison was comforted that since she had forgiven Donald, she didn't have to omit, "Forgive us our debts as we forgive our debtors."

"The Lord is my shepherd, I shall not want," Allison continued, and when they finished that psalm, Allison knew that in spite of their inadequate words, God was aware of the need. As they left the chapel, she was comforted, and the Handleys' concern seemed to have lessened somewhat.

It was midafternoon before the surgeon came into the waiting room, and he looked as if he had been in a battle. His face was haggard, his garments still speckled with Celestine's blood.

"We've finally stabilized her," he said as he sat down near Amos. "We found some medication that clotted the blood but her condition is still critical. We'll have to keep her in the hospital longer than we expected." He stood up wearily. "She will be back in her room in a couple of hours. You can see her there. We'll be monitoring her closely for a few days."

Benton and Allison went back to the office then, but Allison returned to the hospital before she went home for the night. Celestine was sleeping, and so pale that it frightened Allison, but Amos assured her that the worst was over. A container of life-giving blood was slowly transforming Celestine's pallor into a more healthy color.

"I'm so thankful for that," she whispered. "Why don't you and Truman go get something to eat. You need a break. I'll sit with her for a few hours, or I can stay with her all night if necessary."

"We've arranged for a private nurse to stay through the night. The surgeon thought she should have constant monitoring, and it was worth the extra money to be sure she was watched by someone with medical training."

After they had been gone for a while, Celestine opened her eyes, and Allison took her hand.

"Where is Amos?" she asked.

"Downstairs in the cafeteria. I'm pinch-hitting for him while he eats. You've had us all worried today."

"I'll be all right. You shouldn't be here—you need some rest."

Allison squeezed her hand and leaned forward to kiss Celestine's forehead. "I want to be here. You've become an important part of my life."

Celestine pressed Allison's hand weakly. "You're important to me, too. That's why I want you to rest."

She was asleep by the time Amos and Truman returned.

Celestine's improvement was rapid, and within a month, she was able to return to work on a part-time basis. Allison and Benton made one trip to the farm to see Celestine during her recuperation, where they found Celestine being cosseted by her family.

While they were at the Handley farm, Allison and Benton talked with Hannah about publishing her books.

"You realize, Hannah," Benton said, "that we're going to invest a lot of money in this venture, and it will take us several years to recoup our investment. Do you think you can write a few stories a year? Once young readers establish an interest in these characters, we have to keep publishing them."

"I understand. Always before, I jotted down my thoughts whenever I wanted to, but now that I have a purpose in writing, the ideas come easily."

"Have you discussed your plans with your family?" Allison asked.

Hannah lowered her eyes and nodded. "They are displeased and have forbidden me to do this. Perhaps I have a streak of stubbornness, but now that they've taken a stand against me it makes me more determined to follow my wishes."

"I don't want to cause you any trouble," Allison said nervously, with a glance toward Benton, who lifted his eyebrows as if to say, "I told you so."

"You aren't causing the trouble. You wouldn't have known about my writing if I hadn't mentioned it to you. And I hope when they see my books they will know that I'm not writing anything disrespectful." She smiled slightly. "It's strange, but the only one who supports me is Isaac."

"Isaac?" Allison asked.

"The man who wants to marry me. I've avoided giving him an answer for two years."

"If he wants to marry you, it seems he would oppose your career."

"Yes, one would think so, and I was very surprised when he told me that he supports my decision."

On their way back to Columbus, Allison was so concerned about possible trouble she had caused Hannah that she stared out the window, wondering if she had made a mistake. She sat far to the right, expecting Benton to berate her, but he reached for her hand and tugged until she moved closer to him. He put his arm around her shoulders and pulled her into his embrace.

"Don't worry about it. Hannah won't blame you—she told you she was taking full responsibility."

"At least Isaac is supporting her. It must be nice to have someone that supportive."

He gave her a playful slap on top of the head. "As if you don't! I'm supporting you in the project, even though it goes against my better judgment."

"I appreciate it, too, but I've been expecting you to say, 'I told you so.'"

He squeezed her shoulder. "You know I tried to discourage you, so there wasn't any need to remind you of it."

"What if we lose a lot of money?"

"We'll take a tax write-off."

"But if the firm loses money, the employees won't get good bonuses, and they will be mad at me."

"You've made it plain that the amount of bonus depends upon the money the firm makes." Benton pulled off the road into a park 'n' ride, where all the cars were empty of passengers. He put both arms around her and kissed her forehead. "Allison, one of the most important things you

must learn as an administrator is that you won't make excellent decisions all the time, but usually the good and the
bad average out. If you shilly-shally around, putting off
decisions until you're absolutely sure of the outcome, you
will never accomplish anything. And you don't know that
Hannah's books will be a liability. Stop worrying about it.''

Resting her head on his shoulder, she said, ''Have you
ever made any bad decisions, Benton?''

His answer was so long in coming that she lifted her
head. His face was ashen, and his lips trembled when he
finally spoke.

''Many of them, but I can live with most of the mistakes.
The worst one ruined my life.''

He released her and set the car in motion, and she knew
he hadn't been talking about his work at Page Publishing,
but rather some decision he'd made in his mysterious past.
The set, stony look on his face discouraged her from asking
any questions. She didn't see this side of Benton much
anymore. She hadn't asked him to go to church with her
since he had turned her down on Invite-A-Friend Sunday,
but frequently on Wednesday nights he would show up at
the church and sit with her and the Curnutts. He listened
intently to the Bible study, as if he was desperate for answers, but she never saw him there on Sundays.

Within five weeks Celestine was back at work, and on
the following Monday when she came to work, she brought
Hannah with her. But the book publishing hadn't waited
for the author to take up residence in Columbus. Elizabeth
and Pamela had worked overtime to have two of the books
ready for publication by May 1.

Allison was delighted to have Hannah staying at her
home, for she was lonely most of the time. Perhaps after
the series was launched, Hannah could go back to the country to do her writing, but at first it seemed important that
Hannah live where she was in close contact with the editor
and the artist if writing changes needed to be made. Hannah
was slow getting adjusted to city life, and she told Allison,

"I don't have any ideas here in these strange surroundings. When can I go back home? I can work for the Handleys as I've always done and do my writing. City life stifles my creativity."

"You'll need to stay here until we have the series well established," Allison said.

"We've done a lot of advertising targeted at bookstore owners as well as readers, but we still need more publicity," Allison said to Benton, "if we're going to expand our market. I wonder if we could afford a spot on television."

"Don't pay for advertising," he said. "If you approach some of these stations, they'll give you a place in their newscast." Benton was right, for the first two stations Allison contacted agreed to interview Hannah.

The books were ready the same week as Hannah's first interview, when she appeared on the noon telecast on Columbus's largest television station. Hannah's serenity and goodness were accentuated by the simplicity of her garments, and from Allison's point of view, the appearance was a great success. Orders began to pour in from all over the country, and Benton suggested hiring a few new workers for a night shift. Hannah became an overnight celebrity, and she was besieged with invitations to talk shows, but after Allison accompanied her to one of the shows, Hannah refused to go again.

"I didn't mind when they ask me questions about the books, but when they start needling me about my old-fashioned clothing and making comments about my religious beliefs, I've had enough. I'm sorry to disappoint you, but you'll have to cancel the other interview. I've already had a note from my parents that they regard me as a disgrace and don't want me to come back home."

Hannah didn't cry when she admitted that, but Allison did. "It seems so cruel, Hannah. It isn't fair."

"It's to be expected. I knew this might happen, but I didn't know I would have such a sinking feeling in the pit of my stomach. All my breath seems to have been punched

out of me. With one letter, I've lost my friends, and I can't
make new friends here—I'm too different.''

"I'm your friend, Hannah."

"Yes, I know it, and may God bless you for it, but most
people look askance at my odd dress and manners and
won't take the time to know me as a person.'' She paused
then thoughtfully added, "Although I've rebelled at some
of the restrictions I've had to my freedom, I realize now
that it doesn't matter what we wear if our heart is right.''

"I learned that the first day I met you, Hannah,'' Allison
said. "Every day I know you I'm reminded of God's words
to Samuel about David—'The Lord does not look at the
things man looks at. Man looks at the outward appearance,
but the Lord looks at the heart.' That verse reminds me of
you.''

A smile covered Hannah's face. "That's strange, Allison.
That verse has always been my opinion of you.''

Allison knew that Monday mornings weren't good for
Benton, but when he came into his office, she went in to
see him and told him about Hannah's ostracism.

"We knew it was bound to come,'' he said testily. "It
won't hurt the business as long as she continues to write.''

"I'm not concerned at this point about Page Publishing.
I'm wondering what this is going to do to Hannah. She
doesn't like living in Columbus, says she can't come up
with any stories here, but she can't go home again. I should
have listened to your advice.''

"Allison,'' he said, tired, "we've rehashed this so many
times I'm weary of it. Please go to your office and leave
me to do my work.''

His hands shook when he reached for the ringing telephone, and Allison backed out of the office, stunned. He
hadn't been that rude to her before, and although normally
his attitude would have crushed her spirits, she was dismayed over Benton's condition. Every Monday morning he
was morose, but she had never known him to be in such a

condition as this. She wondered about his shaking hand. Could he possibly be an alcoholic?

It was inopportune that Calvin Smith chose that morning to visit her office. The man had really become a pest—contriving excuses to discuss things that should have been handled through Benton, and he always managed before he left to ask her for a date. She had grown weary of that, too, she thought as she answered Calvin's unimportant questions about shipping the new books—all decisions that as supervisor he should make.

He came to the real reason for the interview, when he said, "I've got tickets for a Reds game tomorrow night. I'd like to take you as my guest."

"Mr. Smith, I've tried to be patient with you, hoping you would become discouraged by my lack of response to your attention. You're a good employee, and I appreciate that. Therefore, I've hesitated to be adamant about this. I am not going to date you, so please stop asking me."

His face flushed an angry red, and for a moment, he was obviously too incensed to speak. She hoped he would leave the office without further comment.

But when he got his temper under control, he stared at her a few minutes, then he said, "Very well. Apparently you're interested in my work output, but not my presence. It may surprise you to know that I'm really fond of you. I've not persisted in my attentions because I was toadying to the boss. I'm attracted to you, and given half a chance, I know I could love you."

The hurt in his eyes was evident and Allison was stricken with remorse because of her impatience.

Calvin stood up and paced around the room. "From the first day you came here, I recognized you as a person with poise, loveliness and decency, and I looked to you as the woman who could help me forget my disastrous first marriage."

"I'm sorry, Mr. Smith, but I've made my policy of fraternizing with employees plain right from the first. I haven't misled you.''

He laughed ironically. ''I might swallow that if I didn't know how much time you spend with the Handleys and Benton. You might fool Benton, and perhaps even yourself, but the reason you won't date me is that you've had your cap set for him since you first came here. But let me tell you something—if you think you're going to get Benton, you will be mighty disappointed. Ask him where he spends all his Sundays.''

Chapter Nine

When Celestine came in with the morning's mail, Allison was lying with her head on the desk. Allison had never been so dejected, and she poured out her troubles into Celestine's sympathetic ears. "I've had such a terrible few days," she cried in dejection. "Hannah's family has disowned her, Benton was cross with me when I tried to talk with him about it and just now Calvin Smith said some terrible things to me."

Celestine was moving around the office, watering the planters and opening the blinds, and she said, "Such as?"

"He's wanted to date me for months, and I've refused him nicely, giving as one reason that I didn't want to fraternize with the employees, but today I told him to quit bothering me. He made some spiteful remarks about the time I spend with your family and with Benton, and then he said to ask Benton where he spends his Sundays."

Busy pinching some dead leaves off the fern hanging by the window, Celestine didn't comment.

"I've often wondered about that myself. Where does he go on Sundays?"

Celestine's hands paused, and she moved toward the

door without looking at Allison. "That's a question you'll have to ask Benton."

Allison's dejection was complete. Even Celestine had failed her.

When Benton was short with her, when they had a difficult time with a customer or some problem in the business, he often asked her out for dinner, which he did that evening.

"Benton, I really would like to go, but I don't want to leave Hannah. She was lonely before this. But I want to be with you, too. Why don't you come to the house and have dinner with us. I have time to telephone Minerva. She mentioned having roast beef, and there's always plenty of that."

"I'd love to come. You still eat at six o'clock?"

"Yes," she said, and her heart felt lighter when she lifted the receiver to telephone Minerva.

That evening, after they'd eaten, Hannah elected to take a walk, and Benton and Allison went into the yard to sit on the white lawn furniture. The traffic from Neil Avenue was muffled by the thick shrubbery and the gentle splash of the fountain. "It's almost as private here as being in the country," Benton said. "The air is pleasant, too. I'm glad you asked me to eat here—I'm not in much of a mood to go to a restaurant."

"Then why did you ask me?"

"I was sorry that I'd been so nasty to you today." He put his arm around her shoulders. "I try not to take my frustrations out on you, but I'm not always successful, as you well know."

"But what causes your frustrations, Benton? Aren't we good enough friends that you can share them?"

He shook his head. "When I'm with you, I want to forget the things that frustrate me."

"This may annoy you, but I'm going to ask you something. If it's none of my business, tell me so." Briefly, she recounted her conversation with Calvin today. "What do you do on Sundays that makes you so unhappy every Monday?''

"You may be better off not knowing, although I've been on the verge of telling you dozens of times.'' A ray of sunlight through the trees had turned Allison's shoulder-length chestnut hair into flaming red, and Benton lifted a strand of it to his lips. "But I'm going to tell you.''

He paused again, lifted Allison's hand to his lips and nuzzled it tenderly, nibbling her fingertips with his lips. He didn't meet her gaze.

"You've seen Lois Holmes in my office?''

"Yes, and I've puzzled about your relationship to her.''

"I'm engaged to her daughter.''

Allison felt as if she'd been slapped in the face. "Engaged to her daughter! Why haven't I seen the daughter?''

"Patricia Holmes and I were engaged during our first year in college. She attended Notre Dame as I did, and that's where we met.''

Allison's heart was weeping, but the tears hadn't yet reached her eyes. She had never felt so utterly devastated. Why hadn't he told her?

"Eight years ago when we were sophomores in college, I came to Ohio to meet her family, and we took an afternoon's drive to Buckeye Lake. On our return we were involved in an automobile accident. It didn't seem to be a serious wreck, but Patricia received a head injury, and she's never recovered from it.''

"But where is she?''

"She's in a health care center in western Ohio. For a year I thought that Patricia would recover, and because I felt responsible for not preventing the accident, I promised Mrs. Holmes that I would wait for Patricia until she was well. Everyone except Mrs. Holmes conceded years ago that Patricia would never be any better. The doctors have told her that Patricia is brain-dead and that she should remove the life supports, but Mrs. Holmes won't agree to it.

Occasionally, Patricia does have some movement or a physical change that encourages her mother.''

"What does this have to do with your Sundays?"

"I take Mrs. Holmes to see her every Sunday."

"I'm rather befuddled. Why can't she go alone?"

"She can't drive, for one thing, and although she has
relatives who would take her, she thinks it's important for
Patricia to see me often so she won't forget me. When Mrs.
Holmes comes into the office, she's usually disturbed about
some new problem that's arisen over Patricia's care. The
Holmes fortune was rather large when this happened, but I
imagine most of it has gone to care for Patricia. She often
consults with me about investments."

The gentle flow of the fountain, which had seemed so
restful a short while ago, grated on Allison's nerves, and
even the sharp, clear song of a cardinal annoyed her.

"I take it that Patricia is her only child."

"Yes, and her mother depends on me."

"So what kind of a future does this leave you?"

"None," he said bitterly.

He put his arm around Allison and buried his face in her
hair, but Allison pushed him away. She couldn't deal with
his hurt when she had so many of her own.

"Do you believe there is any possibility that Patricia will
recover?"

"No, but I did promise Mrs. Holmes that I'd wait for
her as long as she lived. I did that in the passion of a
moment when I thought she would be better in a few
months."

"After eight years, why should you be bound by such a
promise? Surely Mrs. Holmes can't expect you to keep
your word under the circumstances."

"She reminds me of it occasionally—quite subtly, I'll
admit—but she makes it plain that she does expect me to
keep the promise. She monitors my extracurricular activities if she can, fearing I'll date someone else. She comes
into the office much more since you've been there."

"But she's using you," Allison muttered, and misery was settling around her heart. The things about Benton that made him such a loyal employee applied here. He felt it was his duty to remain true to a promise, and regardless of the cost to him, he would do what he said he would. "You're trapped just as much as Patricia is."

"Perhaps what you say is true, but I can't go back on my word. So you know where that leaves us."

"No, I don't know where that leaves us," she said angrily.

"I love you, Allison, but I can't offer you marriage, and indeed I've felt guilty the few times I've let my affection for you impair my better judgment. I was indifferent when you first came here. I suppose I resented you. But it didn't take long for me to realize that you are the person I want to share my life with. I won't ask you to wait for me as I have Patricia. That was the reason I didn't speak."

Rejected again! Because she was so miserable, she said curtly, "I always like to know where I stand. It would have been more honorable if you had told me this months ago. I've tried not to throw myself at you, waited for you to take the lead in our relationship, and I think I have succeeded."

He nodded. "I've never considered that you were pursuing me."

"But that didn't keep me from loving you. When I came to Columbus, I was hurting over my severed relationship, which had dealt a disastrous blow to my self-esteem. Right before I learned about this inheritance, I had finally made up my mind to push thoughts of Donald aside and to go on with my life. I didn't want to love anyone again, but I was vulnerable."

She started to cry, and Benton tried to gather her into his arms, but she removed herself from his clasp and stood up. "I had always remembered you, and when I knew you were at Page Publishing, and seemingly unmarried, I'll admit that had a lot to do with my interest in moving to

Columbus. But you're not to be blamed for my foolishness in falling in love. I should have known better than to trust any man." She walked to the fountain, her back to him. "Will you leave now. And in the future, we will be nothing more to each other than business associates."

Without further words, Benton walked around the shrubbery, and when she heard his car driving away from her home and out of her life, she ran into the library and crashed on the chaise lounge, her misery more than she could bear. She didn't know how long she sobbed out her frustration, soaking the chintz covers with her tears, but she heard a sound at the door and looked up quickly, fearing Benton had returned.

"Allison," Hannah said uncertainly from the door. "I heard you crying. Is there anything I can do?"

Allison lifted to a sitting position and wiped her hands across her tear-dampened face.

"Nothing except be my friend and listen to me." Hannah came to sit beside her on the lounge and listened as Allison poured out all the frustration of the past few years—how Donald had treated her, her mother's displeasure because she had accepted Harrison's legacy and moved to Columbus, her difficulties getting started at Page Publishing, her love for Benton and how he was tied to a woman who would never get well. The only thing she concealed was the fact that Harrison Page was her father and how she had found out about that.

Hannah patted Allison's shoulder occasionally as she talked, and she asked a few questions when Allison's narrative strayed, but mostly she listened.

"You don't know how miserable I am, Hannah. None of this wealth means anything to me when I'm estranged from my mother and can't have the man I love."

Hannah walked away from the lounge, fiddled with the items on the mantel, and finally took a chair near Allison. "I can understand your misery," she said, "because I'm very unhappy. I miss my family more than I thought possible." She motioned around the room. "All this is very nice, and I'm glad I had the chance to live here for a while, but this life isn't for me. I had thought that with my income from the books, I could have pretty clothes and an easier way of life, but I've learned the hard way that there's more to life than possessions."

"I'm not that interested in possessions, either," Allison protested, "but what should I have done with the inheritance? I've tried to give away much of the business's profits to others, and I feel as if I'm doing some good with my money."

Hannah nodded in agreement. "You are. I've heard the Handleys talk about your generosity, and God may have put you in this position for a purpose. I could do the same if I make a lot of money on my books, but I don't believe that is God's will for my life. I really thought that seeing my own writings in print would make me happy, but it hasn't. I keep thinking about Isaac. I should have married him, but, no, I had to sow my wild oats. I suppose I'm really homesick."

"But, Hannah, don't you resent your parents for treating you so harshly? After they've been so mean to you, I don't know why you want to go back to them."

"They haven't been mean to me. They're disappointed because I disregarded their advice. So, I'm not angry with them. Besides, as Christians, we're supposed to overcome evil with good, repay mistreatment with kindness."

"Then you think I was too harsh by telling Benton that our relationship was finished?"

"Who's going to be hurt more by that? Every day you see him, your love is going to be like a pin pricking at you. Do you think you'll be any happier if you stop seeing Benton? Perhaps he needs you—his role isn't an easy one. It's costing him to keep his promise."

"Hannah," Allison said quietly, "do you want to stop writing? Is that what you're trying to tell me?"

"Don't think I'm going to back out on my contract. I made a promise and I intend to keep it."

This determination to keep a promise that would ruin more than one life was getting to be an old theme as far as Allison was concerned. She couldn't do anything with Benton's resolve, but perhaps she could help Hannah. "Would your family take you back now if you wanted to go home?"

"Certainly. When I reject what I'm doing now, the door is open for my return."

Allison's appearance when she arrived at work the next morning earned her more than one worried glance from Celestine, because she hadn't slept and even an extra-heavy coat of makeup couldn't hide the weariness of her eyes. Benton didn't look as if he'd rested more than she had, but remembering Hannah's example, she went into his office.

"Benton, will you forgive me for my harsh words last night? I lacked understanding of your problem, but in afterthought, I can see that you have no other choice."

He seemed astonished at her attitude, but he said, "Of course I'll forgive you, but I'm the one who should be asking for forgiveness."

The ringing phone demanded his attention, and she left his office. Stopping by Celestine's desk, she asked for the folder Celestine had prepared on Hannah's contract. With it in hand, Allison started toward the office, but she paused. "Do you know the last name of Hannah's friend Isaac?"

"His name is Isaac Stahl."

"Would he receive a letter if I sent it to the same address as Hannah's?"

Celestine's eyes were full of questions, but she answered, "Yes. His farm adjoins that of her father."

Allison had arrived at a decision on which she wouldn't ask any advice. There wasn't anything she could do about getting Benton to revoke his promise, but she was in a position to help Hannah. Why should both of them be unhappy?

She sweated over her message, fearful that she would make matters worse:

Dear Mr. Stahl:

Hannah Hoptry has been living with me while she works on producing her series of books. She is not happy and regrets the decision she made about coming here. If you should want to come to Columbus, I believe she would be glad to see you.

Allison Sayre

Allison sealed the envelope, affixed a stamp and dropped it in the outgoing mail basket on Celestine's desk before she changed her mind.

A week later when Allison went to the office, Celestine was activating the computer system on her desk. She greeted Allison with upraised eyebrows.

"I brought you some company this morning. I put him in the office."

"Truman?" she asked, for he often came with his mother on his way back to college.

Celestine shook her head. Curious, Allison, opened the door.

The brawny young man dressed casually in jeans and flannel shirt stood when Allison entered, and she was sensitive to his full, generous smile.

"I'm Isaac Stahl, Miss Sayre. I thank you for your letter. I asked for a ride into town with Mrs. Handley this morning because I don't drive in the city. Is Hannah still at your home? Does she know I'm coming?"

"She's at my home, but she isn't even aware I wrote to you. I had expected you to let me know when you were coming so I could prepare her. Perhaps it's just as well this way. Come along, I'll drive you out to the house."

As they crossed the office, Benton stepped off the elevator. Surprise covered his face.

"I need to return home again," Allison said, and touched the button to hold the elevator in place. "I don't know when I'll be back—call me there if you need me."

Isaac was plainly uncomfortable with all the early-morning traffic on High Street, and Allison was worried about Hannah's reaction to her interference, so they said very little during the ten minutes it took to drive to her home. She parked along the street and they entered through the front door. She asked Isaac to be seated in the parlor.

"Where are you, Hannah?" she called.

"In my bedroom."

Allison started up the stairs, and Hannah appeared at the door of her room, a sheet of paper and a pencil in her hands. Not expecting company, Hannah had not yet braided her hair into its customary bun and it hung in waves over her shoulders, adding to the girl's beauty. Allison was happy that Isaac could see her this way.

"Why are you back so soon?"

"We have to talk, Hannah," Allison said. "Let's go into your room."

After she closed the door, Allison paused for a minute. She didn't know how to start.

"Isaac is in the parlor," she blurted out.

Hannah sat down on a chair, speechless, and Allison continued, "Perhaps I shouldn't have interfered, but I wrote and told him that you were unhappy and that you might like to see him."

"Why would you do anything like that?"

"I can't be happy, but I see no reason you shouldn't be."

"I don't understand."

"I'm trying to live by the Golden Rule and operate my firm that way. If anyone could help me find happiness with Benton, I would want him or her to do it. I'm trying to treat you the way I would like to be treated. The decision is up to you, but if you're miserable here and want to go home, I'm not going to stop you. You've written enough stories now for at least a year's worth of books, and if we do those, Page Publishing won't go in the red on the project. I don't want you to let that contract stand in the way of your happiness, so please go and talk to Isaac.''

Apparently not even remembering that her hair was loose, Hannah rushed out of the room and down the stairs. After an hour she appeared on the threshold of Allison's bedroom. Her face was radiant. ''I'm going home, Allison. I feel as if I've gone back on my word, and God forgive me for that, but I'm out of place in the publishing world. Will Mr. Lockhart be very mad at me for not finishing?''

''Probably not as mad as Elizabeth and Pamela, but we guaranteed them only a year's work in their contract, so they'll have no recourse.'' With tearful eyes she hugged Hannah. ''I'm happy for you.''

Hannah returned her embrace. ''Happiness will come for you, too, Allison. I know it will.''

''I'll go to work now, and leave you to your packing. I'll drive you and Isaac home this evening. I want to talk to your parents.''

''Isaac told them about your note, so they won't be too surprised.''

Lois Holmes scuttled out of Benton's office when Allison reached the second floor, so Allison knew he would be alone. She went in, closed the door behind her and leaned against it.

''By mutual consent Hannah and I will dissolve her contract with us after we've published the books that we now have in our possession. The sales will go on for a long time, I hope, so that we won't lose any money.''

''What brought on this sudden change?''

With downcast eyes, Allison said, ''I was in anguish when she came home last week after...after you and I had our conversation, and I unburdened my problems to her.

She confessed that she was miserable, too, being separated from her family and friends. She mentioned Isaac in particular and I thought she loved him.''

"Was that Isaac in the office this morning?"

"Yes. I couldn't do anything about my own misery, but I thought I could help Hannah find happiness, so I wrote Isaac a short note and suggested he come to see her. He didn't waste any time but rode in with Celestine this morning. I took him to the house, and Hannah decided she wanted to go back home—I'm going to take them this evening.''

"Are they going to be married?"

"She didn't say, but I presume so, eventually.''

"Shall I go with you? It will be late when you return.''

She hesitated and threw caution to the winds. "Yes, I would like your company.''

So much for her resolve to treat him as an employee. "I'm sorry I disregarded your advice about publishing the books. Do you think we'll lose much money?''

"I don't think we'll lose any money. If she doesn't write any more, we'll not *make* as much money as we anticipated, but they are good little books and we won't have any trouble selling our inventory, for they will be in demand for a long time. It was a good idea, and I'm sorry I doubted your wisdom.''

His smile made her giddy, but she felt like a child looking at a desired toy in a shop window knowing the door was locked for the night and she couldn't get the toy.

"I'll take my car," he said. "What time shall I pick you up?"

"I'll telephone Minerva and ask her to have dinner at five o'clock, and we can leave at six. Do you want to eat with us?"

"No, I have some errands to do after work. We can stop for a snack on our way home if I'm hungry.''

After leaving Isaac at his farm, Hannah was silent as they drove the mile to her home. Allison asked Benton to wait in the car, and she wondered how she would be received by the Hoptrys, but she didn't want to just dump Hannah out if her parents weren't inclined to receive her.

Dusk was settling around the neat farmstead and scented flowers lined the walkway. Hannah opened the door and stepped inside the kitchen and Allison followed her. Allison quickly surveyed the clean, but unostentatious room. A smooth-shaven man with graying hair was seated at a round table covered with a blue checkered cloth, and the electric fixture above his head cast a muted light on the scene. He held a Bible before him. Two teenaged boys sat across the table from him, but they ran quickly to Hannah and she put her arms around them. A woman in a dress similar to Hannah's stood by the stove, and her worried eyes kept darting from the man to Hannah, and her lips moved noiselessly. Allison wondered if she was praying.

"Pa, I've come home to stay…for good." The man nodded. "This is Allison Sayre. I've been staying with her. She's been good to me. Allison, this is my pa and ma, and my two brothers."

Mr. Hoptry indicated the bench behind the table. "Sit down," he invited.

"Thank you," Allison said, "but a friend waits in the car, and we want to return to Columbus tonight. I wanted to be sure that you would take Hannah in before I left her."

Mrs. Hoptry gasped, and Hannah's father turned amazed eyes upon Allison. "Hannah is our own—we'd not turn her away."

"But you did a few weeks ago."

"If Hannah has come home with a repentant heart, our door is open to her," he answered simply.

"I have, Pa, but it was not bad for me to go to the city. If I hadn't, all my life I would have yearned for the things I had missed. Two months among people not my own taught me what I really value. Isaac is going to speak to you, and with your blessing, we are going to wed."

Allison knew she should leave, but she said, "Mr. Hoptry, Hannah has signed a contract with my company to produce the books she has already written, and I feel that we have the right to publish the rest of those books because it will be a hardship on others if we do not." She took one of the books out of her purse and laid it before him. "I've brought you one to read, to let you be the judge, but I think you will not be disappointed in what she has written. However, Hannah is due a royalty on each of the books we sell, and depending upon sales, it may add up to several thousand dollars. Why would it be wrong for her to receive that money?"

"I will discuss it with Hannah, and she can let you know."

Mrs. Hoptry spoke for the first time. "We thank you, Miss Sayre, for looking after Hannah. We would be glad to have you sit down."

"No, not this time, but I do want to return for a visit. Hannah has been a good friend to me, and I don't want to lose contact with her." Allison hugged Hannah.

"Write to me. I want to know how you're getting along."

Hannah walked with her to the back step. "Will you come back for the wedding?"

"If I can," Allison promised. "Let me know when you set the date."

The following Sunday morning, the phone rang before Allison was out of bed, and she lifted the receiver.

"Hello," she murmured sleepily.

"This is Benton. Did I awaken you?"

"I'd been awake—just dozing now." She sat up and pushed back her hair.

"Mrs. Holmes just telephoned. She has a migraine today and can't go with me to the health care center. I want you to go with me."

Allison's body went rigid. "No," she said without thought. "No, I couldn't do that."

"I know it's a lot to ask, but you'll never really know what my predicament is until you see for yourself. Please go with me."

She remembered what Hannah had said about her being a comfort to Benton. "All right. What time do you want to leave?"

"I'll pick you up at ten o'clock. It's a two-hour drive, and I get there about one o'clock when visiting hours start. That will give us time to stop for lunch."

Allison told Minerva that she was going out with Benton for the day and nothing more, for if any of her friends from church should call, she didn't want them to be worried about her. She dressed in casual slacks and a brown sweater set and waited in the parlor until she saw Benton stop in front of the house, then went out to meet him.

He squeezed her hand when he opened the door for her. "Thanks for going along. I know this puts you in a difficult position, but it's important for me to have you go."

As they took I-70 west out of town, Allison asked, "Why isn't Patricia housed in a facility closer to her home? Surely there are places in Columbus where Mrs. Holmes could visit daily."

"Very few places are equipped to handle cases like Patricia's."

The farther they went from Columbus, the more depressed Benton became; he spoke seldom and stared straight ahead. At times Allison doubted that he knew she was in the car with him, but she really preferred to be ignored today, for she dreaded the afternoon.

They pulled into a fast-food restaurant for lunch, and the hamburger could have been straw for all the taste Allison got from it. Benton called for an extra cup of coffee, but he didn't eat half his sandwich. When they drove into the grounds of the health center, Benton parked in front of a one-story brick building that sprawled over more than an acre of land. He turned off the motor, and his hands gripped the steering wheel so hard his knuckles were white. Releasing a pent-up sigh, he said, "Let's go."

He opened the door for Allison and held on to her arm as they walked up the steps from the parking lot to the main entrance. His hand trembled on her arm, and sensing how traumatic this visit was to him each week, Allison realized now why he was always washed out on Monday mornings. Her heart went out to him and she suddenly felt selfish for the way she'd been focusing on her own emotions. Clearly, Benton suffered great anguish during these visits and his pain was even more acute today, Allison thought, because of her own presence. Benton registered at the main desk and propelled Allison down corridor B. Her steps halted, and she looked up at him with fearful eyes.

"I don't think I can take this."

"I stay an hour or so," he said, more relaxed now than he had been. "If you get too upset, you can go back to the reception room and wait for me."

The door to room 204 was open and Benton walked in first, but he took Allison's hand and pulled her beside him. The room smelled of medicine and disinfectant common to most nursing homes, and Allison drew a deep breath. She caught the back of a chair when she saw the emaciated body of the young woman stretched out upon the hospital bed, her head slightly elevated. She lay motionless and gave no indication of their arrival.

"Hello, Patricia," Benton said, and bent over to kiss her forehead.

Allison cringed at the gesture. Patricia couldn't have weighed more than seventy pounds. Her hair was sparse, her skin as pale as the bed's pristine white sheets. From time to time, Allison noticed her eyes move rapidly beneath closed lids and moaning sounds passed her lips. An oxygen tube was attached to her nose, an IV tube was in her arm and from other attachments Allison could tell that she had no control of her bodily functions.

"She is nourished through a feeding tube," Benton explained, more relaxed now that he was in the room.

"Patricia, I brought a friend of mine today, Allison Sayre. Actually, she's my boss, but we're friends, too." He pulled a chair close to Patricia, sat down and took her hand.

He turned to Allison, who was leaning weakly against the wall. "The doctors suggested when she was first injured that it would be well for us to chat with her in a normal way, talking about everyday occurrences with which she might identify. It hasn't worked, but her mother and I have continued doing it anyway."

Benton didn't seem to be bothered by the girl's occasional moaning and the saliva that dripped from her mouth. Once he took a tissue, wiped her face and continued to talk, but Allison could hardly stand it. She observed an eight-by-ten picture on the dresser, and although she couldn't detect any resemblance to the injured girl, she assumed this was Patricia's picture.

"That's her high-school graduation photo," Benton said when he observed her interest. "I'm glad Mrs. Holmes keeps the picture here—if I didn't remember what she used to be, I couldn't accept what I see today."

Patricia had been beautiful, with short blond hair that framed classic features. In the photo her blue-green eyes exhibited warmth and vitality, and her mouth opened slightly to reveal white even teeth.

Benton continued to talk about the weather, about his week at work, about his bodybuilding exercises at the Y, without any response from Patricia. Allison walked around the room, only half listening to Benton's mundane chatter. Allison's body was tense, her mouth dry, and when the IV bag needed to be replaced and a buzzer sounded loudly, she jumped and knocked a plastic tumbler off the nightstand.

Allison's face flamed in embarrassment over her reaction. She couldn't see that she was being of any help to Benton or to Patricia, and certainly not to herself, and she waved a hand to Benton and walked down the corridor to the reception room. Even after Benton had told her about Patricia she hadn't given up, because if his love for her, Allison, was as great as her love for him, she thought she could persuade him to break his promise to Mrs. Holmes. She admitted defeat now. Under normal circumstances, she could take on another rival, but she couldn't compete with the woman in room 204.

At the end of an hour when Benton joined her, his face was white again, and he had lost the animation he'd exhibited in Patricia's presence. He collapsed on the couch beside her and lowered his head into his hands, gasping for breath. Allison stood in awe of the emotional strain that had made the usually calm, efficient Benton lose his control. Having no idea how to comfort him, she remained silent, but she put a hand on his shoulder and he covered it with his own, his palm damp with perspiration.

After they left the health center, Benton drove for a few blocks and turned into a city park. "Let's walk a bit before we hit the highway," he said.

As they strolled along the graveled path, he said, "What do you think?"

"I can't imagine how anyone in that condition can still be alive, and I don't know how her mother can believe she'll recover."

"Countless specialists have examined her and given Mrs. Holmes no hope for Patricia's recovery. Yet she will not concede that Patricia won't get well."

"But even if she should come out of her coma, would she be the person you knew before the accident?"

"No, I don't think so. I've done a lot of studying on this situation, and people who have been comatose for only a year or so often have changed personalities when they do recover."

"So if she should get better, she wouldn't be the girl you had promised to marry."

"Not likely."

"I think you're being as selfish as Mrs. Holmes, both to me and to yourself, but I suppose I won't be able to change your mind."

"No. If I should marry you and stopped coming up here and she died right away, I would always blame myself. It seems like a no-win solution to me. For the past year, Mrs. Holmes has been pressuring me to marry Patricia as she is—she's worried about what will happen to her daughter if she dies."

"Benton! Surely you wouldn't do that!"

He shook his head. "No, I don't really feel engaged to Patricia anymore, for she isn't the girl I asked to marry me, but I still feel guilty that I might have prevented the accident that caused her injury. I shouldn't expect to find happiness when my failure to prevent the accident might have robbed her of the future, but my guilt doesn't extend to becoming her husband. It would make a travesty of marriage."

They walked in silence, and then he continued, "This is why I stopped believing in God, why I'm no longer the person you met in Indianapolis. I had believed all my life that God hears and answers our prayers, and in faith, believing, I prayed for Patricia to recover. When that seemed impossible, I prayed for God to take her life—I couldn't bear to see her like this. Finally, I shook my fist in God's face and rejected every promise He's made—how all things work together for the good of those who love Him, how if we ask anything in His name it will be done for us, and numerous other prayer promises. They aren't true, Allison. I put God to the test and He failed me."

"But God hasn't failed you. He has the same power He's always had. Your attitude about this alarms me more than your responsibility to Patricia. Please start coming to church with me and give God another chance."

"If I am wrong and God has been there for me all the time and I've spurned Him, it's too late for me to make restitution."

"No," Allison insisted, "God is always waiting to forgive."

Benton smiled wanly. "There have been times when I have experienced an overwhelming void in my life, when I've realized that I no longer have God to bolster me, but I repeat, it may be too late for me to change. I haven't forgotten all the Scripture that I committed to memory when I was working with the crusade, and I often recall a passage from the Book of Hebrews—'It is impossible for those who have once been enlightened, who have tasted the heavenly gift, who have shared in the Holy Spirit, who have tasted the goodness of the word of God and the powers of the coming age, if they fall away to be brought back to repentance, because to their loss they are crucifying the Son of God all over again and subjecting him to public disgrace.'"

If Allison had felt defeated before, it was nothing to the despair she experienced now. Even if Benton were to break his promise and want to marry her, she wouldn't accept his proposal. When she had felt God's guiding hand throughout her life, she couldn't tie herself to a man who denied God. In times like these, she had to fight to hold on to her own faith.

Chapter Ten

After Hannah's departure and her own trip to see Patricia, Allison's spirits plummeted, and she turned down several of Benton's invitations, because she could not bear to be in his company when the specter of Patricia stood between them. Every time she saw Mrs. Holmes in the office, she grew bitter and disillusioned.

Two months after she returned to her parents, Hannah invited Allison to her wedding. "The wedding will be very simple," she wrote, "but it would mean a great deal to me if you would come. Please ask Mr. Lockhart to accompany you."

Benton agreed readily to go, but he said, "Let's go shopping together for a wedding gift, Allison. I've rarely attended weddings and I'm afraid I won't have any idea of what to buy."

"That sounds like a good idea to me. What about Saturday morning?"

"Good, I'll treat you to lunch in exchange for your purchasing expertise."

This was the lighthearted Benton she loved, and Allison wished he could be that way all the time. When he was in this mood, she could forget Patricia Holmes. When he returned to his office, Allison followed him with her eyes, which must have mirrored all her longing for him, because she saw Celestine looking from one to the other in concern.

Benton's mood was still lighthearted on Saturday. As soon as the stores opened along High Street they went to the town center and took the elevator to the household section of the major department store. At the end of an hour, they had decided on aluminum cookware, which they deemed as appropriate for Benton's gift, while Allison bought a sheet set and numerous towels and washcloths.

On the following Saturday afternoon, Benton picked up Allison and Truman, who had come to her house to wait, and they headed toward the Handley farm, where Celestine and Amos would join them.

"I've finally decided," Allison said when Benton gathered up speed as they left the city limits and Truman was raving about the advantages of Benton's expensive car, "why you never let me drive when we go anywhere together. I had supposed you were afraid of my driving, but now I've decided that you're ashamed of my car."

Benton smiled in her direction and was silent, but from the back seat Truman said, "Now that you've brought it up, I've often wondered why you don't buy a new car. You live in a mansion but drive an ancient car."

"I hardly call a seven-year-old vehicle ancient."

"Well, if I were in your place, I'd have a sports model of some kind."

"You sound just like my brother. I don't need another car."

"I think it's stubbornness," Benton said teasingly. "If you and Tim start insisting she should keep the car, she probably would buy a new one."

"Forget I mentioned it," she said smilingly. She wanted nothing to spoil this day.

At the farm, Allison got in the back seat with Truman

and Celestine and let Amos sit up front with Benton so he could guide Benton to the church building.

"It's a small place," Amos explained, "and if their whole congregation is there, we may have to stand."

But Hannah's father stood outside the building, and he ushered Hannah's city friends into the sanctuary and helped them find seats. Allison was glad of his friendliness, for she knew now that he didn't blame her for Hannah's rebellion. The press of the people and their body heat made the tiny room sweltering, but Amos opened a window beside their pew and the evening coolness seeped in.

A young girl dressed in white played soft music on the piano, and when the strains of "Here Comes the Bride" filled the little sanctuary, Hannah walked down the short aisle with her father. Isaac and the minister stood by the pulpit as they approached and Allison's heart ached at the light on Isaac's face. How wonderful to approach an altar with a man like Isaac waiting to offer his love.

Hannah's white dress was as plain as her other garments. She wore a simple veil over her hair and her only adornment was a red rose pinned at her shoulder.

The service was brief. After the minister spoke of the sacredness of marriage and how Jesus had blessed the institution at the wedding in Cana of Galilee, he asked, "Hannah Hoptry, do you take Isaac Stahl for your lawful wedded husband? Will you honor and obey him, succor him in good and ill health and keep yourself only for him as long as you both shall live?"

"Yes, with God's help, I will," Hannah replied sweetly.

As Isaac repeated a similar vow, Allison felt Benton's eyes on her, and she looked at him. His look was tender, intense and so resigned that tears stung Allison's eyes. *God,* she pleaded, *why must our lives be ruined because of Patricia Holmes?*

Allison was instantly ashamed of her thoughts, but why should she be hypocritical about it? If Patricia Holmes had any chance of being well again, she would never have

voiced such a prayer. If the girl died, Allison felt sure that
Benton's faith would be renewed, and they could have a
happy life together. But as she gazed deeply into his ex-
pressive eyes, Benton shrugged slightly, and she quit her
dreaming. This was Hannah's day, and she must forget herself.

At the end of the vows, there was no ring, nor any kiss.
Hannah and Isaac held hands, the minister prayed again and
the wedding service was over.

Hannah and Isaac greeted their friends and neighbors as
they made their way down the aisle. Even though it seemed
contrary to custom, when they arrived at her side Allison
hugged Hannah.

"I'm so happy for both of you," Allison whispered.
"Thanks for inviting us to come."

Celestine hugged Hannah and kissed her, and Truman,
with a roguish look at Isaac, said, "I want to kiss you, too,
Hannah, but perhaps I shouldn't."

The wedding supper was served in a small room adjacent
to the church building, and the fare was abundant—fried
chicken, potato salad, baked beans, homemade bread and a
variety of pies.

Benton and Allison filled their plates and went outside
to eat. Finding a secluded place, they sat down on a bench,
and he took her hand and squeezed it. "I suppose you know
this wasn't an easy experience for me," he said softly.
"I'm almost sorry I came—seeing the happiness of Isaac
and Hannah emphasizes what we're missing. In my mind,
I kept saying, 'I take you, Allison, to be my lawful wedded
wife, to love and to cherish.'" He broke off his words
savagely. "You can't imagine how much I want to love
and cherish you. I tell you if there is a God, He wouldn't
let people suffer like this."

"Let me assure you that there is a God! I get terribly
discouraged, too, but God knows best. I have to remind
myself of that often."

Hannah and Isaac walked to the car with them, and Hannah whispered in Allison's ear, "Don't be sad. Things are going to work out for you and Benton, too. I know you'll be together soon."

Allison had no such hopes, but she loved Hannah for being concerned about her life when she should be concentrating on her own wedding day. Allison nodded, her eyes misty.

Allison had to fight her despondency hard after the wedding, when she had experienced firsthand what a happy marriage could mean, and although she knew Benton was suffering as much as she was, there seemed no way to resolve their problem, and she faced each day with a stoic attitude as summer days faded into autumn. When the first days of cold weather hit the Columbus area, it seemed impossible that she had spent almost two years in this city, and ironically, Allison realized that her condition was much as it had been her last few months in Chicago. The disappointment of losing Benton was so much worse than Donald's rejection, but Allison knew she had to live with her pain. She was determined that she was not going to be hurt three times—her heart had suffered too much already.

If she couldn't have Benton, she didn't want anyone, and since the possibility of marriage with Benton seemed unlikely, Allison had lost any interest in finding her birth mother. Thus it struck her like a thunderbolt when she opened her mail one morning, extracted a small sheet of paper from a legal-sized envelope and read:

If you want to meet your birth mother, come to Antonio's for dinner Saturday, at six o'clock. Ask for Mary Miller's table.

Allison was so stunned for a while that she couldn't move. Now that the time had come, should she respond? She wanted to talk to Beatrice, but when her mother refused to discuss her birth mother, what could she do? Her father would be the perfect sounding board, but if she telephoned him, Beatrice would know. Should she ask Benton? He was the only one besides her parents who knew the facts, but should she put him on the spot about the decision? What about Celestine, who was so understanding? There was no one else she could talk to, and she started toward the outer office, but paused with her hand on the doorknob. Sometimes she wondered if Celestine didn't know anyway, because once when Allison and Benton had been talking about ways to trace one's parents, Celestine had walked in on their conversation. With a dismayed look on her face, she had backed out of the office and Allison wasn't sure how much she had heard.

Deciding not to involve anyone else, she put on her coat, and wrapping a scarf around her head, Allison walked by Celestine's desk. It was a decision she had to make for herself.

"I'm going to be out for about an hour," she said without any further explanation. She walked down the street without glancing at anyone, hardly knowing where she was going, trying to think, but Allison's mind was numb—she couldn't deal with this decision. What she had been wanting to know for over a year was within her grasp now, so why did she hesitate? The answer to that was obvious—fear. What if her mother was a woman of low repute? After all, if she had borne one child out of wedlock, what would have prevented similar occurrences? What if the note was a hoax? And how would she be able to prove that the woman who approached her was really Mary Miller, her birth mother?

Allison sat on one of the benches on the capitol lawn, oblivious to the strong wind blowing around her. The November wind chilled her, and she shivered in her light coat. A squirrel searching frantically for nuts to store scurried up the tree beside her. Out of her reach, it watched her with curious eyes, its long tail switching back and forth.

When the cold began to penetrate and a drizzle started

falling, she walked back to the office, no nearer a decision than before. The rest of the week she halted in indecision, unable to act normally, and she sensed rather than observed the concern Benton and Celestine exhibited. At home, Adra and Minerva weren't so subtle, and after Allison's second day of moping around, Minerva clapped her hand over Allison's forehead.

"I've never seen you in such a mood," she said. "Are you sick or are you in love?"

"I'm not sick, and I am in love, but that's not the problem right now." She patted Minerva's arm and was pulled into a motherly embrace. "I do appreciate your concern, but I can't talk about it at the moment. Haven't you been involved in situations you couldn't discuss with anyone?"

"No, I can't say that I have. But, then, I'm a talker and you're not." She released Allison with a kiss on the cheek. "You know I'll listen when you want to talk."

When Benton asked her out for dinner on Friday night, she turned him down, for she absolutely couldn't be her normal self. She knew she had hurt him by her refusal, as well as by her reticence all week, but what could she say to him? He was sure to ask questions, and when she didn't know the answers herself, how could she respond?

She hoped that she would sleep late on Saturday morning, but she was awake at the usual time, and the hours loomed before her until six o'clock. She considered going shopping, but she had bought a few winter clothes two weeks ago, and she needed nothing else. When Minerva caught her pacing the floor in Harrison's office and threatened to have Adra drive her to the emergency room, Allison vacated the house.

In order to take her mind off the forthcoming revelation, Allison knew she had to do something daring and uncharacteristic. She went shopping for a new car. At first, she had no notion of buying an automobile, but as she went from one car lot to another, she became intrigued with the idea. Her impulsive decision didn't override her conservatism completely, so she turned down the sports models, the full-sized luxury cars with every gadget imaginable and settled on a four-door compact. By the time she had decided on the car Allison was almost back to normal, but she took one more flight of fancy—the car she bought was vivid lavender, definitely a woman's car.

When it came time to settle the deal, Allison haggled with the salesman, until finally at four o'clock, and obviously his quitting time, he threw up his hands.

"Oh, all right," he said somewhat ungraciously, "you win. I should have known better than to expect to best you—I sold Harrison Page a car once, and there's no doubt you're his kin."

There was no doubt that she belonged to Harrison Page, but what about her mother?

When Allison drove into the driveway at her Neil Avenue home, she blew the horn several times until Adra and Minerva came running out. Her purchase didn't surprise them any more than it did Allison.

After arguing with Adra, refusing to let him take his truck out of the garage and put the new car inside, Allison had an hour to reach the restaurant and she rushed to her room.

How should she dress? How to dress for a mother she had never seen? Should she dress to impress her, or wear ordinary clothes in case the woman was a fortune hunter? Although she had never been there, she understood that Antonio's was a ritzy place, so although she decided on slacks, she chose a new pair of Scotch-plaid wool pants she had bought a few weeks before with a golden colored silk blouse and a black wool blazer.

By the time Allison maneuvered her new car into a parking garage, her hands were sweaty, she felt light-headed and her stomach was queasy. She wished now that she had unburdened her problem to Benton and asked him to come along on this occasion. Nothing in the note had indicated that she should come alone.

"I'm looking for Mary Miller's table," she said huskily to the maître d'.

"Right this way. She's waiting for you."

Allison wiped her clammy hands on her slacks and tried to stop their trembling by folding them into fists. Shaking legs did nothing to improve her gait, and she hitched and shuffled along in the wake of the maître d'. She kept her head down, looking neither to the right nor left or even ahead. If there was anyone in the restaurant who knew her, she didn't want to have to speak to him or her, and she put off looking ahead to spot her birth mother as long as she could.

The maître d' stopped, slapped a menu down on the table and said, "Enjoy your meal, ma'am."

Allison lifted her eyes. She didn't know whether to be happy, sad or angry. Slipping into the chair, she looked at her companion with wondering eyes. "Celestine?"

Celestine took Allison's hand in a tender clasp and Allison returned the pressure.

"Mary Celestine Miller is my maiden name."

"All these months we've worked together and you've never told me?" Allison's lips trembled and she put up a hand to control them. "Why would you keep me in suspense?"

"I had promised not to tell, and I wouldn't have, except I overheard you talking to Benton one day about tracing your mother. I knew it would be just a matter of time until you found me, and I wanted to avoid an investigation that Truman might hear about. Then, too, when I was in the hospital so near death I wished that I had told you." She touched Allison's hand. "But how did you find out? Did your parents tell you?"

"Uncle Harrison—" she stopped and smiled wryly "—I suppose I should call him 'Father,' left a letter for me in a bank box. I found it before I had been here three months. I telephoned my mother at once and she refused to tell me anything, for she was very annoyed that he had written the letter."

"And so she should have been. She deserved that consideration."

"I've wanted to know who my birth mother was, but when my mother opposed it, I delayed the search, not wanting to hurt her."

"I want to make my position plain here," Celestine said. "I lost any claim to be called your mother when I gave you up for adoption. Beatrice is your mother, and I expect nothing but to be your friend, but I am grateful to Mr. Page for leaving you his estate because it gave me the opportunity to know you. I hope this won't make any difference in our friendship."

"Does Amos know? He's always been so kind to me."

"Yes, he knows. Since I've come this far, I owe you a full explanation, my dear. I will give you the important details, and you can ask for others at any time." She took a deep breath.

"If it upsets you, I don't have to know."

She shook her head. "Your birth was the result of a onetime encounter between Mr. Page and me."

"Then you didn't have an affair—you weren't his mistress."

She smiled. "Mr. Page wasn't the kind to have a mistress. He was very devoted to his wife. But her disability caused him to live a celibate life. I had been his secretary for about six months, and we were working late one night. I had recently lost my younger sister. She died in a car accident. Something—I don't recall what exactly—reminded me of her and I began crying. Mr. Page tried to console me.

"Before either of us knew what was happening, he started to make love to me. It may be hard for you to imagine, but I was very pretty then."

"That's not hard to believe."

"After the deed was done, Mr. Page was as aghast as I was."

"So my birth wasn't the result of any great love between you?" Allison said in disillusionment.

"No, I'm sorry to say that it wasn't. As I told you, Mr. Page loved his wife very much. We agreed the next day that I would leave Page Publishing and I applied for jobs at other firms, but then I learned I was pregnant and the situation was different. I didn't want to raise an illegitimate child—my pride wouldn't let me—and although I lived to regret losing you, I told Mr. Page that I intended to go away, have the child and give it up for adoption. He wanted a child desperately, but he couldn't let his wife know what had happened, yet he was determined not to let you be adopted out of the family. He approached your mother and father, and Beatrice reluctantly agreed, while fearing that if they took you, Harrison would keep interfering in your life. When he gave them repeated assurances that he would ignore your presence, Beatrice agreed."

"Where were you when I was born?"

"My grandmother lived in Chicago, so I went to her for an extended visit. Harrison paid my expenses and treated me with all respect, and he insisted that I return to his employ. After your birth, I didn't even see you. Your parents came and took you home before I left the hospital. Your birth was never mentioned between Mr. Page and me again, although in an offhanded way, the few times he saw you or if he had a note from your mother that mentioned you, he would make mention of his niece. He always acted guilty in my presence, as if he owed me a debt he couldn't repay. I suppose that's the reason he remembered me in his will."

"Minerva says he always acted guilty toward Aunt Sarah, too."

"Poor man, he paid a heavy price for just once losing the iron self-control he exercised. In a way, it's a rather sordid story and one that may make you feel worse than if you'd remained unaware, but you deserve to know.''

"I'm a little surprised about Amos and how fond he seems of me. I would think he would resent me, but even more than you, he's promoted our relationship.''

"That's true. I intended to maintain a strict employee-employer status with you, but if you remember, he was the one who invited you to be our guest the first time.''

"I'm sorry that you would have preferred to have less contact with me.''

"I didn't say that." Celestine reached out and took Allison's hand. "Believe me, it was for your good that I would have kept our lives separate. After I had Truman and found what joy there is in having a child, every time I did something for him, watched him take his first steps, took him to kindergarten, watched him graduate from high school, over and over I mourned what I had missed with you.''

"And Truman doesn't know?''

She shook her head. "I hadn't dated Amos until after you were born, and when he asked me to marry him, I told him about your birth. He was very angry at first and said he wouldn't marry me, and I couldn't blame him, but a few days later, he had second thoughts. He didn't even object to me remaining with Page Publishing, for it was a good job and he knew there was nothing between Mr. Page and me. I never mentioned you again after I first told him, but he sensed how I felt, and when you came to Columbus, he convinced me that there was no reason we couldn't be friends.''

"Now what are we going to do about it? Shall we tell?''

"I wouldn't. I certainly don't want Truman to know. It will cause more tension if you tell Beatrice what you've learned, and I don't blame her for feeling as she does. It's obvious to me that your parents gave you a loving childhood, more than I could have done if I'd kept you and raised you as an illegitimate child. At the time of your birth, society wasn't as tolerant toward unwed mothers as they are now. Your childhood wouldn't have been pleasant.''

"But I love you and Amos as well as my parents. I don't know why we shouldn't get to know one another and be one happy family.''

"If you make that decision, you might regret it, so consider it a long time.''

"I believe I must have inherited some of your characteristics,'' Allison said, "for although I look like the Pages, I'm not like my brother and sister.''

Before they parted, Celestine said, "Although I don't expect to claim any rights of motherhood, I do want you to know that I'm very proud of the woman you've become, and I love you very much. I will be eternally grateful to your parents for the upbringing they've given you.''

Allison couldn't answer her. This day had been too upsetting. She was glad the mystery of her birth had been cleared up, and in a way that didn't cause her any shame. She could live with the circumstances of her birth, and now if she could get Benton to see his relationship with Patricia in a more rational light, she had brighter hopes for the future. He had been coming to church with her more often, and he had even had some counseling sessions with the pastor. Circumstances were looking up.

But Allison should have known better than to be optimistic where Benton was concerned, for her hopes were dashed again when she went to work the following week. Benton was not there when she arrived, which was not unusual, but when he still hadn't come in an hour later, she and Celestine began to worry. It was not like Benton to be late.

When he arrived at work he looked as if he hadn't slept all night, and he wore the same clothing he had on the day before. His face was haggard, his hands trembled and he seemed on the verge of tears. He sank into a chair near Celestine's desk.

"What is the matter?" Celestine cried in concern.

"Mrs. Holmes," he started, then licked his lips and pulled at his tie. "She died last night."

For a minute Allison was glad that the woman was gone and she wouldn't be plaguing Benton anymore, but why would he be so upset about her death?

"Go on," Celestine urged.

"She had a heart attack, and there was a message on my machine when I got home last night from her lawyer, notifying me to come to the hospital. I telephoned some of her relatives, and I stayed at the hospital until they came. She died soon after her sister arrived. When I was preparing to leave, the lawyer called me aside and told me that Mrs. Holmes had made me her heir, requesting that I use her estate to take over guardianship of Patricia."

"You mean she hadn't even asked you!" Celestine exclaimed. "That was a dirty trick."

Allison had no voice to express her dismay. A black fog seemed to envelop her, and her surroundings receded before her. She didn't even know she had fainted until she regained consciousness and found herself on the floor with the concerned faces of Benton and Celestine hovering over her.

Chapter Eleven

Allison struggled to a sitting position and weakly took Benton's hand. "Please, Benton, don't let her do this to you. She monopolized your life while she was living. Controlling your life from beyond the grave is too much."

"How can I refuse? There's no one else to look after Patricia."

"You said she had aunts and cousins. They can do it."

"You can't think I want this responsibility!"

"As a matter of fact, I think you do. You enjoy being a martyr, trying to prove that your erroneous ideas about God are true—trying to make your point. I thought when Mrs. Holmes died you would be freed from your vow. In spite of what you've told me, I don't believe you've ever loved me at all. You've only used me to fill a few hours when you wanted female companionship. I have no one to blame except myself—I've been the aggressor in our relationship."

Celestine looked stunned at this interchange between them, and she said, "Please, Allison, don't say anything more. You've had a shock. Come, let me help you to your office."

"I don't need any help," she said shortly, and proved it by steadying herself on the chair and standing up.

"Allison, please," Benton said. His voice trembled and his face was stricken. "You ask me to ignore Mrs. Holmes's wishes. It's the same as the inheritance you received here—you wanted to reject it and found you couldn't."

"It isn't the same situation at all. You've dallied around with my heart, and after I fell in love with you, you tell me why we can't be married. Don't you think you owe me any loyalty? You think of everyone but me."

Benton's quiet words stopped her as she staggered toward her office. "I thought you believed in living by the Golden Rule. That's all I've tried to do—to treat Patricia and Mrs. Holmes as I would have wanted to be treated. I'm sorry, but I'll have to go on doing that, no matter what it costs me."

"Or me," she muttered, and went into the office and closed the door. Celestine followed her with a glass of water and a couple of tablets. "Here, Allison, take these aspirin and lie down on the couch for a while. You'll feel better."

"I doubt it," Allison said.

Allison took the tablets, then lay down and closed her eyes. The medicine wasn't making her sleepy, but she did relax somewhat, and she tried to think of this new development in a rational manner. Benton wasn't going to change his mind about looking after Patricia, and she could not stay around and watch him in his martyr role. So what could she do? For one thing, she wasn't going to date him anymore, but how could they function as a team in the office? Too many things had happened for them to continue in a nominal business relationship.

After lying on the couch for a half hour, she stirred into action. Accusing herself of being a quitter, she telephoned Thomas's office and asked for an appointment. When Mary said he could see her immediately, she splashed water in her face, repaired her makeup and left the building.

She decided she hadn't improved her appearance when she entered the lawyer's office and Mary said, "Allison, are you ill?"

She shook her head and walked into Thomas's office. He eyed her shrewdly but asked no questions. She sat in a chair opposite his desk, and clenching her hands, she said, "If we sold Page Publishing and turned the proceeds over to Mount Carmel Hospital, would that be keeping the intent of Harrison Page's will?"

Thomas stared at her, stunned by her question.

"That's a question I can't answer with a yes, or a no. Perhaps you should give me an explanation."

"I don't want to bore you with my personal problems, but it seems I make poor choices when it comes to my male friends. I wanted to leave Chicago because I had been jilted, and I vowed to remain aloof from the opposite sex. I come here and fall in love with Benton Lockhart and find out that he's tied to a vow he made years ago to a girl who is in a coma and will never recover. I can't stand working with him every day and knowing the self-sacrifice he's making."

"So, you're going to run away again," Thomas said bluntly.

If he thought he would jolt Allison into changing her mind by his blunt statement, he was mistaken, for she nodded. "That's right, but if we sell the firm, I would want some guarantee from the new owners, giving job security to the employees. They're good workers and I wouldn't want to abandon them."

"Allison, do me and yourself a favor. Take a vacation. Get away from here for a while. You've been tied to Page Publishing since you came to Columbus. Go on a cruise, whatever suits your fancy. Maybe you could take your sister with you—anything to get your mind off this turmoil. You're going to become ill if you don't.''

Allison didn't want to antagonize all her friends, but she was in an unrelenting mood this morning. ''I came to ask you a question, and you haven't answered it yet.''

''I would have to make some investigation, but if you give the money to Mount Carmel, it seems to me that you would be free to sell the business. I advise against making any such hasty decision.''

After she left Thomas's office, Allison drove south along U.S. Route 23, knowing that she couldn't return to the office in her present frame of mind. Benton had really given her a jolt when he had taunted her about not adhering to her Golden Rule policy. And it hurt even more to realize that he was right. She had actually believed that she was treating others the way she wanted to be treated, while at the same time sitting in judgment on Benton because he didn't share her Christian faith. She had failed miserably in setting an example before him. She had never been a good witness to him, though she had vowed to be one even before their trip to San Francisco. She had never conquered her resentment about the circumstances of her birth—never quite forgiven her two sets of parents. She hadn't had one bit of compassion for Mrs. Holmes, or cared what a burden she had for her only daughter. The more she thought of it, Benton should be awarded a medal for his self-sacrificial efforts to lighten the load of those two unfortunate women. Although it was painful to admit, Allison knew that she had better take a long look at her own heart and life before she tried to straighten out the rest of the world.

Allison had driven more than twenty miles during her deep contemplation, and as she observed the level fields and the neat farm buildings, she had an overwhelming desire to see Hannah, who knew how to forgive. She didn't know exactly where Hannah and Isaac lived, but she could ask directions when she arrived in their area.

She learned that Isaac and Hannah resided in a four-room house on the farm owned by Isaac's parents. Both Isaac and Hannah were at home when she arrived, and they ran down the steps to meet her.

"It's about time you paid us a visit," Isaac said.

"Why didn't you let us know you were coming?" Hannah asked.

But Hannah was quick to read Allison's expression, and she said to Isaac, "Don't you have some outdoor work that needs to be done?"

Isaac looked quickly from Allison to Hannah and left them alone.

"Come in the house and tell me what's troubling you," Hannah invited. The small living room they entered was neat, but sparely furnished when Allison compared it with her ornate furniture. The white lace curtains at the window lightened the rest of the room.

Hannah motioned Allison to a seat on the well-worn couch, and she sat beside her.

Although Allison felt as if she were at the breaking point, she tried to control her voice as she started. She told Hannah the whole story, how she had learned about her adoption, that Celestine was her mother and how much Benton had disappointed her. Long before she finished, her words were coming between sobs. Hannah didn't ask any questions—she simply listened, holding Allison's hand. Her lips moved silently occasionally and Allison knew she was praying.

"So that's the whole sordid tale," she concluded. "It seems everything I've done has turned out wrong. I should have listened to my mother when she told me to disregard this inheritance."

"You've done a lot of good by coming to Columbus," Hannah said.

"I hope so. But right now I'm so full of unforgiveness that I hardly can stand myself. I resent my parents, Celes-

tine, my natural father and Benton, even poor Patricia
Holmes. I remembered how forgiving you were when your
own family turned against you, and I just had to talk to
you."

"You will remember that Jesus said forgiveness was a
necessary action in those who would follow him. The Jews
of His day had a law that you only had to forgive seven
times, but when His disciples asked about that, Jesus said
that the scope of our forgiveness was unlimited. When you
forgive others, it helps you more than it does them."

"I know. I'm miserable inside. I had a terrible inward
struggle until I finally forgave Donald for the way he
treated me, but my hurt seems so much greater now because
I love Benton much more than I ever loved Donald."

"I don't know what I can tell you except to say that God
understands your sorrow. Remember the many times
you've disappointed God and how He has forgiven you.
When I do that I'm always humbled."

Allison reached out and clasped Hannah's hand in hers.
"I know I've disappointed Him again. No one could have
received more spiritual and material blessings than I, and
yet I've been mean-spirited in my relations to others. Right
now, my self-esteem is at its lowest ebb, but it has helped
me to talk to you. I value your friendship."

"Then you'll be pleased to know that my parents have
agreed to let me accept the royalty checks and even to
continue writing."

"Oh, Hannah, that makes me so happy. It's wonderful
that they've been so forgiving."

"After my dad read the book you brought him, he decided that writing is my ministry." She laughed. "He's
taken that book to our church services and told people
about it."

Isaac's steps sounded in the kitchen and Hannah stood.
"Come," she said. "Wash your face and get ready to eat
supper with us. Can you stay the night?"

"Oh, no. I came out here on impulse—no one knows where I am. I will share a meal with you, for I'm hungry, but I'll go back home tonight."

Allison returned to Columbus in a much better frame of mind, willing to forgive Benton for the pain he had caused her, but although the desire to forgive was there, she still couldn't be easy in his presence, so she knew that she still had many changes to make in her own attitude. He tried to talk to her about Mrs. Holmes's affairs, but she avoided the issue, ignoring the fact that he needed the catharsis of discussing his frustrations with someone. All she could think of when she looked at him was the drooling, emaciated girl who was keeping her from the man she loved. As she pondered on this, she realized that she had to exercise some forgiveness where Patricia was concerned, also. She thought Benton resented her avoidance of him and the matters that concerned him, but she had erected a wall between them so that darts of pain would never inflict again.

Thus she was unprepared for Benton's action when he came into the office and handed her an envelope. She regarded him with lifted eyebrows.

"Read it," he said quietly.

She took a sheet of paper from the unsealed envelope and read aloud, refusing to take at face value the words on the page:

I hereby give notice of my resignation as manager of Page Publishing Company, effective two months from this date.

(signed) Benton Lockhart

Allison laid down the paper and stared at him, speechless. Perhaps realizing the jolt he had given her, Benton explained, "I gave two months' notice, for I know that it may take a while for you to find a replacement and for me to teach the things the person needs to know.''

When she continued to stare at him, he fidgeted and continued, ''It might be well for you to consider one of the supervisors rather than to bring in someone who knows nothing about Page Publishing.''

She found her voice at last. ''Please don't do this, Benton.'' The desolation she had felt before her visit with Hannah settled over her so quickly that she hardly knew now that it had ever faded.

''It seems the right thing to do. My presence is obviously unpleasant for you.''

Hardly paying any attention to his words, she said, ''Please don't leave me, Benton. I can't live without you.''

''But it seems you can't live with me, either,'' he said bitterly. ''You avoid me as much as possible, and you won't let me explain my situation in regard to Patricia. I'm leaving because I think it's better for you if I go away, but I'll admit it isn't much pleasure for me to work here when you're in this mood.''

Allison remembered the phone call she had made to Donald three years ago, begging him not to leave her. She had cast her pride before him, and he had trampled it into the ground. Afterward, she had felt degraded and humiliated. Hannah had counseled her to practice humility, but she couldn't grovel before Benton as she had Donald, not even to keep him near her.

Allison folded the sheet of paper and inserted it in the envelope, which she dropped in the top drawer of her desk. Without looking at him, she said, ''Very well. I'll accept your resignation.'' She kept her head lowered, for she didn't want him to see her tears as he turned away from the desk, exited her office and quietly closed the door.

She walked to the window and stared with unseeing eyes at the parking lot, thinking of the future. Page Publishing without Benton held no charm for her. For one thing, she could never rely on another man to handle the business affairs of the firm as she had Benton. Without his guidance, she would lose the company. And she didn't really blame Benton—she had been cold and unapproachable.

She telephoned Thomas's office and soon had him on the line. "Thomas," she said quietly, for she didn't want Celestine to hear, "have you decided if it's legal for me to sell the company and turn the assets over to Mount Carmel Hospital?"

"I've read Harrison's will again, and it states plainly that you have to operate the firm for three years before you can sell it—you've been there only half that time."

"I've always heard that there isn't any will that can't be broken, so please give the matter more thought and research. I won't do anything until after the first of the year."

"What does Benton think of this?" Thomas demanded, obviously displeased at her words. "Have you discussed your idea with him?"

"I don't believe it can be of any concern to him. You see, he handed in his resignation today." She heard Thomas's startled gasp before she replaced the phone receiver.

The next morning when Allison arrived at work, she noted Benton was in his office, and she went in.

Without any preliminaries, she said, "I don't intend to make any attempt to find anyone to take over your position here. I can't operate this firm without you, and you know that as well as I do. If you leave, I intend to sell the company and give the proceeds to Mount Carmel Hospital. Thomas is checking now to determine if I can legally do it in light of Uncle Harrison's will."

"You don't mean it."

"I'm perfectly serious. Whatever our differences in regard to other matters, I need you here. If you stay, I want to make you a partner in the company. You're the backbone of this operation, and not only can't I do it without you, I don't want to. You don't need to give me an answer now, but I would like to have your decision within two weeks.''

He stared at her as if he couldn't believe his ears, but hearing Celestine entering the office, she walked out without giving him an opportunity to respond.

The letter wasn't easy to write, but Allison had finally decided it was easier to write than to telephone, so she took the coward's way out:

Dear Mother:

I don't want to displease you, and I want to thank you now for all you have done for me—your training, the sacrifices you've made and even the times you scolded me for my own good.

I have learned who my birth mother is, and through no effort of my own. I had given up even finding her, for I didn't want to cause you grief. I have been fond of Celestine since I came here, and I have visited her home often, because I am also welcomed there by her husband and son. Celestine wouldn't have told me, but she suspected I was taking steps to have my birth mother traced, and she thought she might as well tell me.

As far as Celestine is concerned, she feels that twenty-five years ago, she gave up the right to be my mother. She regards you and Daddy as my parents, and is content to be my friend. I know you may still harbor resentment in your heart against Uncle Harrison for revealing himself to me, and even Celestine didn't think he should have broken the vow. I like the Handleys, and I think you would, also. It would give me a great deal of joy to bring our two families together as one. I could have kept this knowledge from you, but I have never been deceitful with you and Daddy, and I'm too

old to start now. It's a relief for me to know my roots,
and I hope that you will be happy for me.

Your grateful daughter, Allison

As the holiday season approached, Allison's thoughts
turned to the previous Christmas, when she had excitedly
decorated her house to entertain Page Publishing employees
and their families. Her hands often idled over her work
when she remembered the necklace Benton had given her,
accompanied by his reluctant declaration of love. Though
it hurt to do so, she could not help but recall the hopeful
visions she'd held for their future—a hope that had died
when she learned the reason for his reluctance.

Since Allison couldn't generate any enthusiasm for decorating the house for Christmas, she decided against hosting
the reception again and asked Celestine to arrange for an
outing at the Palace Theatre. Celestine watched Allison
with anxious eyes, but Allison couldn't discuss her unhappiness with anyone.

Although Celestine invited her to have Thanksgiving
dinner with them once more, Allison declined the invitation. She stayed at home with Adra and Minerva, but the
day held little thanksgiving for Allison because she didn't
hear from her parents. She tried to telephone them once
and they didn't answer, so deciding they had gone away
for the holiday without telling her, she deduced they had
been angry about her letter. Was she destined to make
everyone unhappy? She had to do something about her
merry-go-round life. When her parents hadn't telephoned
by evening, she made up her mind to go away for a while.
Only God could bring peace out of the emotional turmoil
sweeping over her, but she couldn't seem to find that sur-
cease in Columbus. She had to be alone to do some soul-
searching.

She got up at her usual time the next morning and packed
a suitcase, and without even having breakfast, she left the

house. She wrote a short note to Minerva and placed it on
the kitchen cabinet:

Minerva:

I'm going away. At this point, I don't know where I'm
going or how long I'll be gone. Don't worry about
me.

Allison

She had considered telling Minerva to telephone the
company on Monday to say she wouldn't be in to work,
but they probably wouldn't care anyway. The place could
operate without her. Having no destination in mind, Allison
started west on I-70, and it was when she crossed the state
line at Richmond, Indiana, that she knew where she must
go.

She checked into a hotel in Indianapolis in late afternoon,
not far from the Market Square Arena. This was where her
infatuation with Benton had started, and perhaps this was
the place to end it.

Minerva found Allison's note about noon, and the message alarmed her so much that she hurried up the steps to
show it to Adra.

"Oh, I wouldn't think anything about it. The girl has the
right to go away by herself. She's been looking a bit worn-
out. A change of scenery will do her good."

"But why is she so secretive about it? I don't believe
she had any intention of going anywhere yesterday."

"Well, it's not our business, Minerva. Just let it alone."

Reluctantly, Minerva took his advice, for she didn't
know what she could do anyway, but when she was in the
parlor running the vacuum, the telephone rang, and when
Minerva answered, the caller asked for Allison.

"She's not here right now."

"Oh, I'm her mother—I didn't think she would be working today."

Minerva hesitated. Perhaps Allison was going to see her parents and wanted to surprise them.

"She tried to telephone you yesterday—I think she was disappointed when she couldn't reach you."

"Our telephone lines were out of order yesterday, and we didn't get service until early this morning. Where is she today?"

"I don't know, ma'am," Minerva said nervously, "and though my husband told me to tend to my own business, I'm worried about her. She left early this morning, leaving a note that said she didn't know where she was going or how long she would be gone." Beatrice's gasp was audible over the phone, and Minerva repeated, "I'm worried about her."

"Is there anyone else she might have told where she was going?"

"Maybe some of the people at her office. I don't know. Do you think I should check with them?"

"How has she seemed lately?"

"Awful down in the mouth. She's not planning to decorate the house for Christmas, and she's not happy and energetic as she used to be. I don't know what's going on."

"Well, Minerva, if you haven't heard from her by morning, perhaps you should telephone some of her office staff."

Benton was still in his bathrobe when Minerva called the next morning, and while he listened to Minerva's concerns, he blamed himself instantly for Allison's disappearance. After assuring Minerva that he would try to find her, Benton paced the floor, praying aloud, *God, where is she? Help me to find her.*

His words stopped him in his tracks. He had actually called upon God—the first time for years. Considering his disregard of God for so long, he was surprised that he hadn't been struck down because of his temerity, but Benton knew now that he had reached the extreme crisis of his life. He was at a turning point—facing a situation that he couldn't handle by himself. If he lost Allison, he had no future. Like a bolt out of the blue, he realized that nothing was important enough to keep Allison out of his life.

Going into his bedroom, he reached on a high shelf of the closet, and from a box of sundry items he hadn't seen for a long time he extracted his Bible. He carried it back to the living room, and it felt like a foreign object in his hand. At one time this book had been his greatest comfort, the guide he turned to in trouble, joy or indecision. How could he have spurned the God who gave him salvation? What had caused him to become a skeptic?

Undoubtedly it was because of Patricia's deteriorating condition that it had seemed to Benton that his prayers had gone not only unanswered, but unheard. He had prayed for her recovery; she had gotten worse instead of better. He had prayed for her to die; she lived on. For the first time it occurred to Benton that he had prayed with the wrong motives and was trying to take God's place, assuming that he knew better than God what should be done about Patricia. He had prayed for God to send him solace, some strength to help him overcome his stress. Now he realized that God had sent him Allison, who could have brought all the comfort a man would ever need in his life, and he had been too tied up in his own distress to see it.

She had accused him of wanting to be a martyr, and she was right. God had disrupted the life he had planned for himself, which had included Patricia, and when things hadn't gone exactly the way he'd wanted them to, he had blamed God. Was God punishing him again for his disobedience by taking Allison from him?

Benton laughed ironically. "There you go again, Lockhart," he said aloud. "Thinking the whole universe revolves around you. Do you think God in His heaven has nothing more to do than punish you? Do you want to blame yourself for Allison's flight so you can play the martyr again?''

He wanted to pray, but his words were meaningless. He turned to the concordance in the Bible and looked up some passages about prayer. What actually were the conditions for effective prayer?

''And I will do whatever you ask in my name, so that the Son may bring glory to the Father. You may ask me for anything in my name, and I will do it.''

It didn't take long for Benton to see how he had erred. He had always claimed the last part of that verse, not realizing that the first portion indicated the chief object of prayer was to bring glory to the Lord Jesus and the Father. Benton Lockhart had been more interested in his own needs than in a desire to exalt God.

As Benton began to look through the Bible, truths that had once been a part of his life began to penetrate his heart and mind. He thought of the many prayers recorded in the Bible that were unanswered, or at least weren't answered in the way the petitioner had expected them to be. Moses had prayed to enter the Promised Land, but had to be satisfied with a glimpse. Jonah had prayed for God to take his life rather than send him to minister to the ungodly in Nineveh, but the prophet had ended up preaching to them anyway. Paul the Apostle had prayed that God would remove his infirmity, but the problem had remained. In the Garden of Gethsemane Jesus had asked to avoid the cross, but He had been crucified.

Benton also remembered the many times God had answered biblical prayers, but not on the petitioner's time schedule. Abraham had prayed for a son, but Isaac, the child of God's promise, was long in coming. Sometimes God answered prayers by permitting situations to become worse before they became better, as had been illustrated in

the mess Abraham and Sarah had made of their home life
by anticipating God and bringing about the birth of Ishmael.

As he read the Bible and meditated on its words, Benton
thought of a quotation he had read somewhere: "Prayer
does not change God, for God is unchangeable, but prayer
changes us into the will of God."

"When you ask, you do not receive, because you ask
with wrong motives." James had written those words, and
when Benton read another passage from the Book of 1
John, he knew that his whole conception of prayer had been
wrong: "If we ask anything according to His will, He hears
us. And if we know that He hears us—whatever we ask—
we know that we have what we asked of Him."

Realizing that he had to make many changes before his
prayer life would be beneficial to others and in line with
God's will, Benton knelt beside his chair. *God,* he began,
and believed that his words were being heard, *I love Allison. Wherever she is, let Your peace bring her courage and
hope. Give her assurance that I love her, and work Your
will in our lives, and in Your mercy and grace, give me
another chance.*

Despite his worry over Allison, Benton was at peace.
God's healing touch had made a change. He was no longer
concerned about the Scripture that indicated if a man de-
serted the faith, he couldn't be forgiven. Again, God had
been merciful.

On that same day, Beatrice, too, was asking God for
another chance. After she had talked to Minerva, she knew
that her obstinacy was the cause of Allison's flight. Why
hadn't she answered Allison's letter? Why did she have to
be so stubborn in a situation that meant a great deal to her
daughter? She'd had the girl for twenty-five years. Why
was she so unwilling to share her with her birth mother?

Beatrice roamed through the house and thoughts of Allison filled her mind. From the hall closet she removed a box filled with items given to her by her children. She found the first Mother's Day card Allison had made for her. The colors of the rose were smeared, as might be expected from a first grader, but the message brought a tightness to Beatrice's throat: "I love you, Mother, bushels and bushels."

She lifted a shell that Allison had found on the lakeshore, and a faded, dried corsage that Allison had sent for Beatrice's birthday after she'd gotten her first job.

Beatrice sat in Allison's bedroom and remembered the times she had comforted Allison when she was ill or unhappy and when she was so distraught over Donald's rejection. She tried to imagine what her life would have been if she had not had the pleasure of seeing Allison every day, and lovingly guiding her growth from birth to adulthood. Why had she been so selfish with all these memories? Why hadn't she appreciated the gift her brother had given her when he had relinquished his daughter into her care?

God, she prayed, *my daughter is more important than my own feelings. Wherever she is tonight, take care of her and let her feel the assurance of my love.*

On Sunday, Benton telephoned Celestine, thinking there was a chance that Allison could be with the Handleys. He noted Celestine's instant alarm.

"Where could she have gone?" Celestine cried. "It isn't like her to go off that way."

"Wherever she's gone—some of us have driven her to it. I've been such a fool. She offered me paradise, and I wouldn't accept it."

"I'll have to take my share of the blame, too. I let her down twenty-five years ago." By those words Celestine conveyed her secret to Benton. He was silent for a moment, wondering why he hadn't guessed that a long time ago.

"Do you think she could be at Hannah's?" she asked.

"That's a possibility. Could you telephone and find out?"

But Celestine soon called back and reported that Hannah hadn't heard from her. "I suppose we can't do anything until tomorrow. Perhaps she'll show up for work as usual."

But when she didn't, and no word was heard from her by the end of the day, Celestine and Benton were terrified.

"She surely wouldn't make away with herself," Celestine whispered.

"Don't even suggest such a thing," Benton said, but his face whitened.

"Where could she have gone? It's almost as though she had to be by herself—that she had to go back to her roots and sort out her life, some place that marked a change in her outlook. A place she had to be alone. But where could that be?"

"I wonder…" Benton said, and then his eyes brightened. "There's one place I can think of, but it seems a little far-fetched. If I knew for sure I'd go after her." Thoughtfully, he wandered into his office, leaving Celestine curious but hopeful.

To Allison's surprise she found that a religious crusade promoting family values was being held at the Market Square Arena, and she went every night. As nearly as possible, she sat in the same section and seat where she had sat almost ten years ago when she had seen Benton for the first time and heard him speak.

Each night the speaker touched on some aspect of Allison's problem—she could identify with most of the illustrations he used. One night he preached about Abraham and Sarah and the conflict in their home. Lack of faith had caused their attempt to force God's hand, and Ishmael's birth had caused a rift in their home. She had tried to persuade Benton to her way of thinking because God wasn't working fast enough to suit her.

Each night brought some healing to her spirit, and she knew that all the trials she'd had when Donald had severed their relationship had been offset by many blessings. How was she so fortunate to be loved by so many people? She felt the security of her parents' love, which had always been readily available to her. Celestine loved her, and Allison felt no bitterness that her birth mother hadn't kept her. Instead of being reared as an illegitimate child, she had enjoyed the happiness of a secure home life. She also felt secure in Benton's love, and she was sorry that she had been selfish and had not understood his problem with Patricia. "You surely didn't set a good example of the Golden Rule," she scoffed at herself. "Put yourself in Patricia's place. If Benton had been engaged to you and you had suffered a similar accident, wouldn't you think it wonderful that he had been loyal enough to keep his promise?"

The characteristics that made Benton sensitive to the needs of Mrs. Holmes and willing to sacrifice his own desires to make Patricia's life more pleasant were the kind of attitudes she would want in the man she married. As the week progressed, despite the obstacles in their way, she believed that, in God's timing, she would marry Benton someday.

On the last night of the crusade, Allison was in her regular seat in the arena studying the bulletin for the evening's program, when someone sat down in the empty seat to her left. She lifted her head to greet the newcomer and looked into Benton's eyes. Surely she must be dreaming.

"How did you know where to find me?"

"Deduction," he said, smiling. "I'm a good detective. But I won't stay if I'm not welcome."

"I'm glad to see you."

The organ and piano prelude started, and Benton lifted her hand and kissed it. "Then let's enjoy the service. We can talk later."

Allison listened keenly to the speaker, believing that God

had sent the message expressly for her and Benton. Mutual love between man and wife was the theme of his sermon. A man was to find his pattern for loving his wife by emulating the love Christ had for the church. Following that example, a husband should set his standard by placing the interests of his wife above those of himself, and the wife was to surrender her will to her husband as he followed the example of Christ. A happy marriage was possible when a man loved his wife as himself and the wife loved and respected her husband. The speaker gave numerous illustrations proving that in almost every situation where a husband and wife had lived together for years, they had worked side by side to develop a good relationship.

During the evangelist's closing prayer, Benton leaned close and whispered, "A lofty goal to work toward, but, with God's help, I'm willing to try it if you are."

"Do you really mean it?" she murmured, and the answer shone from his brilliant gray eyes.

When the invitational service opened and the audience was invited to respond, as one person Benton and Allison rose, still with clasped hands, and went forward to kneel with many others. It was a time of commitment to each other, as well as a renewal of their faith in God.

They left the arena together, holding hands, and Benton said, "I want to talk to you tonight, Allison. I have many things to tell you. Where could we go for a little privacy?"

"Let's go to my room in the hotel. It's a small suite, actually with a comfortable sitting room."

It was a short walk to the hotel, and when they arrived there, Allison got some juice from the small refrigerator in the kitchenette and joined Benton on the couch. He told her about his vigil on the day he learned she was gone and how he had renewed his trust in God. "I made many changes then," he said, "and the chief one is that I want to marry you right away, if you have no objections."

Snuggling closer to kiss his cheek, Allison said sweetly, "I have no objections."

"I've devoted nine years of my life to Patricia, and I have no regrets—even knowing what I do now, I would do it again."

"I know that it was something you had to do, and I love you even more because you have been so faithful to her. I've had a change of attitude, too."

"I realize that my loyalty shouldn't prevent our marrying, but I do feel duty bound to continue to care for her, and I hope you won't object."

"No. In fact, I'll help you take care of her. I don't want you to bear that burden alone."

"And it may become more of a burden, too. After I paid Mrs. Holmes's expenses, she had enough money left to pay for one more year of Patricia's care. When that is gone, there may be some access to supplementary funds for Patricia, but if not, I'll have to take care of it."

"You will have my money at your disposal. When I said I wanted to help you bear the burden, I meant any kind of support you need from me, whether it's financial or emotional."

"When shall we marry?" he asked.

"As soon as possible, although I will want to talk with my parents about our marriage. This week I've realized more and more how much they've done for me. I'm afraid Mother is very angry at me, but I'll telephone her as soon as I get home and try to make amends."

"You're ready to go back to Columbus, then."

"Tomorrow morning." She put her arm around Benton, a teasing expression on her face. "I take it that you are withdrawing your resignation at Page Publishing."

Looking a bit sheepish, Benton said, "You'll never get rid of me now."

Before he left the room, Benton locked Allison in his muscular arms, and she felt the full strength of his love and the physical protection that she could always expect from him. His good-night kiss was brief, but when he lifted his lips from hers, his gray eyes gleamed with intensity and loving promise.

"I'll telephone and let Celestine know where you are, and we'll travel home in the morning. She can tell the McRameys."

"I'm sorry to have disturbed everyone, but I had to have some time alone. Now I know that God was leading me to this crusade, just as He brought me here several years ago. After this experience, I don't believe I'll ever again doubt God's will for my life."

Allison didn't telephone her parents because she didn't suppose they knew she was gone, but Beatrice called soon after she reached her home.

"Belated Happy Thanksgiving, Allison," Beatrice said. "I couldn't telephone on the holiday because our phone was out of commission."

"Yes. Minerva just told me. I needed to get away for a few days."

"It doesn't hurt any of us to sit down and think once in a while."

Could she note a difference in Beatrice's voice—almost as it used to be before Harrison Page had died? Perhaps she wasn't angry after all.

"I'm seldom alone if I want company. Minerva and Adra don't go away very much."

Wasn't Beatrice even going to mention the letter?

"We've been discussing a change in our Christmas plans if it meets with your approval."

Oh, no, they weren't even going to let her come home for the holidays.

Allison was too breathless to answer, and Beatrice continued, "Instead of you coming to Chicago, would you mind if the four of us visit you in Columbus for three days?"

Allison squealed. "Oh, yes, Mother, please come. I would love it. You haven't even seen Uncle Harrison's house. We can have so much fun. Will you drive?"

"We would prefer that. Charles still has a week's vacation, so that will give us some leeway in case there is bad weather."

"Are Tim and Cleta excited?"

"I haven't mentioned it to them yet. I didn't want to have them go into orbit until I'd cleared it with you."

"You couldn't have given me a better Christmas present. I love it."

"And, Allison, perhaps it will be convenient for us to meet your friends the Handleys while we are there."

Allison caught her breath sharply. "Oh, Mother, thank you. God bless you. I'll ask Celestine, and I think she will agree."

So excited she had to share the news with someone, Allison danced up the steps to the McRameys' apartment. "Guess what?" she said. "Mother just called. My family is coming for Christmas."

"That's great news," Adra said. "We like to have a lot of noise in the house."

"You'll have it with Tim and Cleta, as you will remember from their previous visit. Daddy is jovial, too, although Mother is quiet and reserved."

"Like her brother," Minerva said. "I think he would be pleased to know that all of you are under the roof he's provided. Tell me what you want for Christmas dinner, and I'll start planning."

"Please, will you take care of the menus and shopping? I'll want to buy more gifts since I don't have to stop with items I couldn't have taken on the plane to Chicago, and I'll plan to decorate after all. Do you mind taking care of the food?"

"Mercy, no! Though I'm liable to spend more money than you want."

"This is a celebration, Minerva. I want you to spare no expense!"

Allison went to work on Monday determined to persuade Celestine to have Christmas dinner with her family.

"When you have time, Celestine, I'd like to see you in my office," Allison said when Celestine arrived.

"Am I getting called on the carpet?" Celestine asked as she hung her coat in the closet.

"Not unless you've done something I don't know about," Allison replied with a small smile as Celestine followed her into the office. Allison closed the door.

"I wrote my mother about your disclosure."

Celestine stood still, not a muscle moving in her face.

"She didn't answer my letter, but she telephoned last night, asking if the family could come to Columbus for Christmas."

"That should please you."

"Very much, for I've wanted my parents to see my home and this firm. I want them to be proud of me."

With a smile, Celestine said, "How can they help being?"

"You're prejudiced. I don't have such a lofty opinion of myself anymore," Allison said with a grimace. "Mother didn't mention my letter, but she did suggest that this would be a good time for them to meet the Handleys."

Plainly startled, Celestine said, "Wonder what that means?"

"I'm not sure, but I think it's time you met."

"I would agree, except for the effect it will have on Truman."

"Will you come for Christmas dinner?"

"I don't know. I'll have to talk it over with Amos. It's a big decision to make."

"I realize that, but it might be the best Christmas we've ever had."

"Perhaps, but it may also be the worst. At any rate, I won't come unless I've told Truman beforehand. Depending upon how your family treats me, I don't want him disturbed."

"Do what you think is best. I've never doubted your wisdom since I've been here."

Christmas dinner was over. Allison sat at the head of the table with her loved ones around her. She was proud of the large gathering. Five Sayres, three Handleys, the McRameys and Benton had been seated comfortably around the large table. Allison had had a hard time persuading Minerva to sit with them, but still she jumped up several times and rustled around seeing to the needs of the guests.

They moved from the dining room into the parlor and gathered around the tree to open gifts. Allison received a large solitaire diamond ring from Benton, and his box from her contained a legal document recently drawn up by Thomas Curnutt making Benton a full partner in Page Publishing. For a joke, Allison had bought an electrical robot for Truman, and Tim and Cleta had joined him on the floor to figure out how to operate it.

When all the packages were distributed and opened, and paper littered the floor, Beatrice said, "I have two other packages to give if Charles will bring them from our bedroom."

When Charles left the room, Beatrice continued, "First of all, you know now the circumstances surrounding Allison's birth, and I want to apologize for my selfishness in denying her birth parents to have any share in her life. I've recently realized how much I would have missed if I hadn't had her for twenty-five years."

Allison went to Beatrice, sat on the floor and took her hand.

"I wouldn't let Harrison support her or even visit our home and see her. And, of course, Celestine had nothing.

It wasn't only that I was selfish, but I was afraid. I loved
the child so much that I feared Harrison would take her
away from me. With his finances, I knew he could offer
her so much more than we could.''

"Not the love and security of a family, Mother."

"Not only have I suffered because of my attitude, but it
has been a problem to my family. For over a year I've
spurned Allison's pleas to find out about her birth mother.
Today has proven that the Handleys and Sayres have much
in common, and I believe that Allison would have matured
equally as well if she had been brought up by Amos and
Celestine, for they've done well with Truman. And after
meeting Celestine, I know now who bequeathed to Allison
her compassion, gentleness and loving ways.'' With a brief
smile, she added, "She didn't get them from the Page family."

Beatrice took the two packages Charles brought her and
carried them to Celestine. She handed her the largest box.
"In there you will find pictures of Allison from when she
was a few days old until she graduated from college. I've
labeled these so you will know how old she was and under
what circumstances the picture was taken. You know how
she is now, but without these, you would never know what
she looked like when she had pimples, braces on her teeth
and skinny legs."

"Mother!" Allison protested.

Benton went to Celestine's side. "I want to see those
myself."

With shaking hands, Celestine opened the album and
leafed through the first few pages. "I really appreciate
these, and I'll study each one slowly. But I don't have a
gift for you."

"You gave me your daughter. I'll always be grateful for
that."

"And what's in this package?" Celestine asked as she
untied the ribbon.

"That's an original counted cross-stitch plaque. I hope that poem will convey my sentiments."

Celestine lifted the framed sampler from the box, and she read the title, "Two Families," but she lifted a hand to her throat and could read no more. She handed the plaque to Amos, and after he scanned the needlework, he threw a grateful glance in Beatrice's direction, cleared his throat and read:

Two Families

Everyone has a family of one kind or another,
Though some struggle through life without a loving mother,
Never knowing the strength and sacrifice applied
To chart a child on the pathway of life.

Allison, we know, was born out of stress,
In spite of which, she was doubly blessed
With two sets of parents, who each in their way,
Gave her a heritage in evidence today.

One father loved her enough to give her away,
Another one supported her and taught her to play.
One mother trained her and dried all her tears,
The other was denied her daughter, so dear.

The two families caused their daughter much pain
But in God's plan for life, no tears are in vain.
For we know that some ties are impossible to sever
Because God, in His mercy, has brought us together.

Except for Benton and Amos, everyone else was crying when Amos finished reading.

"I'm better at needlepoint than writing poetry," Beatrice apologized, "but you understand my meaning."

Perhaps to lighten the moment, Benton said, "Since this seems to be a family gathering, it's time for me to take care of another matter. I've asked Allison to marry me, Mr. Sayre, and she's agreed, but perhaps I need to receive your permission."

Charles cleared his throat and feigned a pompous attitude. "Well, now," he drawled, "I'm aware of the honor you've paid me in asking for my daughter's hand in marriage, but considering our meeting together here today, I suggest we make this a true family affair. I hereby call a meeting of the Sayre-Handley clan concerning a very important matter. Benton Lockhart has asked for the privilege of marrying our daughter Allison. All in favor, say aye."

The walls of the house resounded with their concerted "Aye," and Benton pulled Allison into his arms and lowered his lips to hers.

"Those opposed, nay." Charles paused. "Being none, the ayes have it."

The assembled clan applauded boisterously, but Benton and Allison were oblivious to what was going on around them—they were still locked in a tight embrace. Finally, Charles tapped Benton on the shoulder.

"Say, young man, the kiss comes at the end of the wedding service, not when we celebrate the betrothal."

*   *   *   *   *

Dear Reader,

Most of the time authors never know how their books influence readers, but a positive response to my first inspirational romance convinced me that the genre was a worthwhile addition to inspirational literature.

When *A Change of Heart* was published by Thomas Nelson Publishers in 1984, the editor told me that one of the reasons for choosing my book was because it dealt headlong with the doubtful practice of sexual relationships before marriage. Soon after the release of that romance novel, I attended a meeting where a woman approached me with the following story:

"I want to tell you something," she began. "When my granddaughter went away to college, I gave her a copy of your book, and she loaned it to a friend. After the friend read the book, she told my granddaughter, 'That book changed my life. When I went home for the Christmas holidays, I had to give my boyfriend a yes or no answer about entering an intimate relationship with him. After reading that book, my answer will be no.'"

After hearing her story, I realized the importance of producing meaningful, inspirational stories. Because reading my book had caused one young woman to retain her virtue for marriage, I considered the tremendous effect a voluminous output of inspirational fiction could have on upgrading the moral and spiritual values of youth.

Both readers and writers owe a debt of gratitude to the staff of Steeple Hill for their dedication to Love Inspired books, providing this increased worldwide circulation of wholesome and entertaining romances.

Happy Reading!

Irene B. Brand

Take 3 inspirational love stories FREE!

PLUS get a FREE surprise gift!

Special Limited-time Offer

Mail to Steeple Hill Reader Service™
3010 Walden Avenue
P.O. Box 1867
Buffalo, N.Y. 14240-1867

YES! Please send me 3 free Love Inspired™ novels and my free surprise gift. Then send me 3 brand-new novels every month, which I will receive months before they appear in bookstores. Bill me at the low price of $3.19 each plus 25¢ delivery and applicable sales tax, if any*. That's the complete price and a saving of over 10% off the cover prices—quite a bargain! I understand that accepting the books and gift places me under no obligation ever to buy any books. I can always return a shipment and cancel at any time. Even if I never buy another book from Steeple Hill, the 3 free books and the surprise gift are mine to keep forever.

103 IEN CFAG

Name	(PLEASE PRINT)
Address	Apt. No.
City	State	Zip

This offer is limited to one order per household and not valid to present Love Inspired™ subscribers. *Terms and prices are subject to change without notice. Sales tax applicable in New York.

ULI-198   ©1997 Steeple Hill

Love Inspired® presents...

THIS SIDE OF PARADISE

by

Cheryl Wolverton

Adventure. Excitement. Romance.

Mild-mannered Jennifer Rose was stranded with a stranger! On a mission to save three orphaned children, she and cynical pilot Gage Dalton had crashed in the dense jungle. Struggling to survive, Jennifer soon found herself on the adventure of a lifetime. For not only was her life in jeopardy, her heart was in danger of being lost to one very handsome man.

You won't want to miss this wonderfully uplifting story coming in September 1998... only from Love Inspired.

Available at your favorite retail outlet.

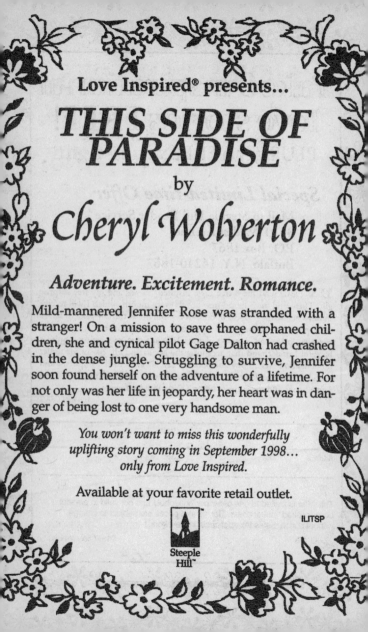

Steeple Hill™

ILITSP

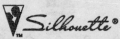

**Available in
September 1998 from**
Love Inspired.®

FOR THE SAKE OF HER CHILD

by

Kate Welsh

Amanda Powers's prayers were finally answered
when she was reunited with her missing son. But
her beloved boy needed her now, more than ever.
As did widower Garth Jorgensen, the man who
had raised her son as his own. Was a marriage for
the sake of their child part of the Lord's mysterious plan?

Available in September 1998
at your favorite retail outlet.

Steeple
Hill™

ILIFSHC

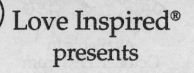